ALONE TOGETHER

Hero sank back against the door. Trapped. They were trapped here. Together. Alone. In one of her sister's fairy tales, they might end up in love and married. But this was not a fairy tale. And Arthur had made it quite plain that he already had chosen the woman he wanted for his wife.

Which, she reflected, meant that she was alone with a man she loved, who did not love her, with nothing to do but wait. Could anything be worse? Only that he might know how she felt. Thank goodness she had not spoken of it last night in the library, tempted though she was.

The silence began to wear at her nerves. "Why do you think Mr. Beasley locked us in here?" She did not dare broach the possibility that the one who had slid back the bolt had not been the bookshop proprietor.

Arthur considered her question carefully before he asked, "Why are you so certain that it was Mr. Beasley? We saw no sign of him when we searched the shop."

This was not what she wanted to hear at all. If Arthur, too, shared her suspicions, then they could not be entirely foolish.

Dear Romance Reader,

Last year, we launched the Ballad line with four new series, and each month we'll present both new and continuing stories set everywhere from medieval England to the American West—the kind of passionate, romantic stories you love best, written by the most gifted authors. At the back of each book, we'll tell you when you can find subsequent books in the series that have captured your heart.

This month, Martha Schroeder and her passionate *Angels of Mercy* are back! In **True to Her Heart**, a beautiful but penniless young woman finds that her sojourn in the Crimea has discouraged wealthy suitors—and that she wants the one man she fears she can never have. Next, the fabulous *Hope Chest* series continues with Paula Gill's **Fire With Fire** as a woman travels back in time only to meet a rugged lawman who sets off an irresistible flame of desire.

In the next entry of the breathlessly romantic *Once Upon a Wedding* series, Kelly McClymer offers **The Unintended Bride**. A shy young woman longs for true love—and when a family friend must offer for her out of obligation, he longs to prove to her that he is the dashing hero of her dreams. Finally, talented Sylvia McDaniel concludes the fresh and funny *Burnett Brides* trilogy with **The Marshal Takes a Wife**, as a female doctor returns to her hometown and discovers that the man she left behind might be the only man to steal her heart.

Kate Duffy
Editorial Director

Once Upon a Wedding

THE UNINTENDED BRIDE

Kelly McClymer

ZEBRA BOOKS
Kensington Publishing Corp.
http://www.zebrabooks.com

ZEBRA BOOKS are published by

Kensington Publishing Corp.
850 Third Avenue
New York, NY 10022

All Kensington titles, imprints, and distributed lines are available at special quantity discounts for bulk purchases for sales promotion, premiums, fund-raising, educational or institutional use.

Special book excerpts or customized printings can also be created to fit specific needs. For details, write or phone the office of the Kensington Special Sales Manager: Kensington Publishing Corp., 850 Third Avenue, New York, NY 10022. Attn: Special Sales Department. Phone: 1-800-221-2647.

Zebra and the Z logo Reg. U.S. Pat. & TM Off.
Ballad is a trademark of Kensington Publishing Corp.

First Printing: July 2001
10 9 8 7 6 5 4 3 2 1

Printed in the United States of America

To Jim, Kristen, A.J., and Brendan,
for all your love and support.

Prologue

"The manuscript is more precious that you can ever know. You must guard it well until the true owner returns for it."

The fire hissed and crackled on the grate for a moment, loud in the silence. "But if he is to be reborn in a different body, how will I know?"

"The flesh does not matter. It is the spirit within that counts. The one himself will give you a sign."

"But—" The burning log shifted on the fire with a startling thump, and there was another momentary silence. "What if he does not come? It has been so many centuries now since Malory placed his manuscript in our ancestor's care."

"He will come!" Silence. A soft sigh. "I know we have waited long for him. Still, I feel he will come during your time at watch. Britain needs him as she has never needed him before—her enemies breathe upon her very neck. Wait for the sign—and do not be fooled by pretenders, no matter how clever they might be."

"And if he does not come while I live? What then?"

"When your life is nearing an end, then you will

do as I am doing now, and pass on the guardianship to one who deserves it. Your son, I hope."

"And if I have no son?"

"You must. There is no one left of our line, our blood. No one who can guard the pages with the same loyalty we have. You will have a son, and you will teach him well so that he can take up the task if—" Silence once more. A sigh. "It is a precious package you guard, remember that and protect it well."

"With my life." Fervent hands clutched tight around the wrapped package of precious, fragile pages. *With my life.* No one would have the book until he proved himself worthy of being recognized as the true, reborn Arthur—King of Camelot, wielder of Excalibur.

No one.

One

London, 1843

Arthur steadied himself in the poorly sprung coach and read the note over again, his fingers trembling.

> *I have the manuscript that will make your quest successful. Peeble's Bookshop. Tuesday. Four o'clock sharp. Be late and you shall never find what you seek.*

There was no signature, and he did not recognize the handwriting, yet he had dropped all to come to London at once. Some might laugh at the melodrama implicit in the short sentences, but he did not. He had been following rumors of this particular book since he was a lad learning tales of knights and ladies at his grandmother's knee.

Most of the time he thought the idea that the original manuscript of Malory's *Le Morte d'Arthur* had survived nearly five hundred years, a rumor that the Round Table Society liked to encourage out of perversity. But some part of him hoped it was true—why else would he pursue each lead as if he might one day end up with the manuscript pages in his very hands.

He looked out the window. The carriage had slowed and occasionally even stopped in the thickening traffic. He was in London proper now and would soon be at his destination.

Today was Monday. He had arrived on schedule. He only hoped that the Duke and Duchess of Kerstone would not be put out with his abrupt decision to visit. Most likely they would be delighted to see him. After all, hadn't Miranda written to invite him several times? He had not come; he had not thought it wise.

But now he had little choice. If Simon found that he had visited London without a visit to the family, he would be mightily affronted. Arthur's heart beat a little faster when he realized that it was the height of the Season and no doubt Miranda's sister Hero would be staying with them in town.

She of all people would appreciate the exciting news represented by the mysterious message in his grip. But should he tell her? Though there was no warning against telling others about the meeting in the note, the abrupt tone suggested caution.

Even as he debated, caught between imagining how Hero's cheeks would flush with delight at the intrigue implicit in the note and the idea that he must once again endure her company without allowing himself to reveal how he felt about her, it was the sweetest torture he could imagine. Still, if he faltered just once and let slip his true regard for her, he would bring them both shame.

Perhaps it would be best not to tell her about the note. It would definitely be best not to see her, but in that matter he had no choice. He could not avoid her; Miranda would notice at once. Though he adored his cousin's wife, her curiosity, once aroused, could not be lulled by excuses or evasions. She would have the truth out of him. And that he could not allow.

He could, perhaps, have stayed with his grandmother while he visited London. That solution, too, had its pitfalls. Grandmama herself was staying as a guest with a friend, in aid of introducing the friend's daughter into society. Gwen Delagrace was a sweet girl, but a visit to her home was fraught with difficulties.

No, staying with Simon was for the best. Since his grandmother had planned, along with Gwen's wealthy father, for him to marry Gwen since before he was in long pants, visiting with her would be even less wise than staying with the duke. If his business was concluded swiftly, he might even avoid the need to visit the Delagrace residence at all. If he was unfortunate enough to encounter them, which would entail an explanation, he would simply tell them he had intended to call the very next day. His grandmother would know better, but she would say nothing to either Delagrace.

He felt a twinge of guilt at avoiding his grandmother, who had raised him after the death of his mother and father. Should he . . . ? He thought of his grandmother's plans for him and shuddered. No, best to keep his secret, play the cool cousin with Simon and his family, and hurry home to the wilds of the North as soon as this business was done.

He glanced at the letter once more. He knew he should not expect this cryptic note to lead him to the manuscript any more than any of the other clues he had followed to dead ends had. But he could not help the quickening of his heartbeat. What if this time the letter held the truth? What if he had finally found the manuscript he sought?

A jeering voice in his head reminded him that he had not truly grown into his name, but he tried to shake it aside. Arthur. He shared the name with the fabled king but not the nature, nor the courage. Sometimes he wished he could change it to something simpler like Edward or John. They were kings as well, but their name did not conjure up the legendary greatness that Arthur's did. The same legendary greatness his family seemed to expect from him, for some unfathomable reason.

Another glance at the note gave him no answers to all the questions rattling about in his head. Could he truly be the man to find the lost manuscript? And if he was, would that make him worthy of his name at last?

Hero was determined that Digby would not catch her alone today. When she saw his card, she flashed a panicked look at her sister. "I feel ill," she said, rising and turning to the door like a cornered hare.

Juliet raised a cool brow and smirked. "Why you fear that adorable man, I cannot imagine, Hero."

She thought of Digby, handsome, scholarly, sincere. "I don't fear him, Juliet. I simply don't know that I feel as strongly as he does."

"So what? He is by far the most promising man to pay you court in the four years you have been on the market. String him along until you find someone who does make that stubborn heart of yours beat faster."

"I would never behave so odiously! Digby is a good man." The truth was, Hero enjoyed talking with Digby, and they shared many interests: a love of the world's literature in its original Latin, Greek, French. He could translate Old English even better than she, and they frequently had entirely enjoyable debates over the pronunciation of some obscure word.

No. There was no doubt she found him interesting. But he was not the husband she wanted, and that she knew down to her very core. Still, common sense made her hesitate to be so final in her judgment. Maybe she was simply not destined for love. Maybe she should settle for warmth and companionship.

"Handsome perhaps. But boring." Juliet flashed her a smile as she added, "Or I would have long ago offered to take him off your hands for you."

Hero could not help the plaintive note in her voice as she asked quickly, "Could you not—"

Her sister stopped admiring the flare of her new skirt and raised her head to pin Hero with a stare. "So it is odious for you to toy with the man but not for me to pretend an interest I do not have?" Juliet's eyes flashed with pique or amusement, it was not quite clear which.

Hero felt herself flush at the accurate barb. "It is not as if you do not break dozens of hearts each Season. Why should one more bother you?" She heard her own words with horror. "It is not even as if I'm asking you to break his heart—only distract it a little, until I can decide what it is I want—or until the right woman for him passes under his nose and he forgets about me altogether."

"I'm afraid I'm already engaged today—to distract that adorable young Lord Wyndham." Juliet laughed. "And anyway, you've already paraded half the eligible misses in London past Mr. Digby and he still seems to want only you, for some unfathomable reason. I don't know if you'll be able to avoid breaking his heart much longer—unless you agree to marry him."

"I cannot—"

"Then you will have to live up to that foolish name Papa gave you and tell him so directly." Juliet patted her hand in a surprisingly empathetic moment. "If anyone can find a way to do so kindly, you should be able to, Hero."

Hero could not answer, as the gentleman in question arrived in the room, his face carrying a smile, his eyes alight with a passion that she wished she could douse as quickly and efficiently as a bucket of water put out a burning candle. Her father should have chosen a different name from his beloved works of Shakespeare for her. Or better yet, Timidity would have suited her best.

She watched, feeling wretched, as Digby quickly greeted Juliet and then turned to her. "Miss Fenster!" He lifted her fingers to his lips and pressed a kiss against her gloved hand.

"Mr. Digby, how kind of you to visit." She noted at once that he seemed to be bursting with some great good news. She only hoped it was not some new reason why she had to question her own sanity. After all, there were already too few good reasons to avoid giving the man the opportunity to ask her to marry him. "Have you had some good fortune?" she asked politely. "You seem elated today, sir."

His smile grew wider. "You know me so well, Miss Fenster." As soon as he spoke—instantly, mysteriously—his smiled dimmed. "I have indeed had some tremendously good news, but I fear I cannot share it with you today."

Hero was puzzled at his odd behavior. What kind of good news would put such a glow in his cheeks, and yet he could not share it with her yet?

He must have observed her confusion, because he said quickly, "Day after tomorrow I will come to you and you will be the first to hear what I hope will be astonishing and delightful news."

"I cannot wait to hear your news, Mr. Digby." For a moment her heart leaped. Had he fallen in love with some other woman? But his gaze into her eyes was as ardent as ever. Hero dared hope only that his words meant he would not be visiting tomorrow. She would certainly appreciate one day alone to enjoy the afternoon rather than dreading what it would hold.

He glanced at Juliet, who had moved off to give them privacy, and lowered his voice. "I had hoped to find some time with you to broach a private matter, but in the light of this impending news, I think I would prefer to wait until next I see you."

She felt herself relax infinitesimally at this turn of fate. For some reason he would not be making any proposal today. She smiled, and dared to tease him. "Then, if you are to keep secrets from me, sir, I feel it only fitting that we read Lord Byron today for our poet. Mystery for mystery, don't you agree?"

He nodded happily. "An excellent suggestion, as always, Miss Fenster."

Juliet came nearer, a mischievous smile lighting

her eyes. "Is she not a paragon of common sense, Mr. Digby?"

With a stern warning glance, Hero said sharply, "Since you agree with me so well, sister, perhaps you would do the honor of reading from Lord Byron's work today?"

But she could not feel truly piqued, even with her sister's deviltry. She had been reprieved and she was coward enough to be happy for it. For he would not attempt to propose today, and she would not see him tomorrow.

"But Lord Byron's words require a deep and masculine voice, don't you agree, Mr. Digby?" Juliet of course knew exactly how to turn the situation to her liking.

He did indeed agree with her, and settled happily to read a selection from the collection that Juliet pulled from the shelf for him. Hero heard hardly a word. Thankfully, Juliet's young lord had not yet arrived, so she amused herself by amusing Mr. Digby with fervor.

Hero's relief that she could put off a decision on whether or not to marry Gabriel Digby shamed her slightly. After all, it was not that he was not a catch. No. There had been girls willing to set their caps for him for as long as she'd known them. Girls willing to go to lectures where he might be, to museums just to chance an encounter with him. She had seen them. It amazed her how Digby himself seemed oblivious to the adoration.

But she did not love him in any way other than as a cherished friend, a sisterly kind of affection similar to that admiration and love she had for her own brother. Perhaps she should be content with that?

But she dreamed of passion. At times she realized how silly it was that she should imagine herself, plain and quiet Hero, evoking that kind of love in a man.

But to feel it herself, that she wished with all her heart. And that was why she had not accepted the few proposals she had gotten these last four years. And why she was so afraid that Digby would be the next to ask for her hand.

Perhaps her brother Valentine and the duke might have encouraged her more strongly to make a marriage if it were not for the fact that the duchess was on her side. Bless her, her oldest sister, Miranda, now the Duchess of Kerstone, had promised that she need never marry a man she did not truly love. Despite all his shining virtues, Digby did not make her heart stir with passion in the least.

Unfortunately for her, there was only one man who had managed to affect her heart thus far in her twenty-four years—and he was as good as promised to marry someone else—everyone in London knew that his grandmother would see the match through before long, despite the couple's own hesitation.

No, though it might have been convenient if Digby could have been the one she wanted with passionate intensity, considering how much else they had in common, it was simply not to be. Her heart ignored her pleas to beat faster when she danced with him, or when they conversed and he said something impossibly witty. She had heard other women refer to his handsome face, claiming he had the beauty of Adonis. And, dispassionately, she could agree that he did. By every measure, she knew she should have fallen passionately in love with the man. But she felt no more for him than she might if he were a brother to her.

In weak moments, she had even been tempted to settle for the amiable companionship that Digby was certain to provide. Yet, watching her sister Miranda with her husband, the Duke of Kerstone, always brought her back to her original conviction—she must marry for love. The couple found more than companionship with each other, despite all the difficulties they had had to combat in their courtship and early in their marriage.

As her thoughts wandered thus, several more callers were introduced to the parlor—all suitors for Juliet, naturally. Hero forced her attention back to the moment. It would not do to insult any of their guests.

Each man took a turn reading from Byron. It was almost amusing to see how each tried to outdo the other in "manly" voice. Only Hero seemed aware that her sister was paying no attention at all. Though she kept each of her suitors dancing to her attention, at the moment Juliet herself was focused only on one—and he had not yet arrived.

How many times had Juliet's eyes strayed toward the doorway? Yet her distraction had not been noticed by her besotted suitors. Such blindness amazed Hero. They claimed to adore the lively and witty Juliet, and yet not one of them seemed to sense her impatience and her lack of attention.

Just as she had the thought, her sister laughed and declared, "How can any decision be made fairly between such wonderfully romantic and emotive readers? I have never heard Byron read so beautifully before."

Apparently, Hero alone recognized that her sister had heard not one word of Byron's beautifully crafted poems. Each man took a turn trying to convince Juliet he was the one who should win the coveted prize—the last of Cook's lemon tarts.

It was no wonder that no man had yet captured her sister's heart for more than two weeks at once. No one had yet seen past her laughing facade to the passionate intensity that lurked beneath the beautiful surface. Woe betide whoever did—her sister would lead him on a merrier chase than she had led the others, no doubt.

When the impromptu poetry competition had been decided in favor of Gabriel Digby—by Juliet, of course—those who had lost graciously left to pay other calls. Which left only Digby, Hero and Juliet.

Her sister's attention was so focused upon the doorway that she was drawn tight as a bowstring—so that even Digby noticed. "I look forward to our next meeting," he told Hero meaningfully as he stood to take his leave, apparently under the impression that he had been thought to overstay. As he did, the footman brought a tray to Juliet with a card upon it.

Juliet leaped from her chair and met the footman halfway across the room. She snatched up the card from the silver tray and read it avidly. A puzzled yet pleased expression blossomed upon her face. Together the girl and the servant left the room without a further word.

Digby's eyebrows rose, and he turned to Hero, an unspoken question in his eyes.

Instantly, she defended her sister's impetuous action. "Juliet is impatient for a visit from someone who has captured her heart."

Digby smiled as if he understood completely. And then his expression shifted, deepened, and Hero's heart dropped to her knees as he said, "Perhaps I am wrong to wait to tell you my deepest secret." He grasped her hands in his. "My dear Miss Fenster, I long to ask you the most important question a man may ask a woman."

She barely had time to panic before her salvation appeared before her like a knight in shining armor, in the shape of Arthur, her brother-in-law's cousin. The very man—the only man—she had ever truly loved.

Two

"Good morning, Miss Fenster, Mr. Digby." Arthur squelched the surge of jealousy that assailed him at seeing the pair in a near embrace. He had no right to be jealous.

"What a pleasant surprise, Mr. Watterly, we were not expecting you to visit during the Season." Hero's face was a study in guilt as she quickly stepped away from Digby upon his entrance into the room. Digby himself seemed to straighten, adding an inch to his already impressive height.

So, that was the way it was? He wondered whether Digby had come up to scratch yet. It was, he knew, only a matter of time. Digby had made no secret of his desire to marry the scholarly Miss Fenster.

But Hero seemed still unused to the idea, given the evidence of her blush. He supposed it was natural enough. She was a shy and modest woman. For a moment he had the urge to reassure her, to back out of the room again, taking Juliet with him so that the couple could have the private time, uninterrupted, that they had seemed to need.

But he was not that magnanimous. Let Digby muddle about just as every other mortal man must. He walked fully into the room, and appropriating the best spot near the fire, accepted Juliet's offer to pour him a cup of tea. "I had unexpected business in town. I could not come to London without a visit to my favorite household."

"We are honored," Hero said softly. She met his eyes briefly, and then hurriedly looked away. Then, with a new blush on her cheek, she turned to her sister. "I will go to the nursery straightaway." She wanted the excuse to leave. He wondered if she was piqued that he had interrupted them so precipitously.

She turned to the men. "You must excuse me, please. Miranda will be dismayed if we do not inform her of this promptly. She will want to greet you as soon as possible."

"No need." Juliet stayed her with a light touch upon her arm. "I have dispatched Nancy to fetch her." She smiled at Arthur, and he could see that she was pleased with herself for thinking of sending the maid before Hero could suggest it. "She is up in the nursery helping the younger girls create a puppet play. No doubt if you are staying for more than a night or two, you will be required to sit through the misery."

"Juliet!" Hero laughed, though her expression hinted of hidden mortification. She met his eyes only briefly as she added, "I am certain that you would be required to do no such thing."

"It would be no hardship, I assure you." He wagged a finger at Juliet in a playful scold. "The play will be delightful, as always." Hero's expression brightened in approval at his willingness to play audience to her beloved sisters.

He smiled in response, unable to ignore the leap

of connection between them. "I trust, as usual, that all of the Fenster misses, even the youngest of them, are more than capable of entrancing their audience."

"I agree wholeheartedly," Gabriel Digby said with a nod of his golden head.

Hero glanced at him and blushed deeply. Arthur thought for a moment that she might have forgotten the man existed, as she quickly thanked him. "How kind of you for saying so, Mr. Digby." But no, her gaze lingered much too fondly on the man.

Arthur was pricked with unwonted jealousy yet again. "Have you seen one of the girls' performances, then?"

"No, I have not had the pleasure." Digby smiled again at Hero. God! Where did one get so many perfect white teeth? "But I am certain that I would be delighted were I to receive such an invitation."

He felt definite satisfaction that things had not yet progressed that far, and said with false solicitousness, "Of course, I forget sometimes that my relationship with the duke puts me at an advantage in knowing all the duchess's sisters well, even to having sat through several plays, musicals, and recitations."

Digby nodded, his impossibly wide smile dimming somewhat. "Not all of us are so favored."

Arthur knew he should leave it there. He had made his point. He knew he was being condescending, even before Hero frowned reproachfully at him, but could not help himself. "I assure you, if you are ever so privileged, you will find that they are talented and lively children."

All three of them stared at him for a moment and then diverted their gazes. He could have bitten his tongue out when he realized how obvious his behavior must seem. Juliet, her eyes narrowed with the pleasure of the tension in the room, said provocatively, "Why, we must see that Mr. Digby is invited to this new puppet show, shouldn't we, Hero?"

Arthur waited with his breath held while Hero gave her sister a sharp glance. Did she rebuke Juliet because she did not want to seem forward? Because she was annoyed with Arthur's foolish gibes? Because she had been hoping for a declaration when he so rudely interrupted them?

Or was it because she did not want Digby's particular attention? There was no way to tell when she answered her sister mildly enough, "That is a splendid idea, Juliet. We should make an event of it. Perhaps your Lord Wyndham would enjoy being invited too?"

Juliet sent her sister back an answering glance that was none too pleased. He wondered if there was some secret prod in the simple enough seeming question, but he could not tell from Juliet's ambiguous aside to Digby when she said, "We shall have to ask Miranda, of course, you understand?"

"Perfectly, I would not wish to impose myself on your family against the duchess's wishes. But—" He smiled again at Hero, and Arthur noted for the first time that the man had a womanish dimple in his left cheek, although, sadly, there was nothing womanish about his broad shoulders or strong jaw and brow. "Please tell the duchess that I could think of no better way to spend an evening than to see young minds at play."

Arthur suppressed his urge to scowl. *Young minds at play, indeed.* With effort, he got his temper under control. He had no business finding fault with Gabriel Digby. The man was perfect for such a paragon as Hero. He was not only handsome but temperate, witty, and a scholar. Drat him! At least he had not yet brought himself to propose. Otherwise, he would no doubt already be treated as a member of the family and invited to such an event without question.

"I will put a word in your favor with the duchess myself, Digby, since you are so eager to see the girls' production." But only if he was assured that he himself would also be present. If Digby were the one to win her, he would not do so with help from Arthur. Even though he was certainly a suitable match for Hero—perhaps one might even say the best match for a woman with the intelligence and wit of this particular Miss Fenster.

Digby, as if sensing Arthur's unspoken challenge, said heartily, "Thank you, Watterly. I am fortunate you chose to visit just now." His brows lifted together as if he had just been struck by a new idea. "Come to think of it, your timing could not be better all around. The Round Table Society is meeting two days from now, and I hope you will be able to come." There was an energy behind his words that Arthur could not fathom.

"I will be in attendance," Arthur answered. "I hope to have some new information to present as well." New information indeed. He intended to turn the staid society on its ear by presenting the original manuscript of Malory's *Morte d'Arthur.* But that he did not say aloud.

"Splendid." Digby's gaze grew sharp with curiosity, but he was too much the gentleman to ask any impertinent questions. "I, too, shall have some marvelous news of my own to impart to the group."

"Indeed?" Arthur felt himself grow wary for a moment, and then he relaxed. The note was safely in his pocket. Digby could not have knowledge of the meeting at the bookshop, could not be about to usurp the find of the centuries. No one else knew a thing about it.

"Oh," Hero said brightly, her gaze focused intensely upon Digby. "So that is your good news, then? Well, I shall hear it at the meeting of the Round Table Society. I will attend as well—they have just accepted me as a member, thanks to your sponsorship, Mr. Digby."

Digby gave Hero a warm glance. "You shall hear it as soon as I am able to tell it, Miss Fenster. And it will be my greatest pleasure to have you in attendance when I report my news to the society."

Arthur glanced between them and was suddenly glad that he had decided not to bring Hero into his confidence. Apparently, though they had not yet become engaged, she and Digby had reached a more intimate relationship than he had realized—he could not jeopardize his find by having Hero blurt it out to her suitor. Especially not if that suitor was Gabriel Digby.

Digby looked to Arthur. "Did you know, Watterly, that the society is seeking a replacement for Phineas Wright?"

"No, I had not heard." The news rattled him. He was not ready yet. He had not found the manuscript. "Is he ill?"

Digby shook his head, and with an apologetic

glance toward the ladies, said, "I believe his wife is a bit younger than he, and she wishes him home more."

"It will be hard to fill his shoes."

"Indeed, whoever takes his place will need to have proved a scholarly ability beyond all others."

"No doubt." He saw Hero and Juliet following the careful conversation with interest and ended the subtle exchange with a noncommittal, "I'm certain the society will be up to the challenge of choosing the best man."

"Beyond question," Digby agreed.

Suddenly impatient for the man to take his leave, Arthur cleared his throat and said ungraciously, "Don't let us keep you, Digby. I'm sure you have other calls to make." He ignored Juliet's quirked brow and Hero's gasp of dismay at his rude dismissal of the man.

Reluctantly, as if he had just noticed the hat that he held in his hand in preparation for leaving, the handsome scholar who had apparently captured Hero's interest bade the room farewell—a little more warmly than necessary to Hero, in Arthur's estimation. After all, she had not yet accepted a proposal from him—and departed.

Arthur sighed with relief. No more Digby.

"You needn't have been rude," Hero chided him. Her cheeks were quite pink and her eyes were narrow with displeasure. He had rarely seen her so put out with him. Apparently, Digby was a serious candidate for her heart.

"I'm sorry, Miss Fenster." Arthur tried to strain the churlish tone out of his reply. "I know Mr. Digby to be a busy man. I did not want to keep him from his business, chatting about the inconsequential."

Perceptively, Hero retorted, "I could almost think you considered him unfit company for us."

Could she see how he felt? "Not at all," he protested, trying to assemble his features into a convincingly sincere expression. "I simply did not want to bore you and your sister with the dull details of the society."

Juliet laughed softly but said nothing. He was relieved that he and Hero were not alone in the room, for he might have been tempted to blurt out something foolish. Something about how Digby was not good enough for her. He was appalled at his own selfishness. He thought he had resolved this issue years before. He was all but engaged to Gwen Delagrace; his family depended upon him for the alliance. He must let Hero have her chance at happiness.

There was no way for him to tell her that he loved her deeply. That he wished circumstances were different. That he had the freedom to choose his own bride. Which did not lessen his desire to tell her, nevertheless, that Gabriel Digby was not good enough for her.

That would not do. For the man was suitable enough, and it was none of Arthur's business anyway, he told himself sternly. But, somehow, no matter how often he told himself so, he could not stop interfering.

He smiled at Juliet, hoping to gain her goodwill, tense as she might be for some reason. He could see that he would need her help to restore Hero to her usual even temper.

Unfortunately, just as he had the thought, the footman presented another card, and Juliet's tense and distant attitude disappeared. She turned to him and began to flirt as only she could. She laughed up at him, her gaze full of admiration, as if he had just said something witty and wonderful. She touched his arm and looked into his eyes adoringly.

Not fooled for an instant, Arthur watched her performance dispassionately. What mischief was she about now? He remembered with a rush how interesting it was to have the Misses Fenster in residence. One never knew what to expect from most of them— except Hero, of course, who was always steady, sensible, and sweet.

"I see, Miss Fenster, that you have found a new suitor in the time I kept you waiting," said a deep voice at his back.

Arthur turned, and bowed slightly to the handsome young blood scowling at him. Would Juliet ever learn? he wondered with exasperated amusement. "You have it wrong, Wyndham. The lady was simply using me as a pair of ears to hear of her great admiration for you."

He heard Hero choke back a laugh, disguising it badly as a cough, and he was certain without looking that Juliet's gaze upon his back would be sharp enough to cut glass. Still, he felt the most heartless flirt of all the Fenster sisters deserved a little of her own medicine back. "She has been waiting for you with bated breath, Wyndham. I hope you have a good excuse for making her suffer so?"

Wyndham, being the young peacock he looked, beamed at the idea that Juliet had been extolling his virtues while she paced the floor awaiting his entrance, and swallowed the improbable fiction whole. His eyes softened as he turned to Juliet and took her hand. "I do apologize for my tardiness, Miss Fenster.

My carriage awaits, if you will forgive me and still consent to go for a drive with me?"

Juliet tilted her head coyly, as if she were contemplating her answer. With a wicked glance at Hero, however, she nodded, and said softly, "I'm certain my sister can entertain Mr. Watterly by herself. He is, after all, a family cousin. And I would be cold-hearted indeed if I didn't give you the opportunity to make amends to me for your neglect."

Arthur realized numbly that she intended to leave with Wyndham. He watched, feeling trapped in an intolerable situation as she called for her maid and her cloak, all the while merrily chatting and throwing pleased glances between her sister and Arthur. The girl knew! She knew how he felt about Hero! No. She couldn't. She was simply being Juliet. A tease. A flirt. A mischievous sprite. Wasn't she?

As she danced out the door, chatting excitedly to Wyndham, he was too cowardly to turn toward Hero and examine the expression on her face. If she knew how he felt, he could not bear it. It was one thing to love her quietly, from a distance, knowing that he could never make her his wife. To have her know this would be like tearing open a barely healed wound.

But she was not the coward he was, it seemed. Her voice was soft but her question sharp as she asked, "Why were you so rude to Mr. Digby? He has never been anything but a good friend to me. Has he done something to you in the past that you should hold him in so little esteem?"

Nothing but win your heart, he thought to himself. Suddenly the words threatened to spill from his mouth without his consent. Such disaster that would cause. To make declarations when he could not do so honorably. To promise what he could not possibly fulfill. No. He pressed his lips together firmly and turned around. He should take his cue from her courage and face her.

To his great relief, Miranda, the duchess, appeared like a whirlwind in the room, holding out her arms to him as if he were her brother, not her husband's cousin. "Arthur, so good to see you. Why didn't you let me know you were coming; I could have had Cook get in some of those mushrooms you like so well."

He laughed at her little joke. He was not at all fond of mushrooms since he had nearly been poisoned to death by them four years earlier.

In his relief at being rescued from his fate, he embraced her more warmly than usual, for him, so that she pulled back and examined his expression carefully. "You have not come for some terrible reason, have you? Your grandmother is not ill, is she? You look healthy enough yourself."

He shook his head quickly. "No, no. All is well. Grandmama is helping a friend bring out her daughter this year. She is here in London, and I have no reason to believe she is suffering any ill health at all. I have come on business. It was unexpected, or I would certainly have given you more notice."

"No matter, you are welcome anytime, as I hope you know. You are, after all, Simon's heir." She said it confidently, as if the fact did not give her any pain.

Arthur's stomach twisted. He did not want to be Simon's heir. He did not want to be duke. Miranda knew that. But she also knew that he was next in line for as long as she and Simon failed to produce a son, and she was determined not to let him forget it.

"That situation cannot last much longer though," he said reassuringly. He knew exactly how unworthy he was for the position, despite the fact that his grandmother believed him fated for it. After all, she had not considered him worth much until Simon's solicitors had found him and informed him of his status as heir apparent.

Miranda's expression darkened, but then she put it aside with a laugh. "It is certainly not as if we need another child in our household."

"You do seem to have more than your share of sisters." Not to mention the governess's daughter and Simon's three American nieces who visited each year. "But I cannot imagine you overset by one or two more." He spoke carefully. At first, after his cousin's marriage, he had been vocal about his hope that the two of them would soon have many children—and many sons. But as the years had passed with not a hint of a coming child, he had grown aware of Miranda's own sadness upon the subject.

She hid it well, but it was still there for him to see, even now. He knew better than to say anything overt, however. Such things must prick a woman's pride awfully. "No doubt ten years from now, we shall both laugh to think of me as duke."

"Perhaps we will." She smiled at him, and then glanced at Hero. He watched her expression shift as she realized that the two of them were the only ones in the room. "Where is Juliet?"

"She went driving with Lord Wyndham. Just now." Hero answered the questions nervously, her palms flattening her skirts at the hip. "She was barely out of the room before you arrived, Miranda. Though I confess I did not think she would go with him, considering how late he was. What a dandy that man is."

Miranda looked hopeful. "Perhaps he has truly captured her affections, then?"

Hero chuckled. "I doubt it. I think that Cousin Arthur was more likely the cause of her suddenly agreeable nature."

"Oh?" Miranda looked puzzled.

"He told Wyndham that Juliet had been eagerly awaiting his arrival."

Miranda smiled, and scolded him gently, "How bad of you, Arthur. You know she will not be pleased with you for that."

Arthur could not help an answering smile. "You should have seen Wyndham, though, my dear cousin. He was pleased as could be."

"Still, as penance, and to make amends for dropping in unexpectedly, I hope you will agree to escort us tonight to the Framinghams for a late supper and a little dancing, as Simon is otherwise occupied?" Miranda's eyes twinkled with mischief, but she was no doubt blissfully unaware of exactly how disastrous her invitation was for him.

Three

Arthur did his best to hide the dread that gripped him at her teasing invitation. It was obvious Miranda knew his first inclination was to offer a polite refusal. But she had made that nearly impossible for him to do without seeming churlish.

"I would be delighted," he lied, with a small bow to both ladies. A small part of him hoped that he would find an adequate reason to excuse himself before the time came.

Unfortunately, he could not even plead a headache. With a smile as genuine as he could contrive, he watched as Hero and her sisters came down the stairs in her finery. Hero's hair gleamed like fine mahogany in the light. The pink hue of her gown enhanced the pale cream of her skin. Too much skin, in his opinion. The fashion—which Miranda and Juliet wore also—was much too revealing in the bosom for his comfort.

To his relief, they donned their wraps, so that he was not tempted any longer to throw his own jacket over Hero's shoulders and spirit her back upstairs for a more modest dress. She wore nothing more daring than any other woman would. It was his own foolishness that made it seem so.

Miranda, sensing his tension, teased him. "Arthur, we are going to the Framinghams, not to the hangman. Please try to enjoy yourself."

"How can I not, when I am with three of the loveliest ladies in London?" She seemed satisfied with his answer and did not quiz him further. Quietly, he listened to their chatter and tried to force his own mood to lighten. But he could only see that Hero would be nearby and yet still out of his reach all evening.

As the carriage moved forward, and he sat uncomfortably next to Miranda, across from Hero, he was struck with a dreadful realization. Grandmama had been to school with Amalia Framingham. He hoped she would not be in attendance, but he dared not ask Miranda, she was much too likely to try to divine the reasons behind his reticence.

It was awful enough to know that Grandmama would now most certainly be told that he had come to London. She would not be pleased to find that he had come to town without informing her. Somehow he must find the time to visit her. What excuse would she accept?

Uncharitably, and not really meaning it, he wished she would come down with the grippe. Then he would have an excuse for not visiting immediately. That way, if he failed in his quest, she would hear nothing of his arrival until he was far away from London and home again.

Unfortunately, Grandmama was in fine health. She had not only received, but accepted, the Framinghams' invitation. Worst of all, from Arthur's perspective, she had chaperoned Gwen Delagrace to the event.

Fortunately, he spotted her from afar, her back to him, as they entered the room. He quickly excused himself from the Fenster women in order to face his grandmother down before she could work herself up into a formidable temper.

Gwen saw him first, and she broke into a smile so genuine that his grandmother instantly turned around, no doubt on the alert for an importunate but dashing fortune hunter. Her expression went from astonishment to suspicion to pleasure in the space of an instant.

He bowed to the ladies. "Grandmama, Miss Delagrace, I have just arrived in London today, unexpectedly."

His grandmother wasted no time with pleasantries and remarked testily, "I should hope it was unexpected, if you have not even notified me."

"A summons I could not ignore." He did not want to say more, but he knew his excuse would need to be extreme in order to turn away her wrath.

"A summons?" Her eyes narrowed. "From whom?"

"A bookseller."

She sighed. "I had hopes of something a bit more exciting. You and your books, Arthur. Well, you are here now, perhaps you can tend to your book business quickly and then work on setting up a household." She added peremptorily, "Why don't you take Gwen out driving tomorrow."

Gwen blushed, embarrassed by the obvious ploy to throw them together. "London is delightful, Arthur. I do hope you will be able to spend some time enjoying it."

"I'm afraid I have no time for anything but what

I've come for. Perhaps I can manage to visit again in a month or so," he said, intending to do no such thing. He liked London for one thing and one thing only—the sheer number of bookshops it held.

"Of course."

His grandmother looked as though she might argue, but then, surprisingly, she did not. "Well, I presume you can at least spare a moment to dance with the girl, then, can't you?"

He saw Gwen blush again and spoke quickly to ease her embarrassment. "Certainly." He extended his elbow for her to take, as he added, "I would be delighted to dance with the most beautiful woman here."

Gwen relaxed her tension, and he suspected she was relieved that the first bit of overt matchmaking was done with. No doubt, being a woman, she did not mind his grandmother's insistence. Fortunately, she had not pushed him, with unspoken pleas, sighing glances, or even—as his grandmother no doubt would have done—with outright demands. She seemed to understand that he was not ready for marriage.

As they moved away from his grandmother and onto the dance floor, he saw Hero already there, dancing with Gabriel Digby, of all people.

Gwen tugged his arm gently. "Is something the matter?"

Surprised to find that he had stopped moving, he began to walk toward the dance floor again. "No." As they reached the perimeter of the other dancers, he took her in his arms for the waltz and began moving awkwardly through the steps of the dance, trying not to pay any attention to Hero and Digby.

"He does dance well, doesn't he?"

Apparently, Gwen knew him too well. She had noticed where his glances fell. But he still pretended to misunderstand her. "Whom do you mean?"

"Gabriel Digby, of course."

"I hadn't noticed."

She laughed. "Well, I certainly have. After all the lessons that Papa and your grandmother have given me, I know an excellent dancer when I see one. And when I dance with him as well."

"So you have danced with him, then?"

"Of course. He is in town and you are not. And, as I said, he is a very good dance partner."

Arthur lost his footing for a moment and then regained it. "Unlike me, you are much too kind to say." He smiled. And then, as casually as possible, he added, "He seems to be set on Hero Fenster."

She stumbled slightly, apparently thrown off by his previous misstep, but recovered quickly. "What makes you say so?"

"He was visiting the Misses Fenster when I arrived today."

"Is that where you are staying, then? With the duke and his family?" He saw the concern in her expression. She knew him well enough to see that being the duke's heir was not something he felt comfortable about. "Do you think it wise?"

"I do not intend to be here long. A day or so, no more."

She smiled, and teased him. "Your grandmother will be disappointed. Each time you come to London, she hopes you will embrace your role as heir to the Duke of Kerstone."

"I hope that the duchess will soon make that role unlikely by providing my cousin with a healthy son."

"I hope the same—for your sake, Arthur." She changed the subject, apparently noticing that his glance had once again strayed toward Hero and Digby. "Do you think Miss Fenster returns Mr. Digby's regard?"

"Yes." He told himself to be honest. "He is an intelligent, sober man with good prospects."

She laughed, a soft sound he was familiar with. She thought he was being obtuse in a scholarly way. "You do not think she sees him in a more dashing light?"

He did not want Gwen to recognize the jealousy that ate at him, so he pretended to an impartiality he did not possess and conceded grudgingly, "Perhaps, he does have a look that some would consider handsome."

She said nothing for a moment as they both danced in the crush, careful of their toes. Then she laughed once more. "If I didn't know better, Arthur, I would say you were jealous of the man."

"Nonsense." Gwen knew him much too well.

"I can understand why," she added, to his alarm. But then her next words eased his worry. "He does seem to have all the characteristics your grandmother has tried to instill in you all these years."

She thought his jealousy was to do with the Round Table Society. And then he realized there was some truth in it. That realization stung. He looked at her sharply, wondering if she had said it because she was angry with him for not declaring for her once and for all. But her look was all sympathy. He said dismissively, "Grandmama has romantic ideals that have not been met for hundreds of years—if they ever were at all."

Her tone was still sympathetic, but her words were not comforting. "She does not think of them as myth, you know."

He lost his step again, and recovered, saying sharply, "Well, she must understand eventually that I will not meet her ideals, no matter what blood runs in my veins."

Her voice was softer still when she replied, "I'm sorry. I did not mean to make our first meeting in London unpleasant."

"I'm sorry." The music ended, and he saw her back to his grandmother. "I don't want you to share my grandmother's misapprehensions, Gwen. You are much too sensible a girl to believe that I will ever live up to the mythic example of King Arthur."

"Oh, Arthur. I know you well enough to understand you. Haven't I known you forever? You are the older brother I never had. The son my father never had. Sometimes I—" Her voice broke off as they neared her father, as if she had meant to confide something else, something more, but did not want to risk her father overhearing.

For a moment he had dared to hope that she would release him from their family's promise. Tell him that she had found another and would love him like a brother but did not want to marry. She did not. Instead, her father took him aside to ask him how long he would be in London. He insisted that Arthur come to dinner the following day.

He wished, miserably, as he sat with the happily chatting Fenster women on the way home, that he had never come to London. It was hell to know it was time to come up to scratch with Gwen, when all he wanted was to spirit Hero away with him into the countryside and never see the city again.

Hero wanted to sleep.

Her bed was soft enough, and she was not too warm. Juliet lay peacefully dreaming across the room, her breathing even. But sleep would not come to Hero.

Unwillingly, when she closed her eyes she saw Arthur dancing with Gwen Delagrace, just as he had been that evening. Gwen laughing and teasing him with utter familiarity and affection. Arthur had been distracted, she would swear it. Twice, she had met his eyes and looked away. Twice, she had found his eyes upon her and then, almost as if she had been mistaken, he had turned his head.

She was making herself into a madwoman with all this useless speculation. Every word, every movement, every look from Arthur Watterly, had suddenly begun to have import to her. Sheer foolishness, but she could not seem to stop herself.

She could not forget how sharp he had been to Digby in the drawing room that afternoon. Almost as if he were jealous. Was it possible? Could Arthur Watterly have some feelings for her? Could he feel the same degree of connection to him that she found in his company?

Nonsense. He regarded them all with affection; that had been clear since the first time she had ever met him. He had been struck nearly speechless with Miranda's spirited attempts to create happy endings for everyone around her, and he was always deft at deflection when Juliet practiced her wiles upon him.

Tonight, at the Framinghams, he had been the conscientious escort and nothing more. He had danced one dance with each of them. No, he had danced two with Gwen, she reminded herself. Only one waltz, but still, two dances. One more and everyone would have been certain he was on the verge of making the proposal that was so clearly expected by the family.

So why did she persist in hoping that he felt more for her than he could say? More than he felt for Gwen. Just because he shared her own delight in the classics, as well as in the tales of King Arthur and his court? Just because he, too, preferred an evening spent in the library to one on the dance floor?

Silliness. He enjoyed their discussions. He found her comments thoughtful and worth listening to. But that was the extent of his feelings. She was allowing her own longings to make more of his irritation than she should. Certainly, he had not seemed to be having a miserable time when he danced with Gwen.

There were times she cursed her own imagination. Tonight, however, it was bedeviling her as never before. Try as she might, she seemed unable to sleep. Every time her head sank into her pillow and her eyes closed, she saw Arthur's face as he danced with Gwen. As he had looked when he had asked her to dance—a waltz as well. As he had looked at Gabriel Digby when the poor man stood in the drawing room right downstairs.

What was it that made him so sharp with Mr. Digby? Even at the Framinghams he had virtually scowled at the man anytime he happened to glance at him. What was between them? Could it be her, or was she foolish to even consider that possibility? She replayed the conversation between the two men, searching for any nuance that could convince her there was more than mere travel fatigue in his animosity.

She had asked him. And she believed he had intended to answer her. A moment more and she might have known why he had been so unkind to Gabriel Digby. Would he have confessed to tender feelings for her? She wished Miranda had not interrupted what he was going to say in response to her questioning his rudeness to Digby.

And then, as she lay there, she realized the extent of her own rudeness. Her entire body flamed with shame. How had she dared ask him that question? And what had she hoped he would say? That he had been rude to Digby because he wanted her for himself?

Absurd. She was no catch, especially not for the heir apparent of a duke as Arthur was. She was only the sister of a baron, with little social grace and less desire to acquire any. She wouldn't even have any dowry to speak of if it weren't for the duke's generous offer to provide one for her—an offer he had made to Juliet and her other sisters as well.

No. She was no catch for Arthur. Miranda may have won a duke, but Hero was not as extraordinary as her sister, and she knew it. Quiet, plain, more interested in books than in the latest fashions from Paris. Even her family found her a puzzlement, although she knew they loved her, oddity and all. She had not really expected to make a match as passionate and loving as her older sister had.

Yet, now that he had come so unexpectedly back into her life, she found that the affection and longing that she thought contained well enough to her fantasies had burst into full bloom at the sight of him. Her feelings for Arthur were shockingly strong, no matter how misdirected. She did not know what to do about them. And as they seemed to be so impossible to ignore, she found herself questioning her reasons to do so.

Certainly, Arthur had never shown that kind of interest in her, despite how often they enjoyed discussing the classics or reading the tales of King Arthur or the poems of Lord Byron. And he had seemed to tolerate the men who courted her, even the ones who proposed and were not accepted. So why would he be put out by a suitor for her hand now?

Never before had she had a suitor as serious as Gabriel Digby in the four years since she had first come out. Could that be what had prompted Arthur's sudden sharpness? Was there any possibility he felt some small tenderness for her? And, if so, what could have prevented him from speaking to her for so very long?

You are dreaming again, she chided herself, sitting up in her bed, thoroughly disgusted with the way her thoughts kept running away from her control. *He is all but engaged,* she reminded herself sternly.

The rumors were that he and Guenivere Delagrace had been promised virtually since their births. No engagement had been formally announced, but this year, after delays caused by first the death of her mother, then the death of her grandfather, she had finally been brought out.

No doubt the engagement would follow on the

heels of Arthur's visit to London. Gwen's father had greeted him warmly. Even Arthur's grandmother had pulled the two together tonight. Probably the announcement would be in the paper in a week or two. Unless something horrible happened to Gwen to prevent it. Hero put aside the uncharitable wish that the girl would somehow disgrace herself in society.

But no, having seen firsthand what flirting near such an event did to her own sister Miranda, she could wish the fate on no one. Not even on the woman to whom Arthur's heart—and soon his name as well—belonged.

There was no question that Arthur needed a woman who could run his estates, preside over his table with elegance and grace, and handle society with the skills that Hero would never possess. She might know obscure historical facts, have a complete understanding of Old English, and have read the classics in their original Greek, but she could not pour tea without fearing that Lady Stirling's dislike of lemon would have slipped her mind, or the spoon in her hand would tumble to the floor with a clatter when she wasn't looking.

She wondered if Gwen Delagrace had ever tripped on her hem and sent a dance partner sprawling? Somehow, though, she doubted it. She had seen her at the balls and parties Miranda dragged her to so determinedly. The girl had probably never tripped in her life.

With a sigh of exasperation, she gave up on the idea of sleep. Hastily, she flung back her covers and threw on her robe as she slid into her slippers. She knew well enough that she would be prey to her churning thoughts until she found something new to focus them upon.

Quietly, so as not to wake Juliet, she hurried out of her room, walking the familiar dark corridors of the London town house as she had done on previous sleepless nights. She could find her way to the library blindfolded. And she could do so silently, so as not to wake any of her sisters. Unfortunately, it was not a sought-after skill for a wife.

There was a light already blazing; she could see it under the doorway as she approached. For a moment she considered turning back, but she did not. It seemed, to her fevered imagination, almost as if fate had intervened to give her an opportunity to speak her mind to Arthur.

Four

She opened the door, her palm so damp it almost slipped from the cool metal of the latch, expecting to see Arthur bent over a book. She was not disappointed.

He looked up at the sound of the door snicking closed. He stood up guiltily, as if she had caught him stealing the silver. "Miss Fenster. I . . . I . . . I was just—"

"Cousin Arthur, you need not explain to me that you could not sleep and came down here to find solace in a good book." She laughed, proud of her unshakable calm. If she could help it, he would not know that being close to him made her heart beat faster. Not unless he clearly wanted to know that fact.

"I have indeed," he said, relaxing almost imperceptibly.

She added calmly, wondering at her own nerve, "I perfectly understand. That is, in fact, why I am here as well."

To prove her words, and conceal her face just in case she was not as good at masking her emotions as she hoped, she went quickly to a bookshelf deep in the shadows.

"I'm surprised to find you still awake after all the

dancing you did tonight." She wondered what to make of his comment. Did it mean that he had been watching her closely? Was it nothing more than a polite conversational statement?

"I could say the same of you." He had danced with Gwen twice. Only once with Hero, once with Juliet, once with Miranda. But he had also danced with his grandmother and several others who had ended up without partners for a dance.

"And yet, here we are, neither of us sleeping. It is the urgency of my business that keeps me awake. What is there that troubles you?"

You, she wanted to say. Instead, she laughed. "Just a slight case of overexcitement tonight, I suppose. I'm certain that after a few pages, I shall be able to sleep peacefully enough."

"A lady's nightcap, then?" He laughed along with her.

She tripped over an object on the floor—a toy that one of her sisters must have left behind—and caught herself before she could fall. "Oh, bother!"

"Are you all right?" He half rose from his chair, but she waved him away.

"Just a doll of Kate's where it doesn't belong," she said in embarrassment, lifting it and waving it in the dark so that he would not think her unbearably clumsy.

"Shall I bring the light?" His offer was the offer any other gentleman she knew might make—any gentleman who had searched many a dark shelf himself in search of a good book.

"No need," she answered hastily before he could make good his offer and shine a light upon her face. She doubted in strong light she could hide her mortification at her own gracelessness. "I know these shelves so well that I could find what I want with my eyes closed."

He sighed. "I envy you, then. I know my own library that well, but Simon's is still a delightful mystery to me."

Hero, putting her hand upon the very book she sought as he spoke, stood still. "I know just what you mean. My first Season, I spent every waking moment here, just working my way slowly through the shelves."

"I would hardly have thought you'd have time with all the invitations you must have received."

"I would rather spend two hours with a book than at a ball, I suppose. It is a good thing that Simon and Miranda were so indulgent of Juliet and me, bringing us here year after year, even though we fail to come away with a husband each time."

She wanted to bite her tongue off as soon as the words left her mouth. Too late. She *had* said the dreadful words. Did he think she was hinting for a declaration from him. Oh, she hoped not. A straightforward, sensible question was one thing, but to have him believe she would try to manipulate him into— no, the thought was too horrible to complete.

He did not seem to think her words terrible though. "As to your sister, however, I confess I despair of her ever marrying—I cannot see the fair Juliet ever choosing just one man to adore her." His smile seemed forced—or else her imagination made it so, however, when he added, "Mr. Digby appears very fond of you. Perhaps this year will have a different ending for you."

She laughed. He had skewered Juliet so wryly—

and so accurately—she could not be offended for her sister's sake. But he had indeed noticed Gabriel Digby's pointed interest in her. "Mr. Digby has been most kind in his attentions."

His expression stiffened slightly. For some reason, she had no wish to hurry to advise him that she did not share Gabriel Digby's hopes, so she added with a smile, "Which is great comfort when all the other callers seem to be in Juliet's court."

"More fool them." There was no hint of teasing in his voice, and her hopes rose. But then he blinked and quickly added, "That one's heart is fully armored against any but the most stalwart attempt to win it for more than a moment. You, I imagine, would be more than reward to the man who dared to try to win your heart. Digby is a fortunate man."

She could say nothing in reply. He thought her love would be a reward for any man. He had said so aloud. She felt almost dizzy from the intimacy of this moment. And then she laughed silently at herself. Only she would consider a moment where she stood halfway across a room from a man, clutching a book amid the deepest of shadows, intimate.

His next question sobered her completely. "Has he proposed yet?"

It was a most personal question. She knew she should not answer it. But there was something about the shadowed room that compelled her to honesty. "No."

"He will. I am certain."

She made herself ask lightly, "Then you believe I should accept his offer if he does indeed make one? You do not think I should hold out for another man?"

The silence of the darkened library deepened. It was time to ask the question fate had given her the opportunity to pose to him. For a moment she had a burning desire to cross the room, to come out of the shadows and stand close enough that he could see the expression in her eyes. Surely if he saw the love that lay resident deep within her, he would feel how strong and true it was—and he would not be able to turn her away.

But she did not have the courage. If he saw, and still thought of her only as a friend, she could not bear it. Her feet were firmly rooted to the floor, her soul too comfortable lingering outside the light of discovery.

His voice cleaved the shadows of her thoughts. "What have you chosen?"

She started, momentarily thinking he referred to her choice to come close to him, to let him see how deeply she regarded him. But then she realized he asked after the title of the book she had selected from the shelf. *"Le Morte d'Arthur,"* she answered, her voice as steady as she could make it.

At first she thought he had not heard. There was a prolonged silence, with his eyes focused on the dark corner in which she stood shadowed from him. And then he said the most extraordinary thing. "What would you say if I told you I have heard rumors that Malory's original manuscript still exists?"

The question was so unexpected, she spent no time softening her answer. "After five hundred years? Impossible." Hearing her words, she reversed herself, feeling as if she were being too harsh. "Not impossible, of course; we have found written records older than that."

He nodded. "Still, you think it highly unlikely."

She wondered if she had offended him. "Perhaps I spoke too soon. I am no expert. But I do know that for the manuscript to have survived, someone would have needed to preserve it with the utmost care. Perhaps even bringing it to Egypt or Africa, where the dry air might prevent the damage our moist English days can cause. It would be a virtual miracle."

"My thoughts exactly. Without someone's care and intent, the manuscript's survival is just a myth."

"How marvelous, though, if it were true," she said quietly, a suspicion forming in her mind. "Do you know who might have it?"

He shifted, and she could sense that he struggled with some internal conflict. His voice was almost strained as he said, "I believe I might, tomorrow. If it is not a myth."

"How . . ." The appropriate word eluded her. Exciting? Astonishing? Marvelous? Impossible? She finished tritely, "How interesting." Which was not quite enough to say about a subject that had managed to completely erase her disappointment in her own lack of courage, despite the endorsement of her plan by fate itself.

He chuckled. "You sound as if you don't believe it possible."

"I'm afraid I could not bring myself to believe it without seeing it myself. After all, miracles are far and few between." Especially the kind that would give a shy mouse the chance to be loved by a man who was not only a great scholar but might one day be a duke.

"I understand. I feel the same way myself. Perhaps I should have stayed at home, not ventured into London. I don't know if any but a fool would even chance that it could be true."

He looked so forlorn, she could not help saying, "Still, I do believe miracles have happened. Certainly to make the attempt to verify the facts would not be foolish."

"Do you suppose so?"

She answered firmly, miserably certain of her answer, "The true fool would be either the one who believed in something without confirmation, or who disbelieved it without examining the evidence to confirm the truth."

"Yes." His voice held a hint of pleasure, as if she had said something that mattered very much to him. For a moment she thought he might say the words she did not have the courage to utter, but he did not.

The silence dragged to the point where she felt the foolishness of her own hopes. Squaring her shoulders as she had learned to do so well all her life when what she wanted was not possible, she said softly, "Well, good night." She turned to leave, sliding out of the shadows.

"Miss Fenster?"

"Yes?"

"My appointment to view the manuscript, if it is indeed the manuscript, is for four tomorrow afternoon—" He broke off and glanced at his pocket watch. "That is, four *this* afternoon. Would you care to join me?"

Arthur spent the day avoiding Hero. He did not precisely regret his invitation. He wanted her company. He wanted to share the discovery of truth or myth with her. But he did not want to divide her loyalties between him and Digby, and that seemed likely now that they both intended to become head of the Round Table Society.

He had penned two notes to cancel the appointment but had burnt them both in the fireplace. The truth was, he did not want to face this alone. With Hero along it became a lark; he could treat it almost as if it didn't matter to him whether someone was playing a prank upon him.

At last, his decision made, he stood waiting, ready to leave. If she did not come promptly, he would instruct the footman to give her his apologies and tell her that he would relay to her his discovery when he returned. A quarter to four o'clock. He checked his pocket watch.

And then he heard her on the stairs and did not know whether to be relieved or disappointed. She was prompt, as always. He could see the excitement shining in her eyes as she came sedately down the stairs, dressed in a darker rose shade today. The color suited her, but he dared not be so personal as to tell her so. He was suddenly happy that he had not left early. Had not chosen to send a note rescinding his invitation and driven away before she was dressed and ready to go.

He could not say what had made him invite Hero on his quest. The hypnotizing quiet and intimacy of the darkened library in the dead of night? Her soft voice? The fact that she had chosen the very title that he quested after? Or simply because he loved her and could not help himself?

Whatever the reason, he could not bring himself

to regret it as he greeted her in the entrance. He noted that she had dispensed with her maid, and raised his brow in question.

As if she could read his mind, she answered him in a low voice, "We are going to a bookshop—Juliet is to drive with Lord Wyndham again. I think that Ellen must go with her. It should be nothing for us to run such a public errand without a maid."

"Of course." She was correct. The intimacy, the danger to her reputation, was in his mind only. The bookshop, a few minutes walk from here, was a destination she could have made on her own, without any maid at all.

But this time she would be going with him. And they might both be the first to see Malory's manuscript in centuries. Save for the mysterious fellow who had sent him the note, of course.

He held out his arm for her to grasp. "Shall we go?"

"Are you nervous?" she asked as they settled into a comfortable stride, neither too fast nor too slow. It pleased him that he did not need to adjust his step to an unbearably mincing pace to accommodate her.

"Anxious, perhaps." Again, he was pleased to be able to share his worries with one who could understand them so well. "Hopeful. But as you have already said, the idea that the original manuscript survived all these centuries is difficult to believe."

"Still, you must have good reason—"

He laughed shortly, and she blinked in surprise, stopping there on the street, oblivious to those who had to dodge around them. "I'm sorry. Sometimes I think my Arthurian quest is more of an obsession. And obsessions do not require reason, logic, or possibility to drive them." Uncomfortable with the looks they were drawing from passersby, he tried to urge her forward. Oblivious to his efforts, she remained, stubbornly unmoving.

She looked at him, a dawning sadness on her face as she said, "No, they do not indeed." Her expression made him wonder if she, too, had a secret obsession. The sense of a shared quest almost made him bend the barrier of propriety and ask her.

But then she seemed to pull herself together and put her sadness away. "What convinced you that this information might be genuine despite your doubt?"

How could he explain such a thing to her? There was so little time before they must make the appointment. He reached into his jacket, pulled the note out, and showed it to her.

She took her spectacles from her pocket and set them upon her nose to read the note. They sat slightly crooked, and he had the overwhelming urge to straighten the wire rims upon her face. But he did not. After she had perused the note for a while with a thoughtful frown creasing her brow, she looked up at him and commented, "How mysterious!"

"Therefore suspect, of course," he answered. This time when he urged her to walk, she took his arm and they resumed their pace. "We can both see that. If I were of sound mind, I would no doubt have ignored it—" Above all, he did not want her to think him a fool.

She protested, "How could you? No matter how likely that it is a hoax, you would always wonder what you would have found if you kept the meeting."

"True enough." And that was indeed the reason

he had come such a distance just to follow the cryptic instructions on an unsigned note. It pleased him that she understood the draw of the thing so well. He had allowed himself to forget how well he liked being in Hero's company.

He wished his grandmother understood the draw that Hero presented him as well. But she had her heart set on his marrying Gwen. It was a marriage that would solidify a bond between their families. His grandmother and Gwen's father had planned this for so long. His bride was even to bring a specially made round table to the marriage.

Idly, he wondered what his grandmother would do if he confessed he loved another woman. If he simply told her how he felt and insisted upon having his own way in the matter of choosing a bride.

Perhaps then she would not be insisting that he marry Gwen. Not that Gwen wasn't a wonderful girl. But she was more suited to be the wife of a man who was interested in society and its goings-on, and he was never going to be that man. Even if misfortune struck Simon and Miranda and they never had a child. Even if he did become the duke. He knew it in his heart.

A woman like Hero would be relieved that he would not be duke, would not have a title and responsibilities. A woman like Hero would appreciate his need for scholarly activities. A woman like Hero might even come to love a man like him, despite his unheroic nature.

But Grandmama would be furious. Gwen's father would be apoplectic. And Gwen herself would no doubt feel that he had betrayed her in a most unforgivable way. Fortunately, his contemplation of this outcome was brought to a halt when they arrived at the bookshop.

They stopped short, staring in dismay at the shop front. Arthur checked his pocket watch again. Five minutes to four. But what did that matter? The sign on the shop door read "Closed."

Five

After a moment, Hero said hopefully, "The note says four o'clock and it is not quite yet time. Perhaps the shop will open then?"

"Perhaps." But he did not want to stand in the street, waiting to see if that was to happen. "Or perhaps Mr. Beasley, the shopkeeper, simply forgot to change the sign. He is quite elderly, after all." With only a slight hesitation, he reached forward and turned the knob to open the shop. The door was not locked.

He looked at Hero. Her mouth gaped ever so slightly in astonishment. He pushed open the door, stepped back, and said, "After you, madam."

After a bare hesitation, she entered. It was not her first time in this establishment, but for some reason nothing looked familiar. Perhaps it was the fact that she knew she should not be here. The shop held the musty odor of old books. Hero felt a shiver run down her spine as they entered the darkened premises.

"Is anyone here?" she asked nervously. "We really should not trespass this way."

"Mr. Beasley!" Arthur called out. "Mr. Beasley." The proprietor was not about. He did not come at their quiet calls. Nor when they made their voices louder.

"I have occasionally had to track Mr. Beasley down among his shelves," Arthur said. But she could see by the slump in his shoulders that he now believed himself to have been thoroughly duped.

Her heart sank. For a moment she had allowed herself to hope that Arthur's note was not a hoax. He deserved to be the one to find the original manuscript. He was an even better Arthurian scholar than Digby himself, though the Round Table Society didn't seem to realize it.

"Let's look, then. He is an older man, and I don't think he hears as well as he used to." Carefully, they searched the stacks of shelves. There were marvels and treasures that Hero would have loved to stop and browse, but no hunchbacked, white-haired shop proprietor.

At last they met each other in the middle of the shelves. "No one seems to be here. We should leave." She touched his sleeve lightly, in sympathy. "I'm sorry. I know how disappointing this must be."

Just as Arthur opened the door to the shop for her, a breeze caught a slip of paper lying upon the floor. Upon it was a very familiar scrawl. Hero felt a chill pass through her. "Arthur, look," she called out as she bent to pick up the paper.

It was another note.

She held the note out to him and they read it together. "Climb to the heights to win your treasure." It was as cryptic as the first note, and made little sense.

"What do you suppose it means?" she asked.

"Climb to the heights? Should we look for the nearest hill? In London?"

He did not answer. He did not laugh. He simply took the note from her fingers and searched it for any clue to the meaning of the phrase scrawled upon it.

While he stared unbelievingly at the piece of paper in his hand, she said softly, "It is the same handwriting, I'm sure of it."

Still without a word, he took out the other note and they compared the two side by side. He nodded. "There is no doubt, I agree." Unmistakably, the same hand had penned both notes. He said quietly, "Perhaps the note refers to the upper level of the shop? I should—"

Hero felt as if someone were staring at her from behind, but when she turned to look behind her, there was no one visible. "Mr. Beasley?" she called out.

There was no answer. She turned back to face Arthur. "I don't like this at all. The shop is closed but the door unlocked. The note left where anyone could find it."

"True, but who would look at it twice but the one it was meant for?" he asked.

She read the message again and understood what he meant. No one else would think twice about such a short, seemingly nonsensical note. "And where is Mr. Beasley?" Despite the note, despite the confirmation that both notes were from the same hand, she had a deep dread sitting like a lump in the pit of her stomach. "I don't like this," she repeated.

"I don't like it either," he agreed. "But we have

come this far; are you suggesting we abandon the quest?"

She nodded. "I think we should just go, now." Cowardice, she supposed, but it made her hope that Arthur would refuse to play the note sender's game any further.

"I did not realize there would be more games once I reached the shop." He sighed. "I am sorry I brought you into this. I will take you home immediately."

At once she felt guilty. It would not be that difficult to climb a few stairs to make certain that the manuscript was not up there, with Mr. Beasley. "Nonsense, I lost my courage for a moment, but I have gained it back. No doubt Mr. Beasley is up those very stairs, waiting for you."

He was not fooled by her show of bravado. "Then I will return shortly to deal with him, after I have seen you safely home."

That would not do. "And what if he is gone, then?"

She could see that he considered it a real possibility, but he did not let the fact sway him from his resolve. "If he is, then I will accept that I have been fortunate to have avoided being taken in by a hoax."

"But you will come back to check after you bring me home?" She could not bear it if he lost the manuscript. But this situation did not seem to bode well for that hope.

He nodded and then stopped. He turned his head. "Do you hear that?"

"What?"

"A knocking sound?"

She paused to listen, enveloped by a sense of coming doom. Hoping for a terrible moment that she would hear nothing because she wanted nothing more than to leave this shadow-strewn shop behind. But the sound was clear, even if it was faint. Reluctantly, she nodded. "Yes, I do hear it."

"Wait outside while I check to make sure that Mr. Beasley has not fallen or hurt himself in some way."

She knew well enough that he worried the shopkeeper had been hurt by the one who had left the note for them to find. "I would prefer to go with you, I think," she said.

He looked as if he might protest, his lips parting to allow him to speak. However, having learned a trick or two from her sisters, she quickly began to ascend the stairs before he could voice his agreement or disagreement with her wishes.

"It would be wiser if you waited outside," he said as they climbed the staircase.

"Then I am not being wise today," she answered sharply. She had no intention of wandering idly through the other shops on the street while he might be facing a madman alone.

They followed the sound up a flight of bare steps, through a wide door with a padlock hanging loose, and up a final rickety flight of stairs that creaked ominously under the weight of their careful feet.

"What do you think it is?" She asked the question only to break the dreadful silence that made her want to scream and run. "Perhaps," she offered, "it might be a loose shutter. Or a roof board."

As if he sensed her growing unease, he added sensibly, "Or perhaps Mr. Beasley came upstairs, fell, and now cannot get down the stairs by himself to seek help."

"Or call out?" She didn't mean to sound doubtful. "He is elderly, I know, but surely we would hear his voice calling by now?" She pictured the man lying injured upstairs, the victim of the note writer who was tormenting Arthur.

They opened the last small door and ascended three final steps, finding themselves in a small, dustless chamber lined with yet more books at the top of the shop. Mr. Beasley was nowhere to be found—injured or well—in any of the rooms.

One small octagonal window let in light. Somehow Hero was comforted to see the patch of blue sky above them. It almost seemed that their journey up the stairs had taken them hours rather than minutes, that she should see stars through the windowpane.

"There's no one here," she said with relief. And then she realized that the rhythmic sound had in fact stopped. She looked at Arthur and saw that he, too, had realized . . . and then the door behind them slammed shut.

At first she thought it an accident. She had begun to speak, expecting that Mr. Beasley had somehow sneaked past her notice. The sound of a bolt being slid home sent a cold chill up her spine.

She raced for the door. "Mr. Beasley, there's someone up here, don't lock us in." Silence.

"Mr. Beasley!" She pounded on the door. The elderly proprietor of the shop was nearly deaf. Now was not the time to be ladylike. Nor was it the time to wonder if her jailer was Mr. Beasley—or the one who had sent the notes.

Arthur joined in, and the door rattled slightly under their joint efforts. But Mr. Beasley did not appear to rescue them.

After a moment she stopped, her fists aching from the force of the blows she had been raining on the door. "Do you suppose he did not know we were here?"

"We did ascend quietly." Of course they had, they didn't know who or what they might face when they reached the top, no matter that they spoke as if whoever had locked the door must be Mr. Beasley, even now.

"What shall we do?" Hero glanced at Arthur.

"I suppose we are trapped here until he comes back to unlock the door."

So they would pretend it was Mr. Beasley, still. She could not refrain from a sharp question. "The shop usually closes at six in the evening—and often enough of late the last few years, he closes early because of ill health—it is more than possible that he might not return until tomorrow morning."

His gaze met hers, shocked at the implication. He shook his head. His voice was filled with frustration. "But that is simply not acceptable."

He scanned the room carefully, his gaze focused and intense. "There must be some way to escape. If only Beasley had conveniently left an ax up here—" He lapsed into silence, but his gaze was searching and pensive at the same time.

Hero sank back against the door. Trapped. They were trapped here. Together. Alone. In one of her sister's fairy tales, they might end up in love and married. But this was not a fairy tale. And Arthur had made it quite plain that he already had chosen the woman he wanted for his wife.

Which, she reflected, meant that she was alone with a man she loved, who did not love her, with nothing to do but wait. Could anything be worse? Only that he might know how she felt. Thank goodness she had not spoken of it last night in the library, tempted though she had been.

The silence began to wear at her nerves. "Why do you think Mr. Beasley locked us in here?" She did not dare broach the possibility that the one who had slid back the bolt had not been the bookshop proprietor.

He considered her question carefully before he asked, "Why are you so certain that it was Mr. Beasley? We saw no sign of him when we searched the shop."

This was not what she wanted to hear at all. If he, too, shared her suspicions, then they could not be entirely foolish. "He could have been hidden somewhere."

"We looked thoroughly through the shop."

They had, she could not argue. He had even laughed at her for checking inside a large cupboard. "You know he does not hear well, perhaps he did not hear us calling"—a new hope struck her—"or perhaps he just stepped out for a pint and just now returned."

"That is possible enough." Arthur paused to consider her premise. "But why not leave a sign to say so?"

She sighed. He was so particular in the details. Most of the time she loved that about him, but not now. "Perhaps he forgot—he must be nearly eighty. Perhaps it was blown away, or stolen by a prankster."

"Perhaps."

Mr. Beasley locking the door unwittingly was one thing. But it if were someone else— "Who else could it have been?" She hoped he would have some other answer than the one that was sending chills down her spine.

"A thief? Perhaps Beasley was robbed—"

"There was no sign of a struggle," Hero said calmly, though she felt anything but calm at that moment. "We saw most of the shop while we were searching for him. Do you suppose—"

She could see that he was reluctant to say aloud what she was thinking. After a moment, she said quickly, "Could it have been the one who sent you the message?"

The question hung in the air between them as they both considered its implications.

At last, slowly, reluctantly, he asked, "But what motive would—"

She said quietly, knowing that it would hurt him, because it would mean that the manuscript had been a maliciously illusive lure, "To hurt you, perhaps? To make a fool of you?"

"How?"

"Someone will have to release us, after all. We shall have to explain how we came to be here. . . ." The full implication of what she was saying began to dawn upon her, and she trailed off.

"True. I should have known it was a hoax." He put his hand to his temple and squeezed his eyes shut. "And now I've involved you in a foolish mess. I apologize, Hero. I should never have trusted—"

"Nonsense, you did what any good man on a quest would do—you followed your instincts and checked up on a lead that was slightly improbable but not outright foolish." Which was not to say that her own thoughts had not become distinctly foolish as she realized he had called her by her first name.

Apparently, he had not even realized he had done so. If he had, he would have been appalled, he would have apologized. Still, she had heard it herself. She knew it meant nothing. He was distraught. He was confounded. He had called her by her name, and it sounded so right from his lips, her heart was swelled with joy, and she dared not look at him too long for fear that he would see and understand how she felt about him.

He ruffled his hands through his hair until it was so untidy, there were wisps that actually stood straight up. She had a strong desire to run her fingers through the locks to calm them. But she did nothing of the sort. Instead, she turned her attention to the books.

She must not think about his slip of the tongue. Must not think it meant anything at all. If she was not careful, she would say something she would regret forever. She needed a distraction. "Well, I suppose we are locked in for a while, then. Why don't we see if there is a good book to read?"

She began to browse the shelves. There were large and small books, seemingly all on one subject, judging by the way Mr. Beasley had organized them. She was grateful that they had not been locked into an empty attic room—with nothing to look at but themselves. Though, of course, she wouldn't have minded looking at Arthur for hours at a time. If only she weren't afraid she might blurt out something of her feelings she believed he would rather not know.

She put on her spectacles to look more closely at the books on the shelves. Oddly enough, many had no titles visible on the spines. The other titles were not ones she recognized. She chose a few at random and began to leaf through the pages rapidly. Some were illustrated as well, she realized.

Several were even illustrated in hand-painted color, she noticed as she chose one book and opened it idly to thumb through it more carefully. And then one illustration in particular captured her attention. She gasped. "Oh, my."

The book would have slipped from her fingers to the floor if Arthur had not caught it. His expression grew horrified and then quickly blank as he, too, saw the drawing on the page that had made her fingers lose grip.

"I did not know Beasley sold books like this," he said sharply, without looking at her, as he replaced the book on the shelf.

"I didn't know there *were* books like that," Hero replied shakily. But the illustration was burned into her brain. A man and woman. Undressed. In each other's arms. She looked at the walls and their shelves of books. Were they all like this one? Curious, she took another from the shelf and flipped it open. Yes. This illustration was not in color, but the india-ink sketch left no detail to the imagination.

If Miranda had not already been quite clear and explicit about what happened between men and women when they married, this sketch might have sent her into hysterics. She snapped the book shut, remembering Miranda had promised that though it sounded awkward and painful, it wasn't. For one moment, though, she found herself doubting her normally truthful sister.

She looked up at Arthur. They were trapped in

this room together. Alone. In a roomful of books
that illustrated what a man and a woman could do
together, did they dare.

Trapped for how long? With books that made her
imagination run wild—even without opening them
for more than a second or two. She fluctuated rapidly between wanting to laugh until her breath came
in gasps and to cry until her tears were spent. Could
anyone have devised such a perfect torture for her?

She hoped none of her feelings showed upon her
face as she said numbly, "How long do you think we
might have to wait?" She lifted the book in her hand
in a wordless gesture, and then said only, "I don't
think this reading matter will keep us suitably occupied."

He was staring at her with an intensity that made
her wonder if he might not be sharing her wild imag-
inings. But that was impossible. She repeated her
question slowly, as if he were not able to hear her.
"How long do you think we will have to wait here
before Mr. Beasley comes back?"

He shook himself out of his trance and looked
around the room at the shelves of books. He shuddered. "We have to get out of here," he said, renew-
ing his assault on the door until he suddenly stopped
mid-blow and bent to examine one of the hinges.

After a moment, he said, "I think this is loose; can
you find something flat—wait." He pulled a page
cutter from his pocket and worked at the hinge.
Within a few moments he gave a cry of triumph and
a wrench of his arm. The hinge hung loose in his
hand, and the door gaped open slightly.

Six

She stood watching as he went to work on the second hinge, thankful that they would soon be free. For some reason, he had been the object of a malicious prank. But now they would soon be free to return home as if nothing untoward had occurred.

With a little more effort, Arthur had the top hinge undone as well. "Well done," she said approvingly as he pulled the door away and they hurried down the three little steps into the darkened outer room—where they were promptly stopped by the larger door.

"I cannot believe this!" he exclaimed in frustration.

Hero stared at the door, unwilling to believe what her eyes told her. Earlier, she remembered, the padlock had hung loose, but now the door was securely fastened, and apparently padlocked from the opposite side again as well.

They both stared at the second door in dismay. There were no hinges on this side at all. And, just as solid as the smaller door, it did not give way to their blows. Nor did Mr. Beasley come when they called.

Trapped again. Hero noticed that the light was

quickly fading away, and she climbed back up to the small room to see, through the octagonal window, that the sky was darkening to dusk. Juliet would be home from her drive by now. Miranda would be frantic when she realized Hero was missing.

Had she told them she would be going to this bookshop? She couldn't remember if she'd been specific. The secrecy of their quest had been foremost in her mind. What detail had she given her sister? Her maid?

She sighed, looking at the walls of books. She could hear Arthur moving things around, looking for some way to open the second door. She wanted to read, to lose herself in someone else's story and forget her own predicament. But the books she had looked at—

She moved toward the shelves, browsing only titles. Surely not all the books were like the two she had perused. Her eyes lit on an innocent-sounding title, *A Milkmaid's Life*. That might pass the time well enough until Arthur either found a way out for them or gave up, as she had.

Arthur could find nothing suitable to batter the door, to pierce it, or to pry it. His knife had worked well enough on the hinges of the smaller door, but there were none to be found on this larger door. And the smaller door itself was too unwieldy to be used as a battering ram in the confined space.

After some time spent assessing the situation, the quiet of the room intruded into his consciousness, and he looked around him in the gloomy semidarkness. He realized that Hero was no longer in the larger room with him. Somewhat apprehensively, he climbed up the three steps to the smaller room, prepared to find her weeping uncontrollably on the floor.

Instead, he found her curled up against one shelf, reading. Apparently, she had managed to find a book that was suitable for a lady to read. Her face was held close to the page to compensate for the dimming light. She started in surprise when Arthur began to speak. "Night is fast approaching. I do not think Mr. Beasley is likely to be back tonight."

She looked up at him from the book she had been reading, closing it over her finger to hold her place. In the dim light, he thought her cheeks might hold a guilty blush. "I confess I came to that conclusion some time ago."

"I have had no luck finding a way through this door as yet. I will not give up, don't worry."

"I'm sorry, Arthur." Her voice held more sympathy than he thought he deserved. After all, the note had been addressed to him, he had not needed to drag her along with him to the shop. "I'm sorry it was all a hoax."

A hoax. Yes. But a malicious one that had hurt her as well. "I'm sorry that a simple afternoon's outing has turned out so unfortunately for you. Your sister will be frantic with worry."

"Yes." She sighed, not nearly as distraught as he had expected she might be. "I will have a great deal of explaining to do tomorrow, I suppose."

"Tomorrow?" He was confused for a moment.

She looked up at him, as if surprised that he did not understand her. "I am afraid we are destined to spend the night here, unless Mr. Beasley decides to return tonight." Her lips curved into a smile. "No doubt he is now at his dinner."

Spend the night? Alone with Hero? It was impossible. Could anyone have devised a torture more horrible? Arthur wanted to groan at the thought. He wished fruitlessly that he had come alone. A night on a wooden floor trapped here would have served him right for believing in a foolish myth. However was he to see to Hero's comfort, never mind her modesty?

But what choice did he have? He had been the fool to get her trapped up here with him among the finest books in the world—most on the subject of lovemaking. Illustrations and all. "I suppose you are right to be practical, but I will hope to get us free before we come to that extreme."

She shrugged. "I don't mind. It's almost an adventure, don't you think?"

"An adventure?" He looked at her in surprise. He would not have imagined that Hero's cheeks would flush, nor that her eyes would sparkle at such an "adventure." Perhaps the shock of their predicament had addled her wits? Or perhaps this Miss Fenster was not quite as different from her sisters as he had supposed.

He watched her, standing demurely in the attic room, her eyes huge as she surveyed the rows and rows of books. A waning ray of light from the small window had caught in her hair, so that it glinted with coppery highlights.

Demure or not, she did not seem horrified by the type of books in the room, and the shock that had caused her fingers to lose their grip had passed so quickly, he had to wonder whether it was the book itself or simply the unexpected illustration that had made her grip suddenly nerveless.

She had not fainted at the illustrations in the book after all. She had even glanced at yet another of the erotic books quiet Mr. Beasley had collected through the years before she realized the true nature of the book.

From nowhere came the quite wicked thought—perhaps, if he asked, she would welcome a kiss from him. After all, if Mr. Beasley was not the most discreet man in London, the gossips would say that they had done more than share a kiss this night. Could it hurt if they did kiss—just once?

"Are you hungry?" she asked.

The question brought him back to his senses immediately. How dare he think of kissing her when he could not even meet her most basic needs. "I'm afraid we must remain unfed tonight."

"Go to bed without our supper for our mistake, you mean?" She smiled, and he had the distinct impression that she had seen and understood his impulse to kiss her. But that, he reassured himself, was his imagination.

He did not return her smile. "We are not children. But my actions were foolish enough that I should be considered no better than a green boy, I admit."

Hero could see Arthur was struggling with his guilt over inviting her along on what had promised to be a mysterious yet simple errand. For once, however, she could live up to her name. "Well, you should be glad you asked me along, then. For I have supplies for our adventure."

"Supplies?" His expression was one of outright disbelief. And then, more quietly, "Adventure?"

"Yes. Adventure," she insisted. She wanted to think of this as an adventure. And she was determined to do so. An adventure in an attic full of books she dared not read. With a man she dared not approach, for fear he would see in her eyes the feelings she had kept hidden for so very long.

"And supplies." She fished through her pockets, pulling items out and making a neat pile in front of her on a makeshift tablecloth. She stepped back. "See?" she asked with a flourish. For once, she felt enterprising. Before her lay a treasure trove of food to serve as their evening meal: several wrapped biscuits and a handful of dried apples.

Arthur had stopped his pacing at once when he saw that she had laid everything out neatly on a clean handkerchief. "Wherever did you get all that?"

"With so many younger sisters, one learns to travel prepared," she laughed. The servants hated the task of cleaning her pockets, she knew, because of the crumbs. However, it had saved her temper many a time when she could pull out a biscuit or an apple to soothe a tired, hungry child. And now she had managed to impress Arthur.

"You Fenster ladies never cease to amaze me," he said in wonderment, looking at the few trifles as if they represented the greatest feast he had ever seen.

Looking at her makeshift dinner table, she realized that something was still missing. "Well, I have provided food. Unfortunately, I cannot provide anything to drink."

His eyes lit up, and he smiled unreservedly for the first time since they had begun this adventure. "I can, however."

"Don't we make a resourceful pair?" she could

not help but ask, although she wanted to call the words back as soon as they were spoken.

"We do," he agreed, pulling a flask from his coat pocket. He raised the flask in a toast to her and went to take a sip. He halted the flask at his lips and glanced at it, a look of dismay on his features. "I'm afraid I can only offer to share with you in the most primitive fashion," he said apologetically. "As I do not have any cups on me."

Hero felt a flash of daring she quickly suppressed. A flask meant whiskey or brandy. Dare she? "I'm not thirsty. You go ahead."

He lowered the flask and said quite firmly, "No. I could not if you do not."

Well, who could argue with that logic? She must take a sip, if only for his sake. "Then I shall be honored to share your flask, Mr. Watterly."

He sat across from her. Between them, the meager meal on its festive tablecloth looked even less impressive. He set the flask beside the biscuits. She appraised everything as it was laid out and wanted to laugh at first, and then to cry. Her skills as a hostess were sadly lacking. And yet she did not care that the meal was small. Why on earth did such a thing seem so special? She knew the answer: because she was sharing it with Arthur.

They bowed their heads briefly and then she played the lady, serving him two of the biscuits and most of the dried apples. She did not know what to do about the flask, so she left it alone.

"You haven't given yourself enough food," Arthur protested.

She would have argued that he had been the one to pry the door open, and he had been the one to try to open the larger door, so he should get the lion's share of the food. She knew, however, that he would not accept that logic. "I am not very hungry," she lied.

"Nor am I, then," he said gallantly. "Why don't we save some for our breakfast tomorrow?" Quickly, he wrapped a biscuit and half of his dried apples in a clean handkerchief.

"Do you think . . ." She didn't dare complete the thought. Would they be rescued tomorrow? She almost didn't want to know that it wasn't a surety.

He seemed to read her mind, for he lifted the flask in a salute and said, "A toast! To a fine hostess who knows how to set a table without a raft of servants to help her." He held out the flask toward her and she reached out, took it, and sipped quickly, before she could lose her nerve.

There was no sting of alcohol. Definitely not whiskey, not brandy. Yet it was not water, either. The taste was familiar and yet not quite.

She handed it back to him and watched as he took a sip for himself. "What is that?"

"It is a concoction that Katherine, your sisters' governess, gave me the recipe for after I ate those poisoned mushrooms. As I recall, it is tea strongly steeped with currants, lemons, rosemary and honey."

"I had thought it might be whiskey or brandy," she confessed, wondering if he would be shocked.

He was not. Instead, he grimaced, as if he had done something wrong by not supplying her with spirits. "I'm sorry, but I have nothing stronger than this mixture. I suppose most men carry such things in their flasks. But I find this settles my nerves, soothes my throat, and quenches my thirst much more satisfactorily."

"It is refreshing. I think I shall get the recipe from Katherine for myself." The governess had been a village herbal healer before taking up her post. Perhaps she might even have some potion to calm a wayward heart as well.

For such a small meal, it did seem to take forever to consume. They told stories, considered the expression that Mr. Beasley would wear when he opened the door in the morning to find them there, and spoke with endless disdain of the prankster who had written the notes to Arthur and led him on the hunt for the manuscript of *Le Morte d'Arthur.* They did not discuss, not even once, how they would explain things to Simon and Miranda.

At last, Arthur stood, brushing crumbs lightly from his clothing and bowing graciously to Hero. "I must thank you for an enjoyable dinner, Miss Fenster. I beg your leave to wish you a good night before I retire."

She was confused. "Retire?"

He indicated the other room that they had come through to reach this tiny attic room. "I think it would be best if I slept in there and you in here—for propriety's sake." He looked at the door he had taken off its hinges. "I can replace that—"

"Don't be silly. It is much too late, and getting much too dark for such work." In fact, she could see only a silhouette in the dark where she knew Arthur to be.

"I would not feel comfortable treating you with such disrespect—"

She dismissed his objection. "I shall be fine. I trust

you are a gentleman." Most definitely she did not want to confess her true fear—she was deathly afraid of sleeping alone in this dark, strange place. The fact that she had so many sisters had always ensured that she slept with at least one other person each night. Sometimes, during thunderstorms when the lightning was fierce, they had all six curled up in bed together. She could not admit that humiliating fact to Arthur, however.

He stood quietly for a very long time, and then he said firmly, "I think it would be wiser for me to be in the next room."

She wished suddenly that she could see his face. His tone held an odd note that she could not decipher without looking at his expression. Perhaps, she told herself, to suppress further objections, he was thinking of how he might explain things to Gwen when next he saw her. "As you wish."

"Very well, then," he said. "I shall bid you good night." He left the little room. Hero realized that it was absurd for her to feel alone when he was just a few steps away. She fought her fear valiantly. She arranged her cloak as comfortably as possible and leaned herself against one of the bookshelves for support.

Her position was not the most comfortable she could find, but she dared not lay flat on the floor; she felt too vulnerable. Vulnerable to what, she could not say. She trusted Arthur. It was just that the dark felt like a real thing as it fell. An entity that could threaten her.

She scoffed at her own fears, listened to Arthur's movements in the other room for confirmation that he was still there, and tried to remind herself that she was an intrepid adventurer who could withstand this tiny hardship.

If only there were enough light, she could read more of *The Milkmaid's Tale* to take her mind off her circumstances. Arthur had said nothing to her about the book; she hoped he thought it as innocent a tale as she had when she first began reading it. Did milkmaids truly have gentlemen who admired them so? She blushed, remembering the escapades of the simple dairy girl. Of course, she was a simple, *beautiful* dairy girl.

Thinking of how it would feel to have Arthur lying beside her in the dark, to have his arms around her. To have him kiss her as the milkmaid's admirer had kissed the milkmaid—Hero blushed to think that those kisses had not just been on the mouth . . . But she stopped the direction of those thoughts, which made it impossible to sleep. She closed her eyes and tried to count sheep.

That, of course, became difficult when the silent darkness settled around her like a cloak and the scurry of mice unsettled her. She jumped each time she heard a rustle, or a squeak, real or imagined. Unfortunately, her imagination was quite lively, and she did not seem to be able to keep still.

Once, a mouse ran over her foot and she screamed. It was only a little scream, but she heard Arthur stir next door, and the next minute heard his tread on the stairs. "Hero? Is something wrong?"

"A mouse just ran over my foot, I am fine." She tried to sound brave, but her efforts sounded pitiful in her own ears.

He moved across the floor steadily, quietly. She realized he had removed his boots. To her astonishment, he settled himself beside her. "Would it help if I hold you and guard you against the mice?" Her heart squeezed with a regret so sharp, she had not realized how very much she had come to care for him. His offer was a gesture she wished with all her heart had been elicited by more than his impatience with her squeamishness.

For a moment, she resisted. "I am fine, truly. I was only startled."

"Are you certain?" He leaned in close to her.

"Yes."

He moved away, and without thinking she reached for his arm to pull him back. She had felt so safe with him warm against her.

He sighed and settled back against her. "You have been brave enough tonight, Hero. Let me fight the mice for you."

"And the spiders?" She asked it only to lighten the humiliation she felt at exposing her cowardice.

He laughed. "Come here," he said. "And the spiders. They will not bother the two of us if we huddle together."

She came willingly enough into his arms. For a moment she wondered if he truly thought she would believe his comforting yet untrue statement. She hoped he did not honestly think her such a lackwit.

He made her a little bed with his jacket and her cloak. But in the end, she was not able to settle until he had snuggled her tightly in his arms in assurance. "No mice will get up your skirts tonight, I promise. Go to sleep, Miss Fenster."

Not that she believed he could keep the promise—not unless he himself . . . but, no, that thought was unworthy. Which did not stop it from circulating through her brain as she softened and slept beside him, warm and comforted in his embrace.

Seven

Arthur himself did not sleep so easily. But it seemed a small price to pay for such a gift as Hero Fenster in his arms, no matter how chastely. She felt as he had always imagined she would. Warm and real. His.

But she was not his. Not truly. Not yet. He marveled that fate had given him the opportunity to hold her as he had wished to, and he wondered if he owed cowardice or heroism to his ability to defy temptation to do more. She did not deserve to be treated with disrespect. He could not consider himself honorable if he used their circumstances to take advantage of her.

As he lay sleepless, contemplating the future, he realized that he had little choice but to marry her. Whoever let them out of the attic the next day—if anyone did, which was not a thought he wanted to examine just then—would be privy to scandalous knowledge.

His grandmother would be devastated. Gwen . . . Perhaps she would not mind as much as his grandmother, or her own father. She had always been a social creature. Everything he had heard indicated she was enjoying her entrée into society and all that

London had to offer one of her temperament. His grandmother had written him weekly of the beaus Gwen had gathering at her feet.

He had read the letters with a totally inappropriate lift in his spirits. He knew that Grandmama hoped that would bring Arthur to the point of a formal declaration, but it had instead made him hope that he would escape from his family obligation to marry Gwen without having to make his own wishes take precedence over so many others.

That did not seem to be a possibility now.

But what about Hero's wishes? Had she hoped Gabriel Digby would speak soon? She had treated the man with clear affection. It was more than possible she had been dreaming of a life with Digby. He tightened his hold on her until she protested, and then loosened his arms.

No matter the circumstances, would even Gabriel Digby be willing to give her his name if this night became fodder for the gossips? As much as Arthur hated to admit it, he knew that was a possibility. And not one he wanted to allow.

The only question remaining to be answered was what did Hero want? The answer was obvious to him when he compared himself to Digby. Arthur was the better scholar, though not by a great deal. Digby, however, was the better material for husband, for father, for man of the world. How could he doubt which man she would choose if given the chance?

What a mess he had made of her life with his simple request that she accompany him on this misbegotten quest. It would be his responsibility to straighten it out as well.

He bent his head against hers and inhaled the

pleasant scent of rosemary from her hair. So the question for him would come down to whether he was selfish enough to keep Hero for himself, or let her go to Digby with a blot on her reputation.

Oddly enough, the answer seemed heavily weighted to one side, no matter how he played with the options. He closed his eyes, knowing which way he would decide without question. And wondering if Hero would be the one to pay the price for his arrogance.

He wanted her, there was not even the tiniest doubt in his mind when he allowed himself to contemplate the matter. So he was to be selfish. But what did he owe to Hero if he followed his own desires this once? She should not be forced to endure marriage to a man who was a pale shadow of Gabriel Digby.

He thought about his foolish quest. It was time to give up such things. It was time for him to do as his grandmother had been asking him to do for so long. He would have to find some way to finally make his mark in the world. To live up to his namesake and his legend. It was the least he could do for Hero, when he was taking the biggest decision of all away from her.

He slept at last, to dream of the Garden of Eden. Hero was Eve, but Adam's face was obscured by mists.

The morning light streaming in from the little window woke Hero. She enjoyed the feel of being cradled against Arthur. He seemed more slight of build at a distance, but up close he was warm and solid.

She could feel the muscles in his arms flex as he held her safely against him.

She lingered in that timeless place between sleep and waking, not moving. Part of her wished she could stay in such a state forever. She sprang fully alert, however, when he shifted and she knew he was already awake.

She wanted to do as the milkmaid might have—turned lazily, with her head still resting in the crook of his arm, to look up at him. But she was not that bold. Instead, she pulled away from his warmth, hiding her reluctance as best she could as she tidied her hair and her clothing with a flurry of little pats.

"Good morning," she said. And then, in the awkwardness of the moment, added, "I don't quite know the proper morning greeting in a situation like this."

"Good morning is quite proper, I expect. Although I know nothing of such things either." His return glance was warm, but he made no move to embrace her, so she decided it was just her imagination at work again. "Perhaps in this situation we should make our own rules."

Again, she sensed that there was some deeper meaning beyond the surface of his comments. Uncomfortable with the serious tone he was introducing into the morning, she said lightly, "Well, then, good morning, Mr. Watterly. I trust you slept well."

"As well as can be expected in the circumstances, Miss Fenster," he replied with a smile.

She was inordinately relieved to have the tension of the moment dissipated and was most reluctant to ask her next question. "I don't suppose you've heard Mr. Beasley moving around downstairs yet?"

"No, I've heard no sounds at all from the shop,

although the street is abustle." He stood and began tidying himself, pulling his pocket watch from his vest as he spoke. "He should be arriving soon, I expect."

Where last night had seemed a romantic adventure, this morning their predicament seemed more serious. She went to the open doorway to study the one that had been so firmly padlocked. "Do you suppose he unlocks these doors first thing?"

He contemplated her question for a moment before answering, "I certainly hope so. We cannot stay here forever."

The thought had never occurred to her, for some reason. "We certainly cannot!" If Mr. Beasley took days to open this door, it would be too late for her, and for Arthur. They would die from dehydration even before they starved to death.

Even as she had the awful thought, her stomach began to grumble with hunger. She glanced at him in embarrassment, but either he had not heard or he was too much a gentleman to comment upon the complaint of her unmannerly midsection.

But no, he had heard. For he said, "Perhaps we should have some breakfast while we wait for him?" He unwrapped the biscuit and apples he had put aside last night.

"You take it," she said quickly. "I am not hungry."

He shook his head. "We are in this predicament together, Miss Fenster. There is no help for it but that we shall breakfast together." Without further words, he snapped the biscuit in two and handed her half, along with several dried apples.

"Thank you." Despite her hunger, she nibbled at the food without much enthusiasm as she stood staring at the locked door, wondering how long they would have to wait for rescue.

Nervously, she reassured herself, "He no doubt has a routine for the shop. I expect we should make ourselves as presentable as possible. I fear we'll give the man quite a shock when he finds us here."

"I expect he will survive us. We are quiet enough sorts. I certainly have no intention of jumping out and howling like a ghost. Have you?"

"No. Although I confess to having played such pranks as a child, I have long since put them away." She smiled at the thought, remembering how she and her sisters had loved to frighten one another into screams, which quickly dissolved into fits of giggles, as children.

"I myself intend to wait patiently until I hear the tread on the stairs, then calmly stand and wait for the door to be unlocked."

The room seemed so small today, where yesterday it had only been intimate. Hero began to pace. Twenty paces lengthwise, ten paces crosswise. She must simply refuse to believe they would not be rescued. "If he comes to open the attic door today."

He must have heard the panic in her voice, for he took her shoulders and said firmly, "We will get out of here today no matter what."

She did want to believe him. But— "How? If—"

He said confidently, "I will rip a board from the shelves and batter the door down if I must."

"Can you do that?" She recognized, only after she spoke, however, that her astonished tone was far from a compliment to his abilities.

He laughed abashedly, as if he, too, found the

thought incredible. "I know I'm not your typical warrior, but I think I could manage it."

"How long should we wait?"

"An hour or two, perhaps? No more. I simply hate to be so destructive if it is not necessary."

An hour or two. The scene back home, where Miranda and Juliet, and even calm and lordly Simon would be frantic with worry. She needed to get home, to let them know she had not been abducted. Had not been hurt.

Nervously, she began to pace. And then a possibility occurred to her. "Mr. Beasley should be in the shop by now, wouldn't you say? Perhaps he has already come and gone and we are free and don't even know it?"

He looked dubious. "I have heard nothing on the stairs."

"Still, it does not hurt to try," she said, hurrying down the little steps and into the other room. He followed somewhat reluctantly.

Quickly, they tried the door, but it was quite solidly locked and did not even rattle in its frame when Arthur pounded upon it. No treads sounded up the stairs when they called for Mr. Beasley, even though they did not give up until their voices were hoarse and their fists numb from pounding.

At last, exhausted, they turned and leaned their backs against the door, catching their breaths side by side. Arthur said, "We are simply going to have to wait a bit longer. This does us no good at all."

"I'm sorry. Suddenly, all I could think of was how frantic everyone must be at home, to have us both missing at once."

Another worry occurred to her. "Do you believe

Mr. Beasley will be discreet? About the two of us being here all night?"

He did not meet her eyes. "I suppose we will know soon enough."

She began to pace nervously as the consequences of this night began to become even more real to her. "I don't want Simon to find out. He is quite a stickler for such matters, you know."

"I'm certain he will understand," Arthur said quietly.

"Perhaps, but it would be better if he did not know. He might even"—she laughed nervously— "expect us to marry if he were to find out."

Arthur smiled in response. "What? Just because we spent the night together—alone."

"I realize that such a priggish attitude is absurd to the two of us. But I fear it is not to Simon. In fact"—she lowered her voice as she continued—"I know that is the only reason he married Miranda— even though he loved her quite desperately, of course."

He seemed quite unshocked by the news. "I had heard the rumors, but I did not want to credit them as the truth. It seemed none of my business. They are, after all, quite well suited to each other."

"Exactly. Which is why their misadventure did not become a disaster." She dared not pause for breath, for fear that he would argue that they were indeed well suited—or for fear that he would not. So she continued, "We must swear Mr. Beasley to silence and we must agree to it ourselves."

"Do you believe that we can trust him with such a scandalous secret?"

"We must." She paced in agitation. "My family

would be quite distressed if they knew the truth." She tried to make light of the potential for disaster. The last thing she wanted for him to feel was a sense of obligation to her for this predicament. "Could you imagine—Juliet would not be pleased if my misadventure became known and resulted in her number of suitors being so drastically reduced."

"Mr. Digby would be distressed as well."

Digby. "But he will know nothing if we do not tell him. Our family is another matter. They well know we were not at home as we should have been last night."

Abruptly, Arthur grew grim. "Don't worry about your reputation—or Juliet's suitors." Then he added, "No one will know of this. I will pay what I must to make certain of that."

"And Mr. Beasley—"

"Mr. Beasley will have no choice," he said with a rather grim expression. "Especially since we can tell of this interesting collection he has up in his attic. Such news would likely reduce his clientele quite sharply."

"Do you suppose he would get in trouble?" Hero looked at the books, and blushed at the thought of what she had seen. Of what she had read in *The Milkmaid's Tale*. Perhaps she should have read more of that book, scandalous though it was, rather than bring up the subject of how to deal with those who might question them.

He shook his head firmly. "No. He would simply find that the young ladies who visited his shop no longer were allowed to by their parents. But perhaps he would gain some clients as well."

"Yes, it would be quite awful if—do you think Miss

Delagrace would be too upset with you?" She wondered if she had been too forward, the way he looked so forbiddingly at her at the mention of Gwen Delagrace's name. It was not yet a formal engagement, but the gossip had them on the verge. Perhaps she had overstepped by mentioning it aloud?

His answer struck her like a blow. "No more than Mr. Digby would be with you, I imagine."

Hero realized that she had made a decision sometime in the night regarding Gabriel Digby. He was not the man for her. Nevertheless, she felt obliged to defend his character. "Mr. Digby is a sensible man. He would believe me when I told him that we were as safe together as brother and sister."

He grimaced. "Miss Delagrace would no doubt require some gift to help her recover from her pique. But her father and my grandmother are quite set upon the match, and I do not think they would let her cut me dead." He seemed about to add something to that sentiment, but then he did not.

Hero quashed her hope that he would tell her that he no longer wanted to marry Gwen Delagrace, that he wanted to marry her instead. "That is well, then. But it would be best, still, if we could sneak home and not have it remarked upon."

He looked at her in astonishment. "Do you think your family will not know you have gone?"

She answered miserably, "No. I expect they are scouring all the bookshops in London right now to find me. But once I explain the whole situation, Miranda will understand that it must be handled discreetly."

"Are you certain?"

"Yes, I know my sister. She would not want to have

me gossiped about for something I had no control over, especially considering what happened to her."

"So you will prefer Digby not know ever, then?" She could not tell if he disapproved of such a plan or not.

"No. I will tell him." Hero bowed her head to hide her expression. If fate were truly kind, Digby would rail at her and refuse to speak to her ever again. But no doubt he would believe every word she said and forgive her without question—except for asking her to marry him, of course. And then she would be in a pickle. How could she justify refusing to marry a man who showed such faith in her as that? She didn't know the answer, only that she would refuse him, sensible or not.

"That is brave of you. He could choose to believe you lied. That something had happened between us." Wickedly, she wished that she *did* have something to regret from this night alone with Arthur. That he had opened one of those books and they had spent the night wantonly trying each and every illustration's pose. She blushed at the thought, the india-ink images so clear in her brain suddenly superimposed with her face—and Arthur's as well.

Stop it! She ordered herself. "Digby will believe me. He is just that kind of man." What had put such thoughts in her head? She was no beauteous milkmaid with gentlemen in pursuit. On the other hand, she had spent the night in his arms. Of course, she could dismiss it as a kindness . . . except . . . she had felt something more and she had thought he had also felt it.

Apparently, Arthur had no such thoughts, however, because he said quietly, "Digby is the right man for you, then. He will make you happy, I have no doubt."

"No doubt at all?" Did he feel nothing, then? She tried to examine his expression discreetly.

"Why? Have you? He is a paragon, is he not?" She was wrong, she realized. He was not unaffected by the books surrounding them. His expression was odd. His face was ever so close to hers as he spoke, and she could see something behind his eyes. Something puzzling. Something that stole her breath. Even as he said the words, practically pushing her into Digby's arms with each one, Arthur leaned forward and kissed her.

As naturally as taking a breath, she responded to his kiss and lost herself in the feel of his lips pressing warm against hers, their spectacles clicking gently together. At her response, his arms came around her to hold her tight to him, and his mouth slanted hard upon hers, demanding a further response, which she gladly gave.

After a frenzied moment, their spectacles clicking together furiously, he pulled away, tearing her spectacles from her face so that she couldn't see him properly, only a blurry face she knew was Arthur's. She reached to retrieve the pair of eyeglasses from his fingers where they dangled.

His hand closed over hers, squeezing her fingers. "I shouldn't have done that," he said on a rush of breath.

"No," she agreed shakily, though inside herself she acknowledged that she had been wanting him to do just that for years. "You shouldn't have."

There was a glint of recklessness in his gaze. "I want to do it again." He took off his own spectacles and tucked them in his vest pocket. "Properly, this time."

Hero dropped her own pair into her pocket with trembling hands. "Then do." She closed her eyes, sure that she would explode with tension if she watched his face draw nearer, anticipating the kiss.

"Are you certain you will not regret it?" he whispered, and she sensed he spoke of more than a simple kiss.

"I'm certain," she answered, though she was anything but.

"I will be gentle this time, I promise," he whispered.

She smiled, preparing herself for a gentle kiss. But it never came, because the sound of boots pounding up the stairs broke them apart in guilty haste.

Eight

Arthur stood fighting the rush of blood in his veins. One moment before, he was reacting to the stir of desire, and now danger had triggered an even more violent urge. He pushed Hero behind him and struggled to reclaim his spectacles and put them in place, so that he would be able to see what he was up against. The strong footsteps pounding up the stairs did not suggest the elderly, hesitant Mr. Beasley.

The lock rattled as someone began to undo it from the other side, and he checked the room for a weapon. There were no good selections, so he chose a particularly hefty, sturdily bound book and held it at the ready as the door swung open.

To his astonishment, the man who stood in the door frame was none other than his cousin, the Duke of Kerstone, Simon Watterly. He set the book down and moved aside so that Simon could see Hero was safe. Unfortunately, he could do nothing about the fact that she looked like a woman who had been quite thoroughly kissed not long before. In some primitive way it even pleased him.

"Arthur." His cousin gazed at him with a puzzlement that mirrored his own.

"Simon." He wondered if there was anyone in

London he wished less had been the one to find them in this delicate predicament.

The duke's eyes focused on Hero, and then he glanced around the room as if he expected to find another person with them. At last he gazed back to Arthur and asked brusquely, "What are you doing here?"

"We were trapped here overnight. Someone locked us in—" He broke off, suddenly wondering why Simon had searched for them here. "How did you know—"

"I received a note." He looked between Hero and Arthur again for a moment, his brow creased by a frown. "Is Gabriel Digby not here, then?"

"Digby?" Arthur did not understand. What did Digby have to do with this?

Impatient with the confusion in the room, his as well as theirs, the duke snapped, "Yes, Digby. I received a note saying that I would find Hero here with Gabriel Digby. Instead, I find you and no Gabriel Digby at all. What is going on?"

"Someone sent you a note saying I would be found here with Mr. Digby?" Hero interrupted. "I don't know why that would be. I have not seen Mr. Digby since the day before yesterday." She moved slightly farther from Arthur as she spoke, putting even more distance between them than she had when Simon came into the room. "Arthur and I came to search out a book and were locked in."

"Overnight?" Simon was barking out questions now, barely waiting for an answer, a habit left over from his army days.

"We were locked in—" Hero began an explanation.

Simon interrupted with another question. "How did that happen?"

"I had hoped to pick up a book here." Arthur wondered what he could say to ease his cousin's wrath. He had been foolish to ask Hero to accompany him. He did not want her to be in trouble with Simon for agreeing.

"And I wanted to browse, of course. When do I not want to visit a bookshop?" Hero laughed just a trifle nervously, but Simon's eyes were sharp upon her.

"And Mr. Beasley?"

"He must have locked us in, not realizing that we were up here."

"And what were you doing up here?"

"Looking for Mr. Beasley, as it happened. We looked all over the shop for him and could not find him, and then we heard a banging sound from above and we thought it might be him . . ." Hero's words trailed away as she seemed to become aware of her own nervousness and exactly how intensely Simon was assessing them both.

"Mr. Beasley is at home with the grippe," Simon said in clipped tones. "I saw him when I had to get the keys to come into the shop. He was in no condition to have climbed these stairs to lock you in, I assure you."

Arthur realized, with a sudden start, that there now could be no doubt that it was not Mr. Beasley who locked them in the attic. No, it had to have been the note sender. But why? What could possibly be gained. . . .

Simon looked at the pair of them with fury. "Do you know how frantic Miranda has been?"

As if she had been prodded by his statement, Hero hurried through the door, saying, "We can discuss all this later, Simon. I must see her without delay so that she can see with her own eyes that we are fine."

Arthur stopped the supposition tumbling through his mind for a moment, aware that he needed to deal with Simon at once, before his cousin expired of apoplexy.

He patted his cousin's shoulder stiffly. "Never fear, old man, you are not undone. I will make it right with her." Simon did not look particularly convinced of the truth of that statement. And who could blame him? After all, Arthur had compromised Hero, and his cousin was more than aware of the fact. He knew he had to reassure him immediately. "All will be well, Simon. I will do what is necessary."

"You will?" Simon seemed to relax as he nodded once firmly. "I would never have doubted it, cousin."

The words were kindly meant, although Arthur wondered how true they really were. But he could not blame the man. He would have felt the same if he had found Hero here with Digby.

And why had the note suggested that she would be here with him? It was a puzzle that he would have to solve. But not until he had set things right by marrying Hero.

His grandmother would not be pleased.

Hero felt as if she had stumbled into a nightmare. Could there have been any worse savior for them than Simon himself? She loved her sister's husband dearly. He had been nothing but kind to her. But his notion of how to fix this mess diverged wildly from hers.

Miranda had been overjoyed to see her alive and well, but no one had even given Hero a chance to change into clean clothes and wash up before the decision was made. She and Arthur were to marry.

She protested, but the duke was adamant.

She reminded him that they had been lured to the attic and locked in. But he did not count that fact as important. No, he still insisted she marry Arthur. No matter that they had been locked in the attic overnight and it had been done deliberately.

Simon had shown them the note he received. The handwriting matched that of the two notes sent to Arthur. No one could argue that it was deliberate. Yet Simon still urged marriage as the answer. And Arthur did not argue.

Hero wanted to cry. She wanted to stamp her feet in a temper tantrum worthy of her youngest sister, Kate. But her fate and Arthur's hung in the balance of making Simon understand why he was wrong. Now that they knew for certain it had not been poor Mr. Beasley who had locked them in, there was little doubt who had arranged for it. But why? What game was this note sender playing that the play should rest upon the marriage of Hero Fenster and Arthur Watterly?

She would not be used as a pawn in so vile a way. She felt the innate stubbornness that she had inherited from her father take hold of her. She looked her brother-in-law and her sister full in the eye, one after the other. "This is absurd. You cannot think to force me to marry a man because we were tricked into an unfortunate circumstance."

She took a breath. She was making the argument of her life; she could not afford to be less than compelling. "No one will know of this incident, and we can assure you that there is no reason for any hasty decision upon the subject of marriage." She looked at Arthur and felt herself blush hotly from the neck up as she remembered the kiss.

She might as well have not even spoken. Simon was adamant in his reply. "That argument is no more persuasive than it ever was." He glanced at Miranda as he spoke, and Hero saw an exchange of understanding pass between them. "You must marry."

"To build a marriage on something so flimsy is more than foolish, it is heartless."

"Is it so flimsy, then?" He stared at her, but she had a feeling his gaze was somewhere in the past. And then he snapped back to the present and his eyes bored into hers. "I don't understand why you even argue over the matter. You and Arthur get along well enough."

"Get along well enough!" What an argument. "Is that what a marriage should be?"

He sighed. "All I meant was that you both seem to enjoy puzzling around dusty bookstores and reading the writing of men long dead. I've seen marriages based on less do well."

For a moment, though she had been relieved to arrive home safely, Hero wanted to return to the bookshop. It might have been preferable to dry up into dusty, neglected mummies than be foisted upon a man who had told her not that long ago that she should marry someone else. "But, we—we were innocent. It was a mistake."

Or if not a mistake, then certainly a misunderstanding. Arthur did not want to marry her, no matter what he said now. His motive was her reputation. And who would speak of it, really? Arthur? Mr. Beasley? Certain not Simon, Miranda, or Hero. No, he was simply being chivalrous when there was absolutely no need to be.

She ignored the tiny part of her that wanted to agree. What woman in her right mind would wish for a husband who married her out of a misguided sense of honor? She could only remember how certain Arthur had been that Digby was the right husband for her. Those words were not the words of a man who wanted to be her husband himself.

Kiss or no, he had been clearly disinclined toward marriage. It was only the influence of those dratted books that had made him so bold. She could not hold him to a lifetime of marriage over one kiss. She would not.

"You have spent the night alone with a gentleman, Hero. It does not matter what transpired between you." The duke's eyes swept over her disarranged hair, Arthur's loosened collar, and his lips tightened. "You will marry."

Arthur's eyes held only sadness and regret when he said firmly, "We will do what is right, Simon."

"No—" Hero protested. *What is right.* Not what he wished to do. What he must do. She hated to be thought of as an obligation to be met satisfactorily.

Simon, who was usually quite the perfect brother-in-law and duke, was unfortunately more interested in what Arthur had to say about duty than what Hero had to say about common sense. He nodded approvingly at his cousin. "I know you will, Arthur." He hesitated briefly, and then asked quietly, "Your arrangement with Miss Delagrace . . . was that ever . . . confirmed?"

"No—it was an understanding between my grandmother and hers." Arthur shook his head. She wished she could tell from his voice or his expression if he was heartbroken not to be marrying Gwen Delagrace, but it was impossible to say. "I know Grandmama had hoped that I would come up to snuff this year, but I have made no formal request for Miss Delagrace's hand, so there is no impediment to an immediate marriage between Miss Fenster and myself."

Simon nodded and took Miranda's hand. They both looked to Hero as he said, "Good, I will secure the license immediately, and we will hold the ceremony in a week's time."

"I will not agree."

"I think you will see reason by the time the ceremony arrives," he said blandly.

"I think it will cause exactly the scandal you wish to avoid when I do not appear at my own wedding," she retorted, turning on her heel and exiting without another word.

For the next few days Hero continued to try to change the duke's mind on the subject of marriage. She refused to cooperate with fittings and choices for flowers and seating for guests. No matter that she made no decisions, everything was planned and decided around her as if she were a mere stone to be shifted about.

It was almost a relief when it was time for the meeting of the Round Table Society. She and Arthur—with the fair Juliet for a chaperone, much to her distress since she found the idea of an evening devoted to Arthurian discussion intensely boring—left in the carriage.

As she sat across from Arthur, she could feel his worry. In sympathy, she said, "No one knew you hoped to have something to present tonight."

"That is some consolation," he agreed. And then he added, "Of course, I will be able to announce that I am to be married."

She felt a quick rush of dismay. "Must you?"

"I cannot see the reason to put it off."

"Why do you not believe I will refuse to speak vows with you?"

Juliet interjected, "Because, Hero, you have always done what others expected of you. Why should we think this temper will last, never mind that it will cause you to embarrass your entire family by standing up your groom."

She looked at Arthur. "Can you tell me this is what you want? Not out of duty, but because it is best for both of us?"

He looked at her miserably. "It is the right thing, Hero. I know it. We will come to accept it. I promise to make you proud to call me husband, even if I cannot do it tonight."

His quiet worry about the evening finally reached through to her. Why was she arguing the matter here, when he had other issues on his mind? Her own troubles paled in comparison to his. Not only was he in the same predicament as she, he also had to face the society without the manuscript he had hoped to have in his possession.

"I'm sorry. I know this isn't the right time for this discussion." However, as they climbed out of the carriage, she stopped him with a hand upon his arm.

"Please, do not make any announcement about us. I still hope to make Simon see reason."

Before he could answer, Arthur Digby greeted them. "Watterly, Miss Fenster. So good to see you."

"And you, Digby," Arthur said in an utterly unconvincing manner as he led Hero into the meeting room for the first time.

The members crowded about an inadequate round table. Some eyes grew larger with shock to see Hero—a woman—invade their sanctum. But more had voted to allow her to join. She was glad that Digby had helped her with the scholarly paper required to meet membership. This looked like an exacting crowd. She hoped that they saw clearly that Arthur would make a good leader for the group. He was more devoted and more knowledgeable than any Arthurian scholar she had ever met before.

She would never know whether Arthur would have honored her request not to announce the impending wedding. For, with Digby standing at her elbow, a man she had never met before, but who obviously knew Arthur, said heartily, "Congratulations, Watterly, I hear you and Miss Fenster are to be married. Lucky man."

He gave Hero a friendly look, completely unaware that she wanted to kick him in the shins until he was forced to hobble out of her sight.

Digby's face grew pale. "Is this true?"

Recognizing with sick horror that Juliet was right, Hero could not humiliate Arthur or her family by denying such a thing, she said in a low voice, "Yes." She wanted to explain, but not here, not in a crowded room. "It was most unexpected."

Before he could reply, the sound of a gavel striking

silenced the members, and they all began to file toward the society's round table.

Nervously, she took a place beside Arthur. Juliet, fortunately, had elected to sit in an anteroom, as she was not a member—and not in the least interested in the proceedings either. She had brought a popular novel to keep her from being fatally bored. But there was a look of mischief in her eye that Hero hoped would die out before being acted upon. At least, she comforted herself, her sister had not seen her confess to the wedding. Juliet had an unfortunate tendency to crow when she was proved right.

An older man with flowing silver hair and a tunic of deepest blue stood to speak, and all the members grew quiet. He began by welcoming the new members; there were two in addition to Hero. A small knighting ceremony was held, and then the important announcement that all the members had been waiting to hear.

"As you know, I must retire. We must find a new Arthur to head this group." He inclined his head toward the four men sitting at his right. "Sir Launcelot, Sir Kay, Sir Galahad, and Sir Gawain will make the final decision, along with me, about the man who has proved himself worthy of the honor."

"The membership must ratify," said a portly man. Hero recognized him with a start—Fenwell Delagrace, Gwen's father. He was sitting next to Digby, and the look he gave to Arthur was none too friendly. Apparently, he, too, had just learned about the engagement.

With quiet dignity, the white-haired man said, "Of course, the chosen member must be accepted by all. But which of us would not accept the candidate who has accepted and performed the three challenges required? It is a rare man capable of such feats."

Hero wondered what the challenges were, but dared not ask Arthur. His attention was focused upon the speaker with complete gravity.

"The challenges of Honor, Chivalry, and Valor will begin at the end of this meeting. Each of the two candidates for head of the Round Table Society must meet each challenge, as well as prove that they have met each at our assembly here, in three months' time."

"Three months' time! That is too long." Again, Fenwell Delagrace interrupted, ignoring the black glances being sent his way by other members.

With patience, the speaker said, "One month for each challenge, that is the way it has always been, Fenwell, do you dispute it?"

He sat back in his chair, obviously not pleased, but he muttered, "No, my liege."

"Good. Then it is decided. In three months' time we shall decide who is worthy to be the new Arthur. Gabriel Digby, Arthur Watterly, are you prepared to meet the challenges?"

Digby stood, and said in a strong, carrying voice, "I am."

Arthur stood. His voice was quieter, but just as certain. "I am."

The look that the two men gave each other made Hero's heart drop. This was more than a quest to be leader of some dusty old society. This was a personal matter of honor. And one of them must be beaten in the end.

Nine

Once again, Hero attempted to halt the wedding plans. Now that she understood how betrayed the Delagrace family felt, she could not stand by and allow Arthur's chances for success and recognition to be lost because he had had the misfortune to be locked with her overnight in a bookshop attic. Truly, it was ridiculous.

She made a desperate attempt to explain it to her brother-in-law and her sister once again. "Please, I beg you. Arthur has been all but promised to her for years. Her father will never forgive him."

Simon sighed. "Arthur knew that when he agreed to marry you, Hero. He accepted it."

"This is not fair. Certainly you understand how foolish this is. No one knows—" She broke off. Simon did not look as if he could hear a word she said; it was obvious he had made up his mind before she had begun speaking, and nothing she could say would change it.

She looked to her sister for aid. Miranda, of all people, must see how impossible this whole situation was. "We should not hold Arthur to this promise. It was made out of guilt."

"Why would he feel guilt if all was as innocent as you say?" he probed.

Hero did not want to follow where that path led. "I know we will all regret this if we proceed."

Miranda clucked softly, her face a study in miserable sympathy—but she said nothing in Hero's defense when Simon said harshly, "I know, Hero. Your sister knows. I'm sorry if you would have preferred someone other than Arthur for your husband. But I am sure the two of you will suit well enough."

Suit well enough? What did Simon know? She would gladly have married Arthur—if he had wanted her.

"I will not do it." She crossed her arms stubbornly in front of her. "I will go back to Anderlin if I have disgraced your household. But I will not marry when I have done nothing to warrant a hasty marriage. Valentine will understand."

Miranda laughed softly. "Don't count on our brother to do anything but support Simon in this decision, Hero." Their eyes met, and Hero remembered with a rush that Valentine had supported the marriage between Simon and Miranda even against Miranda's wishes . . . at least, at the time.

"But—"

Miranda shook her head and said sympathetically, "He is quite fond of Arthur. And everyone with eyes can see how well you two get along. No one can sensibly object to the union, especially knowing that your reputation is at risk."

Her reputation. What a useless thing that was. She almost thought she'd be better off without it. It would solve so many of her problems. Even Digby wouldn't propose to someone who had been quite thoroughly, openly, ruined. "I don't need a reputation—all I need are my books."

Her sister smiled, almost as if against her will. "You believe that now, perhaps."

"I do. With all my heart."

"But one day you will want children. I think then you will be glad to have a husband you can be proud of. A husband you are not ashamed of. One whom you can talk to when you worry." Miranda's eyes were shadowed.

Children. Hero's imagination raced ahead to a future surrounded by little boys who looked like Arthur. She would read to them. And Arthur would listen raptly—

What a fantasy her mind could conjure! Arthur did not want to marry her. "What of your promise that I should marry only for love?" she asked her sister in a last challenge. Miranda did not make promises lightly. Would she keep this one no matter what Simon wanted?

Miranda hesitated then, glancing at Simon. For a moment Hero thought she would speak up at last to stop this travesty. But instead, she turned her gaze back to Hero. With an impatient sound, she grasped Hero's arm and pulled her away so that they could talk privately.

Hero waited to hear her sister tell her that she would help her avoid marriage. Instead, Miranda said sharply, "Tell me that you do not love Arthur, and I will intervene with Simon for you in this matter."

Hero sighed. Of course I love him, she thought. But she dared not say it. Not to Miranda, with her romantic heart and belief in happy endings. "Arthur does not love me."

Unfortunately, her sister was not satisfied with the evasion. "I am not speaking of whether Arthur does or does not love you. I am speaking of you and your heart."

She did not want to answer. Her sister had always treated her well and she had never lied to her before. Yet to tell her the truth was impossible. "But—"

Miranda put her hand gently upon Hero's shoulder and pressed lightly but firmly. "Tell me that you do not love Arthur and I will see this ceremony never takes place."

Her throat dry as dust, Hero stared at her sister. She must make herself tell the lie, or she would regret it forever after. "I . . ."

Miranda sighed. "You love him." She paused and then shook her head. "I am sorry that he has not shared similar feelings with you, but he is a man and he felt obligated to the Delagrace woman before. Now his obligation to you comes first. He is willing to marry you, declarations of love aside."

Willing to marry. Declarations of love aside. How noble of him. Hero simply could not allow this to happen. "I—"

Miranda pressed a finger to her lips to silence her. "You will marry him." Her command had all the force and majesty of a true duchess. "You will love him, as you have for so long already."

"I do love him. But he—"

Miranda shook her head. "Useless worry, Hero. Time will determine whether he loves you or not. I am certain that he will treat you well, no matter whether he feels a touch of regret for the marriage."

That stung. Thinking of Arthur harboring regrets, yet behaving with perfectly husbandly grace. No doubt he would. Which meant that she would have to be the temperate wife, expressing no love of her own except the most gentle and responsible kind.

As he stood, waiting to take his vows, Arthur wondered how quickly Hero would regret the marriage. She had fought it strongly enough that he suspected it would be within hours of the ceremony. And yet he still felt a touch of pleasure himself that he would have her for a wife. If only he were not disappointing his grandmother—not to mention Gwen and her father.

He'd have to do his best. And while he was smoothing over the troubled family waters, he'd give her time to accept the idea. He would not push her too fast or too far. It was not worth the risk of losing her love forever. He did not want a dutiful wife, he wanted a loving wife.

He had had some concern when she arrived at the chapel just a little late. But Miranda quickly whispered to Simon, and his cousin advised him not to worry, that she had been searching for a set of pearls gone missing.

He thought her the most beautiful woman he had ever seen when she appeared. Her expression, however, was as melancholy as he had ever seen it. The smile she greeted him with was obviously contrived.

His bride spoke her vows clearly, though she was pale. Only he was close enough to see how her fingers trembled. He could not resist pressing her hand in his own briefly. More than anything he wanted to tell her that he loved her, that he would make their lives together as happy as he could. But he did not want to overwhelm her when she had already faced so much. Better to tell her in a few months' time. He offered a smile, not certain if it would reassure her or send her deeper into despair.

Everyone congratulated him as they stood in the receiving line. No one seemed to look askance at the hasty marriage. At least, not to his face. Perhaps, if they were fortunate, there would be no gossip at all. After all, Hero was hardly the talk of society, and he had been considered ineligible by most husband-seeking misses, by rights of the unwritten agreement between his family and Gwen's.

He saw Hero's face flame with embarrassment at the gentle teasing she received from those married women who passed through the line. He knew he must let her know that he would not press her to act the wife just yet. They both needed time: she to adjust to the idea of being a wife when she was not expecting it; he to make a place for himself in society, so that she could say she was proud to be his wife.

He was quite pleased with his resolution. So much so that he took her aside to let her know what he had decided. He expected it might ease her mind, help her enjoy herself a bit more during the celebration. To his astonishment, however, when he explained the matter to Hero, she seemed to be put out.

"You were in such a rush to marry me, and now you want to treat me as if nothing has changed?"

"But, my dear, I just wanted to comfort you. I know that you must have time to adjust to these new circumstances of ours." He smiled. "Your life doesn't have to change."

Her response was a stare that made him wonder if the top of his head had flown off. "Of course my life has to change. I am a wife now."

He had hoped he would not need to explain to quite this degree. Why couldn't there be a sort of silent communion between them? He sighed. Evidently, that was not to be. "Nonsense. I will leave you here. I will not trouble you."

She looked decidedly wary. "Not trouble me? What does that mean?"

He explained, certain that once she understood, she would be pleased. "I must return home to take care of business, but there is no need for you to accompany me. You stay here, enjoy the Season, I know that Miranda and Simon will be content—"

"What business?"

"Something I must do." He evaded a direct answer, not wanting to let her see how important tracking down the prankster who had turned his dreams upside down had become to him.

"You would humiliate me so?" Her temper was rising decidedly.

He tried to soothe her. "I do not intend to humiliate you, what I intend to do—"

"Find the person who did this to us?"

He wished she were just a little less perceptive sometimes. He could not lie, though he wished he were able. "Yes," he answered reluctantly. "I do want to see if I can find out who it was who played so cruel a prank on us."

"Very well." She nodded in satisfaction. "I want to know as well. I will help you."

He blinked. He could not have heard her correctly. "But you also need time to adjust—"

"I will come with you."

"That is impossible!" he argued. "What I must do could be dangerous—"

"Why?"

"Mr. Beasley could have been killed—" The bookshop proprietor, they had discovered, had not been ill. He had actually been poisoned so that he would not be able to open his shop on the day of Arthur's appointment. Because of his age, the man could have died if the poison had been even slightly more potent.

"So I should be a good wife and let you go off to risk your own life while I am safely sipping tea and counting Juliet's suitors?"

For some reason, she seemed to find that thought infuriating rather than comforting. He tried to make his tone utterly reasonable. "I would prefer you stay here, out of harm's way."

"How unfortunate for you. I intend to accompany my husband on whatever quest he has set for himself."

"I'm afraid that is impossible." He thought of the primitive travel conditions, the haste with which he would need to travel, the kinds of people he would contact for information. No, she could not come with him.

"We shall see," she answered with a lift of her brow, turning away from him to rejoin her sisters across the room.

He was still watching her, wondering how long she would remain angry and unreasonable, when someone spoke from behind him. "Well, Arthur, I assume you are pleased with yourself now? I would have hoped you could do at least one thing right, but I see my hopes were in vain."

Arthur turned and bowed stiffly. "Grandmama. How good of you to come to celebrate my wedding with me."

"Celebrate? Mourn is more like. Do you think it a mistake that I wear black without relief today?" She toyed with the lace at her throat. "Even my lace is black in mourning for what you have done."

"I have simply married a wonderful woman, Grandmama." He said it as forcefully as he could, knowing his grandmother rarely understood another's point of view if she held a differing one.

"What have you done, Arthur?" she asked, sighing and shaking her head. "Hero Fenster could never be a good enough duchess for you. Look at her sister if you doubt me. I shudder to imagine what people must think—"

"I admire Simon's wife very much, Grandmama. But I do not ever expect to become duke, so Hero's suitability is not really important to me." He realized that his statement could be construed as an insult to his wife, so he added, "Not, of course, that I don't think Hero would make a fine duchess."

She might be miserable in such a life, but she would certainly do her duty, of that he had no doubt. Had she not just told him she would accompany him on his quest for the prankster because she was his wife and it was her duty?

His grandmother sighed noisily. "When are you going to accept your destiny, Arthur? I know your mother did a poor job of raising you, coddling you and your sniffles—"

Wearily, he said, as he had been saying for years, "I will not listen to you defame my mother." Now, he realized, he had a new refrain. "Nor will I argue about my wife."

"Gwen—"

"Will make a good marriage. We had an informal understanding—not between us, but between you and her father—she has not been harmed by my marriage, despite what you say."

"If you think that, you are mistaken."

"Nonsense. We are all reasonable people."

She stared at him in astonishment. "Fenwell is furious and Gwen could barely bring herself to show her face today after such a rousing humiliation. You are fortunate indeed, because if they didn't think of you as family—"

He interrupted her. "Grandmama, I am heartily sorry that I cannot live up to the example of my father and be a legendary warrior. I am a scholar. That has its own merits." It was enough he had a wife who would have preferred to be exiled to the country rather than be married to him. He had hopes that he could make Hero proud of him. He was not as certain where his grandmother was concerned.

She sniffed in disdain. "Perhaps I would agree if you did something to show your blood was true. I hear they are looking for a new head of the Round Table Society. Are they looking to you?"

He had not wished her to know, but he could see no point in lying. She would have the truth out of Fenwell soon enough. "I am in the running."

Her brow quirked in a question as she asked

sharply, "In the running? Who else would they consider?"

"Gabriel Digby."

Her smile was bitter. "Of course. I have heard of him. In fact, if it were not a horrible thing, I might wish that he were my grandson."

"Grandmama," Arthur warned her from the topic. It was enough that his wife would have preferred Digby for a husband. Now his grandmother wished for him as a grandson. Had he made a mistake marrying Hero? No, he refused to believe it.

His grandmother sighed. She, of course, would not be warned away from any topic she felt she needed to remark upon. "I could almost think that Mr. Digby was your father's child, switched in the cradle while you were both still babes. Well, I hope for the family's sake that you win the position. It would go far to erase this disgrace."

"My marriage is no disgrace, Grandmama. I hope someday you will see that." He added, "As to the leadership of the Round Table Society, I hope to deserve it soon."

Her gaze sharpened. "Have you some feat in mind to prove your worthiness? What is it?"

He nodded. Before she could ask a question, however, he held up a finger to his lips. "I prefer to keep it to myself for now, I think."

She nodded, surprising him by not pursuing the matter. Instead, she gave him a little prod with her fan and indicated Gwen, who was making her way toward them on the arm of her father. "You smooth things over with her, my boy. Her father has been a good friend to our family."

He turned to greet the couple with dread. When

he glanced back, he could see his grandmother was heading straight through the crowd—straight for Hero. He hoped she would say nothing to his bride about the Delagraces' anger. But he did not expect such restraint, not from Grandmama.

He watched for a moment as his new bride greeted his dragon grandmother with a sweet smile. Sighing, he turned away to deal with Gwen and her father. Hero would have to learn to deal with his grandmother, just as he had been forced to ever since his mother's death long ago.

Hero had greeted Arthur's grandmother in the receiving line, and knew the woman was not pleased about the unexpected marriage. She had blushed when the older woman had leaned close to whisper confidentially, "There best not be a babe in less than nine months' time, or we'll never live down the scandal."

Still, she was surprised when the older woman accosted her upon the fringes of the dancing crowd with the bluntest of questions. "So, you have him, do you? Think you're worthy?"

What diplomatic answer was there to such a frontal assault? "I hope to be."

"I tell you that you are not." After a quick up-and-down check that, judging by her expression, left Hero coming up short, Arthur's grandmother stared in challenge. "What do you make of that, miss?"

Ten

Hero stood rooted to the spot, hoping the woman's challenge had not attracted undue attention. She would not want to be the subject of more gossip than she no doubt already was.

Arthur's grandmother stared at her with unfriendly eyes, obviously expecting some sort of reply.

Would she be a better wife to Arthur than Gwen could have been? She had no answer to give to the question. She had thought that the Dowager Duchess of Kerstone was a forthright woman, but Arthur's grandmother put her to shame. She darted a quick glance around the room, but there was no one from her family nearby to rescue her from this situation.

Impatiently, Grandmama—could she ever dare call her that, as Arthur had suggested?—said, "Well? What do you have to say for yourself? Are you proud to have followed your sister's lead and tricked a good man into marriage?"

The woman was small and delicate, with snow white hair. Alarmingly, she had color high in her thin cheeks. Her voice rose to a shrillness that she would no doubt have deplored in anyone else. Her outrage was obvious to anyone in close proximity. Unfortunately—or perhaps fortunately, considering the possibility of eavesdroppers—the only one so close was Hero, the source of her great displeasure.

Knowing that she would gain nothing by further alienating the woman she would soon be sharing a home with, Hero said quietly, "My sister and her husband are quite happy together, I assure you. As for myself, I realize that you are disappointed in the way matters turned out. But I promise to make your grandson a good wife."

Disdainfully, the woman sniffed. "Good wife? Arthur needs a *great* wife, my dear. A strong woman to bear him sons. To support him in his quest. Can you say that you are up to such a challenge? Can you help him fulfill his destiny?"

His destiny? Knowing she should not ask, nevertheless, she could not help herself. "What destiny shall I help him fulfill, exactly?" Did his grandmother know about the book? Had he confided in her and was that quest the one she spoke of, or was there yet another?

His grandmother did not answer. Instead, she glanced at the dance floor and said, "That destiny, of course."

Hero looked over to where, she saw, Arthur and Gwen were now dancing. They did make a perfect-looking couple. Gwen was small, and her blond hair shone in the candlelit ballroom. The best she could offer was some small comfort for the future. "She will make a good match, even though it will not be with Arthur."

"They were destined for each other, stupid girl. Look at them!"

She watched them dance again for a moment. "They do dance beautifully together," she assented reluctantly. Perhaps she should have run away rather than let her family persuade her that marriage would be the right thing to do.

"He could have been a great man if he had married her. She was the key to his destiny and he threw her away for you!" In disgust, Arthur's grandmother flipped her fan in rapid strokes and turned away from her grandson's new wife.

With relief, Hero watched her walk away to join friends of her own. There was little choice but that she would have to live with the woman. But, for now, she would simply be thankful that she had been rescued from further tirade.

She turned back to watch her husband dancing with the woman his grandmother called his fate. It was not possible to tell whether Arthur mourned the loss of his long-intended bride. He danced with Gwen as he did with any other woman—politely attentively, respectfully.

She might have taken that as a good sign. But it meant nothing. So he danced with Gwen politely. Just as he had danced with her earlier that evening. Indeed, just as he had danced with his grandmother.

But if Arthur seemed his usual self, the same could not be said of his partner. Gwen was quite unhappy. Her porcelain skin was flushed with heat and her eyes were reddened slightly. She had obviously been crying, though she had tried to cover the signs.

Hero sighed. Could no one have what they wanted tonight, then? All because she had to accompany Arthur on his quest to the bookstore. All because she had been fool enough to follow him up the stairs, too bound up with curiosity, and the thrill of being with the forbidden man who made her foolish heart beat too fast to think of the consequences of her actions.

Of course, she would not have gone—he would not have gone—if it were not for the note. Or, more properly, the mysterious person who had written the note. She had to wonder if that person was now laughing to see the hasty wedding.

Or was he, perhaps, chagrined? There was no way to tell what had been intended. Hadn't the note Simon received suggested that she would be found with Gabriel Digby? That was a puzzle that had yet to be solved.

Could the note sender have achieved his goal? Would the tantalizing hope end now for Arthur? In the week spent preparing for the wedding, there had been no more notes. Arthur had tried to hide his agitation from her, but she felt the tension of waiting as keenly as he.

He had joked that the prankster was through with them. Somehow, though, she did not think that the note sender was finished with them. The only way to be certain was to do as Arthur intended and find out the identify of whoever was behind the cruel hoax. The thought of what could be next had made her toss sleeplessly in the night. That, and the thought of marriage to Arthur.

Arthur refused to discuss the possibility of future notes, or the possibility that the manuscript might still exist, no matter that the note writer had not shown it to him. He seemed to feel that he would hear no more—or so he said. She was glad to know that he intended to find out who it was. But still, she intended to see the quest through. After all, it was what had forced them together forever in the first place.

Such a little thing to have made such a change in her life. Without the notes, they would not have been married.

But she had meant what she said to him tonight. She intended to accompany him on his quest. If they were married, they might as well share everything—including unlikely adventures and strange notes that moved them like pawns on a chessboard.

The question that his grandmother had raised revolved in her thoughts—was Arthur moving away from his destiny or toward it? And did she have a destiny herself?

She felt a headache coming on at the thoughts that swirled in her mind. The air suddenly seemed stifling. She moved to the balcony and stepped outside to the raised terrace. The gardens of the London town house were small, but still carried a refreshing scent on the breeze.

Other couples came and went, looking for a brief respite from the dancing that crowded the room indoors, a cool breeze, a breath of fresh air, just as she had. She sat, secluded, in the shadows, watching the stars in the sky, listening to the whispers. The future seemed so uncertain, she took comfort in the steadfastness of the night sky.

Once, she thought that one of her sisters approached, but she was too lazy to turn her head to see, and the person walked away without saying a word. She noticed a faint, familiar scent but could not rouse herself from her reverie to place it in her memory.

Gradually, she realized that there were no more

whispers, laughs, or footsteps. Everyone had gone inside—to dance, to eat, to talk. The quiet was unsettling, and for the first time she realized how dark it was in her little corner. Even the stars seemed to have deserted her.

Suddenly, she felt vulnerable. Felt a need to escape back indoors, where her sisters were. Where Arthur was. As she stood, she heard someone again come up behind her. Nervously, she turned. She saw no one there.

Instinct urged her inside, where there were lights and music and people. She rose, intending to indulge her nerves, though she often did not.

Before she could, however, she felt a sharp push at her back. For a brief moment she fought for balance, and then, losing the battle, she toppled down the granite stairs that led into the garden. Dazed and stunned, she lay for a moment without moving, until she heard someone calling her name.

Juliet. And then Miranda called too.

"Here I am," she answered. Her voice sounded shaken and weak to her ears. "I'm here," she called more loudly as she struggled to get to her feet.

"Oh, my dear!" Miranda found her. "What happened?" she asked as she helped her back to the bench she had been sitting upon earlier. Juliet disappeared back into the ballroom for a cup of punch.

"I fell," Hero said, not wanting to admit that she might have been pushed. She could so easily have been mistaken in the shock of the fall. Really, who would want to push her?

Miranda clucked sympathetically. "No wonder,

someone has put the torches out over here. It is a lucky thing you didn't break your neck."

"Yes." Hero began to shiver. "I must look a fright." She had scraped herself in several places, and the sting of the scrapes were making themselves known now that her shock was lessening.

Miranda cradled her protectively in a sisterly embrace. "Let us wait out here for a little while, and then you can go in through the library entrance and up the back stairs so that no one will remark on your condition."

Hero nodded, unwilling to allow Arthur's grandmother to see her like this. No doubt the woman would see it as a further sign of her unsuitability to be Arthur's wife.

Her sister took her arm in her hands and examined it carefully, flexing both the elbow and the wrist, probing at the rapidly developing bruises. "No bones seem to be broken. I will send the maid to get you ready for bed and ask Katherine to apply some salve to your cuts and scrapes."

Bed. The very word made her remember that tonight was her wedding night. She wondered if Arthur would be gentle, or if he would be as passionate as he had been for that one kiss in the bookshop? It could not bode well for her that he had earnestly assured her that he would prefer she stay in London.

As if her worried thoughts had summoned him, Arthur appeared on the balcony. His expression was concerned. It was only her weakness that made her wish it held more.

His gaze fell upon them, and he came to her and

knelt by her side to look into her eyes. "Are you injured? Juliet said you had a fall."

"I am perfectly well. Just a bit clumsy." With his face so close to hers, all she could remember was the attic and his kiss. She wondered if he could see what thoughts turned in her brain. Even now, feeling the pain from her injuries, her main thought was only that tonight she would share the same bed as Arthur. As her husband.

Miranda stood. "Arthur, sit here with her while I get her a cloak from inside."

He looked at her, shaking with either the cold or a reaction to her fall, and protested, "Shouldn't we get her inside?"

"I'm going to take her in through the library doors so that she does not have to go through the main room," Miranda answered, and then she left them alone.

He made no move to sit next to Hero as Miranda had instructed. He liked kneeling before her, looking into her face. He touched the torn sleeve of her gown. She shivered again, and he put his arms around her gently and pulled her to rest against his chest. "What happened?"

She leaned against him, not answering, and he savored the feel of her in his arms. There was no one to shake a head at their actions. He was perfectly within the rights of a husband to comfort her when she was in distress. This, of all things, was what made the marriage endurable. He could touch her, she could touch him. They could pass their strength and comfort to each other in a way they had not been allowed to before.

After it became clear to him that she would not

answer, he took her chin in his fingers and turned her to look into his eyes. "Tell me what happened," he ordered gently.

She hesitated before answering. "It was the oddest thing. I thought for a moment that someone had pushed me." She sighed and closed her eyes. "No, that can't be right. I must have imagined the feeling of being pushed. There was no one else out when I fell."

"Are you certain?"

"Yes." She started to nod, winced, and then thought better of it. "I turned to see because it felt as if someone was there, staring at me. But there was no one."

He was not quite as convinced. After all, his grandmother and Fenwell Delagrace were furious. "Where were you?"

She patted the stone bench upon which they sat, describing her examination of the stars, and the sudden unease that had made her rise to go back into the ballroom.

"And you saw no one there? Could there have been someone deep in the shadows?"

"I think I would have sensed anyone standing there." She tried to discount the shove. "I must have imagined I felt a shove, just because I hate to be so clumsy. I'm sorry to be such an embarrassment. Gwen would never have fallen down the stairs on her wedding day."

He smiled. "No, I doubt she would—I doubt she *will.*" Gwen had been upset this evening when he danced with her. But not upset with him. Instead she was suffering from the aftereffects of a tongue-lashing by her father. Apparently, Fenwell Delagrace blamed her for letting Arthur slip away.

"I am so sorry." Hero began to cry, burying her head against his jacket. "So sorry for this whole mess."

"Don't cry." He moved to sit beside her, to comfort her, but when he sat down, there was something else on the stone seat. Rising again, he turned to stare at the bench.

"What is it?" Hero had stopped crying when he had made a sound of surprise. She watched him, tears still shining in her eyes.

His lips pressed tight together, he pulled a piece of very brittle paper into the light spilling from the ballroom. "What is this?"

She removed her spectacles so that she could dash the tears from her eyes and look at what he held. "I don't know, I haven't seen it before."

He read it with difficulty in the poor light. " 'I entrust you, my friend, with this precious manuscript. I know you will know how to care for it, until the time comes that the true King reclaims it.' "

He read the last again, and then looked toward her once more as he said in disbelief, "It is signed, 'Yours ever, Sir Thomas.' " He held it out to her.

"Another hoax?" she asked as she took it from him. The paper was fragile, and she used care as she examined it. Read the handwriting. Looked at the bench where it had lain. "How did this come here—"

"You did not see it when you first sat down?"

"No, it was not there then, I am certain of it," she said, shaking her head and wincing again. "I always make certain to sweep the bench clean of leaves and berries so that I do not ruin my gown. . . ."

She stared at the spot where the note had been as if it might give up a secret to her. And then she gasped, "I remember—I thought that Juliet or Miranda had come out to join me, and then decided to go away without saying a word."

"Did you ask either of them if they had been outside earlier?"

"No. I did not." She said, "I did not think it was important."

"You should ask, then, to make certain."

"I will." She looked at him, shock in her eyes. "Perhaps it was not either of them at all. Perhaps the man who is sending you all these notes—" She broke off, he could see that she was trying to make sense of events.

The anger that was rising in him was intense. "He does not stop at locking us in an attic, then." Had he pushed Hero down the stairs, or had she merely lost her balance? Did it matter? Surprisingly, he found that it did matter very much. Hoaxing him was one thing. Hurting Hero another.

"I will find him. And he will pay for pushing you down the stairs." He would let no one hurt her. These games had to stop.

"That makes no sense though." Hero challenged him. "Why would he push me if he had just left the note by my side with the intent that I would find it—"

Just then Miranda returned with the cloak.

"I will discover the answer, I promise you." He saw that his words worried her, but he would not waver.

In frustration, she protested, "Do not be foolish on my account. No doubt I was just clumsy and tripped on a stone. After all, I have been known to be ungraceful and trip in the past."

He understood that she would prefer such to be the case rather than think there was someone out there who would push her down the stairs as easily as they dropped a piece of paper on the floor. He would prefer that as well. But it was becoming more unlikely by the minute.

He offered Hero his hand and pulled her to her feet so that Miranda could wrap the cloak around her. "Miranda, did you come out on the balcony to speak to Hero and then leave without saying a word?"

"No," she answered gravely, and he knew her well enough to realize that his query had opened up a curiosity in her that would soon result in a torrent of questions.

Knowing that he had no answers for her—yet, he turned to Hero and said quietly, "I apologize for the fact my quest has caused you injury."

She protested, "I merely tripped—"

"If so, the facts will tell us quickly enough, don't you agree?" And what if they pointed to the fact that he had made her a target for a madman by marrying her? What would he do then?

"I suppose you are right." She glanced toward Miranda, and he knew she was thinking about the fact that it was highly unlikely that Juliet would have come out to the balcony and left without saying a word.

"Let your sister take you through to the library now, and you get yourself seen to. Katherine's herbs will have you better in no time, I am certain of it." She looked so forlorn, he could not help himself. He embraced her once more, briefly. He said quietly, against her ear, "I cannot tell you how much I regret that this marriage was forced upon you. I know I am not the man most women dream of, but I hope to be an adequate husband."

Eleven

Hero was puzzled at his vehemence. "And I hope to be an adequate wife as well." She decided that it was only his guilt over her accident that made him say such a foolish thing.

Arthur politely disagreed. "I cannot imagine you being anything less than a perfect wife."

Hero had to laugh in a self-mocking way. "As long as you only wish someone to read to you, and not someone to take care of your home."

As Miranda took her arm to help her through the dark to the library entrance, Hero felt as if she needed to know one thing immediately. "Do you think the letter is real?"

He answered quietly, "As real as the shove that sent you down the stairs, I'm afraid. But I will know more after I do a thorough examination."

"You will examine it tonight?" It was a foolish question, and she could feel the suppressed excitement within him. He would not be able to rest until he knew as much as he could about the letter itself. She only wished that he felt some of that same anticipation focused upon their upcoming wedding night.

He nodded. "At once."

"I will wait up for you." And then, realizing that could be construed as forward, even for a bride, she added, "I cannot rest until I know what your examination reveals."

He seemed taken aback by the idea that he would see her again before morning. Halfheartedly, he protested. "It is late, you will be retired by the time I have completed my testing—"

"When you come to our room, I will be waiting to hear the news." She considered a moment. "And if I am not, I would ask you to wake me."

"Wake you?" She could see by his shallow breathing that he had not truly considered what change the marriage had brought about. They now shared a room. He could indeed wake her. For they would share the same bed tonight. "Of course," he stumbled. "If I am not all night at my examination."

"I hope you are not." She dared say nothing more direct, though she wished she had just a touch of Juliet's boldness about her tonight of all nights.

She was not asleep when he returned, though it was very late. The accident, the ache of her scrapes, the newness of knowing that Arthur would be coming through the bedroom door at some point, the note . . . There was nothing that inclined her toward sleep tonight. So she read, instead. *Le Morte d'Arthur.*

As if she had begun to take on his obsessions with his name in the marriage ceremony, Hero could not stop thinking of the myth. Could someone truly possess the original manuscript? Who would it be, who would not have presented it to the Round Table Society, or a museum? And if the manuscript did exist, why, then, tantalize Arthur with the letter but not deliver the manuscript? Was the possessor driven only by mercenary desires?

Eventually, she slept, though only lightly. She awoke when the door to her room opened. To their room, she amended to herself. He came in quietly, and she suspected he had no idea how to handle waking a wife. She listened as he paced about the room, obviously still agitated. After a bit, she realized that he had no intention of waking her.

She sat up in the dark. "Arthur?"

He turned, startled by the sound of her voice, or perhaps by her presence. Had he perhaps forgotten once again, in the excitement of the purported letter from Sir Thomas, that she would be there waiting for him tonight?

"What did your tests reveal?" she asked. "Is it real?"

He paused before he answered. She could feel his suppressed excitement fill the room. "I believe it may be authentic."

She closed her eyes. *Authentic.* He thought it was most likely truly a letter from Malory. "Incredible." Almost as incredible as the fact that he was there in her room tonight. Her husband.

He answered briskly despite the lateness of the hour. "Indeed." She could almost believe they were in the library holding this discussion, rather than the bedroom. "I will want to confirm my analysis, of course."

"That will take time," she said softly, hoping that he would light the lamp and look at her. Surely he could not see her lying there and still talk as if they were colleagues rather than a man and his wife on their wedding night?

"It will take some time, but it is worth the effort."
He went into the dressing room, his voice carrying
in the quiet of night with a faint echo. "Barnestable
is a noted expert on such matters. I will have him
take a look. That way there will be no question."

He sounded confident of his findings. "But you
do believe it to be genuine by your own testing?"

"I do."

"Which means," she pointed out quietly in the
darkened room, "that you are not pursuing a hoax."

The lamp in the dressing room lit, and he appeared in the doorway to say cautiously, "Perhaps.
Or perhaps this letter is all that remains after so
many years."

"Do you believe that?"

His expression was bleak. "I do not know what I
believe. Except that I must pursue this further. I need
facts, not notes sent to me anonymously that draw
me to London, trap me in an attic, and force us to
marry."

She felt vulnerable, suddenly, in the bed, in the
gown that had been chosen especially for her wedding night. The bitterness in his voice left her no
doubt that he regretted the necessity to marry her.
She closed her eyes against her own sadness. "So far,
he has certainly made us dance to his tune, has he
not?"

"And all without confirmation whether the manuscript exists still, or not," he agreed, his voice clearly
carrying his frustration.

"We are his pawns, even now," she said sensibly,
wishing it were not so.

"No longer." He stood against the doorjamb and
looked out into the darkness at her.

Did he intend to abandon the search, then? "How—"

He interrupted her question to say with heat, "I will not let him treat us so one moment longer. Tomorrow he will find his game has changed."

"What does that mean to us?" Would they speak of the manuscript no longer? Assume that it no longer existed? Could he do that after so long a time? After seeing the letter from Malory?

"What it means to me is that I must pursue this matter immediately. But I will not simply pursue the manuscript any longer. I will also pursue the one who is sending me the notes. The one who left us Malory's note to find." He sighed, adding, "As soon as I decide which avenue holds the most promise to shed light on our newest clue."

He struggled with his jacket. Without a valet he was having difficulty with his clothing, she realized. Without considering her actions, she hurried to help him shed his jacket and waistcoat. As he stood in his shirtsleeves before her, in their bedroom, the intimacy of the moment nearly made her forget the letter. She had not fully accepted that he was her husband until that moment.

He, however, appeared to think nothing of her assistance. She could as easily have been his valet.

"I told you that I intend to go with you," she warned. If he were going soon, they must have this argument resolved or he might very well leave without her. She could not bear it.

He paused to look at her gravely. "Given this new development—the danger to you—I would prefer that you stay here, with Simon, with . . ." His voice trailed off and his eyes focused on her fully for the first time since he had come into the room.

"What is wrong?" she asked as she unfastened his collar and began to unfasten his shirt as well.

"What are you doing?" He had grown still under her ministrations. His expression reminded her of the time in the attic, right before he had kissed her. She realized with a pleasurable jolt that he no longer thought of her as simply a stand-in for his valet.

As if she did not realize the intimacy of her gestures, she answered innocently, "I am helping my husband disrobe so that he might retire, of course."

"I can manage this part by myself," he said, trying to brush away her hands. But his gaze was focused on her, and she could not hear any conviction in his tone. He had, at long last, realized what the marriage meant: that she was now his wife, that she was here in this room with him for the night. She waited with bated breath to see how he would act upon that knowledge. Would he refuse further help? Or would he kiss her?

Arthur wanted to kiss her. She stood there in her nightclothes. Inches from him, warm and open. Her hands were hovering gently over his chest as she unfastened his shirt. Such an intimate gesture. But not an unusual one for a wife. His wife.

All at once he didn't care about the letter or its supposed authenticity. He just wanted to fold her into his arms and kiss her breathless, as he had in the attic of the bookshop. His conscience warned him that he had promised earlier that evening that he would not rush her. The question was, could one kiss be considered breaking his word?

He touched her cheek, lightly, so that she met his

eyes. "Would you mind very much if I kissed you right now?" He added hastily, so that she would understand, "Just a kiss, I will not insist on anything more. It is much too soon."

Her breath was sweet when she breathed out her answer. "I would not mind if you kissed me." She reached up to remove his collar as she spoke. "I would not mind at all."

He closed his eyes against the rush of desire he felt at her response. He must be tender with her; he did not want to frighten her, to cause her to regret the marriage any more than she already did. But as he moved to embrace her, she winced away from him slightly.

He stopped short, opening his eyes to see where he had hurt her. Her arms were bare in the lamplight as they stretched up to allow her to reach his collar. She was beautiful, perfect. And then he saw the darkness of the bruises.

At first he did not understand, and then he remembered that she had fallen right before they found the letter. Apparently, it had been much more than a little trip, as she had told him. He could see the injuries she had incurred clearly because of the revealing nightdress she wore. A frisson of guilt crawled up his spine that he had not noticed before. He had been too distracted by the sight of her breasts rising from the top of the nightgown, just barely held in by the lace.

But now he saw the damage that she had done to herself in the fall. The injuries. He stood, unable to take his eyes from them. Her forearm was horribly scraped, and several bruises lay purpled upon her skin. He stared at her arm, realizing fully for the first time how close she had come to real injury, possibly even death. And there was a possibility that she had not fallen but had been pushed.

Hero saw where his gaze rested and pulled back her arm so that the loose silk and lace of her sleeve covered her arm. "It is nothing, I caught myself before I had fallen too far." He understood how seriously she could have been hurt, despite her protest. "I am fine," she assured him again.

But it was too late. He knew what the silken sleeve now hid from his view. He had seen the huge raw scrape on her arm from her fall—or push—down the stairs. And he knew it was his fault.

He touched her arm gently, above the scrape. "Nothing. You could have been killed if you had not caught yourself." Had that been the intention? Was her life in jeopardy now because of his quest? Or had it been an accident?

A primitive urge came up within him. He would not let anyone hurt her. She was his. He crushed her against him, kissing her without the gentleness that he had first intended. She did not respond as she had when they were trapped in the attic. Instead, she stood quiet in his embrace but did not try to escape.

He broke away from her with a groan and buried his face in her neck. "I am sorry. I cannot bear to see you hurt."

"I will heal," she said, her arms coming around his waist. The feel of her warm arms, through only the thin material of his shirt, made him wish he had not made the resolve to wait. But he owed her that much restraint, and more.

"I know you will heal." He set her aside gently, adding, "And I will give you time to do so."

"You will not leave me here?" He heard the unhappiness in her voice, but he could not tell its source.

Should he take her with him? His instincts warred with each other. He needed to keep her with him. He needed to protect her. A fierce swift anger against anyone who might hurt her flooded through him.

Reason spoke to him once the flood of rage subsided. She did not want to be his wife. She was merely being agreeable. Perhaps even trying to escape any gossip that might result from their hasty wedding.

He had no right to drag her across the countryside with him. She did not want to go with him on an uncomfortable journey chasing will-o'-the-wisps and shadows centuries old.

"You would be better off here, with your sisters. You would be comfortable. You would be safe." Safe. He wished he could be sure of his words.

He wished he could know what was best. If he left her here, would whoever had struck . . . if someone had struck . . . try again? Or was he the true target? Perhaps once he was gone, there would be no more danger to Hero.

She closed her eyes. He savored the feeling of holding her arm lightly in his fingers and looking down upon her serene face as she considered his words. "Safe. Is there such a thing?" She seemed to doubt it as much as he just then.

Her eyes opened and she looked at him. She was not wearing her spectacles and he could see the clear determination shining in her eyes. "No. I want to go with you. I want to know what is happening just as you do."

Part of him was jubilant. Another part was horrified. How dare he believe he, Arthur the scholar, could protect her against true danger. He might not even be able to prevent her from getting a paper cut. "When I know, I will tell you."

She smiled as she shook her head. "I am not so patient as you think. Besides, I might be able to help you puzzle this out." She took his hands in her own and gazed directly at him. He could feel her conviction as she spoke. "No. We were both affected by the game. We should both try to find out who had done this to us, and why."

He could not deny that it pleased him she would be so insistent. And so reasonable. There were no tears. Only logic. Pure logic. What joy. His grandmama used imperious commands and icy fury to get her way. Gwen had a habit of pressing tears from her eyes without making a sobbing sound. And her father blustered about everything.

Hero's calm logic was everything he could wish for. It would be an easier journey with her along—for him. Still, it was only fair to let her know what she was facing. "The travel will not always be comfortable. For a young woman gently raised—"

She smiled. "That is a small enough objection. You needn't worry about me, Arthur. I will take what comes without complaint." He could see that she believed what she was telling him.

The question was, should he?

He nodded, placing his pocket watch down upon the nearby table. "Very well. If you decide you want to go home, you need only let me know. I do not want you to suffer on my account."

"I will bear that in mind. Not, of course, that I ever intend to ask to go home." She added with a touch of shyness, "I do not want you on your own."

"I don't deserve you," he said softly, bending to kiss her temple. Her hand rested against his chest, warm and soft.

"When do we leave?" Her voice was breathless, and her fingers slid up to caress the back of his neck.

His palm pressed against the small of her back. "I thought we might use the next two days to prepare, and then begin."

She touched his cheek, urging him toward her mouth. "Do you know where you head first?"

Lost in the kiss, he did not answer for a while. "I want to be methodical about this, so we will travel from the closest place to the farthest."

She gave a soft sigh and pressed her lips against his jaw. "Where is the farthest?"

He did not protest when her hands moved to slip the shirt from his shoulders, allowing it to fall carelessly to the floor. "I cannot say at this point. It could be Constantinople for all I know."

"Constantinople!" She pulled away from him in shock.

He smiled, coaxing her back into his arms. "I'm sorry, I'm just being ridiculous. No doubt we will find confirmation of whether what we seek truly exists or not before we would need to decide to leave England."

He was kissing her. And he was going to take her with him on his quest. Hero allowed the bloom of triumph to fill her as she returned his kiss, as she dared to do as the milkmaid in the book she had read in the bookshop attic might, and run her fingers across the bare skin of his chest, feeling the tight run of his ribs.

His kiss became more passionate, and his arms grew deliciously tight around her. "Shall we retire, then?" she asked shyly when he had moved his lips to her neck.

He did not respond, and she was afraid he thought her too forward. She did not want him to know that she was anticipating this night because of the book she had read in the attic. In fact, she did not want him to know she anticipated anything at all.

Hastily, she added, "That way we can better rest in preparation for our journey?" Not that she hoped they would rest.

"Perhaps we should—" He did not finish his sentence with words but with kisses. For a moment she thought he would lift her and carry her off to the bed.

But then he pulled away abruptly. "Wait." He turned his head, stilling as if listening for something.

Hero quieted herself as well. All of her senses were focused as she listened, hoping to hear nothing at all that would pull them away from the delightful things they had been doing. A sound outside the door made her tense with dismay.

A soft sound at the door, almost as a cat might scratch to gain entrance. But the knob did not turn. She wanted to open the door, but she could not; she was frozen, watching as something began to push through the gap between the door and the floor.

The white square of paper was becoming increasingly familiar.

Her hand tightened upon his arm as she whispered in dismay, "Not another note!"

Twelve

Arthur hurried over to throw open the door and glance into the hallway. "No one," he said, his fingers brushing through his hair in agitation as he closed the door once more. And then he bent to retrieve the note where it lay beneath his foot.

He moved to the dressing room, where the light still burned, and read the note carefully.

Hero was afraid to ask him what it said. Afraid to cross to him and read it for herself. The one who had sent it knew this was their wedding night. And still he had left a note.

"He could not have known we were still awake, Arthur," she said nervously. "He must not have expected us to find the note until morning."

"Good," he answered. "That will put us closer to his heels than he meant us to be." He looked up at her, all signs that he had been on the verge of taking her to bed gone. He sounded determined when he said, "Perhaps it will make him easier to catch."

As she watched, he began to dress himself in the clothing she had just managed to remove from him.

Her disappointment was a sharp and lonely feeling deep inside her. She forced herself to ask calmly, "What are you doing?"

He looked up at her in surprise, as if he had expected her to understand. "We must leave."

Astonished, she could not help a plaintive question. "Now?" He expected her to pack for a journey in the time that she had been hoping to be sleeping with her husband, in a real bed instead of a makeshift one on an attic floor?

He frowned, as if he did not understand her objection. "Certainly now."

"Wouldn't we be better served to wait for daylight?" After all, it was only a few hours away.

He spoke patiently, as if to a student or a child. "As you said, he did not expect us to find this note until morning. Would you have us turn away an advantage such as this just for a few hours' sleep?"

"Of course not." But for a chance to spend her wedding night with her husband in a real bed, she might. She did not say so, however, because it was obvious he did not feel the same.

Hero stayed motionless with disappointment for a few moments longer, but then she, too, began to dress. All she could think of, with faint bitterness, was that the note had arrived too soon. For it had arrived before she could find out what her wedding night would hold. And now, apparently, it would hold a midnight ride to some unknown destination.

At least, she comforted herself, he was taking her with him. There would always be tomorrow night. Hopefully, that would go more successfully than tonight.

When he had shrugged into his jacket, he said, "I will call down for the carriage," he said. "And ring for your maid to help you finish dressing and pack."

"What about your things?"

"I have not yet unpacked from my visit here," he answered distractedly. She could see his mind was on the coming travel. And perhaps, upon what he would do when he found out who had been sending him the notes.

It seemed to take no time at all for them to be packed and ready to go, a true miracle. Whenever her family would go anywhere, it would take hours, sometimes days to get all their supplies together. Packing for one was much less arduous.

Hero spared only one glance for the bed she had hoped to share with her husband tonight. And then they slipped out while the rest of the guests were sound asleep.

As they crept quietly down the staircase, he asked, "Shall we have Miranda awakened?" His anxiety was palpable. "I do not want her to worry after you again, so soon."

"I have left her a note explaining everything," Hero offered. "I see no point in upsetting her at this late hour."

"Will she be furious with me?"

It was amusing to see him so worried about her most forgiving sister's reaction. "Miranda?" She decided not to tease him but to ease his mind. "No doubt she will be delighted that we are to spend time together. My sister believes in happy endings in the most unlikeliest places."

"I will do my best to see that they do come true for you. You deserve them."

"I'm not so romantic as my sister," she demurred. Mentally, she added, most of the time. For some reason, she persisted in seeing Arthur in a most unrealistic light—as a knight in shining armor who would wear her colors and pledge himself to her forever, as Launcelot had done for Guinevere. Although, come to think of it, they hadn't been married. Perhaps that was a bad example.

He answered more seriously than she thought the conversation warranted, "Still, I owe you that, seeing as how I took you from the man who should have had you."

Astonished that he would say such a thing, she would have questioned him on that statement. Unfortunately, the library door opened at just that moment, interrupting the conversation.

"I'm surprised to see you both awake at this hour." Digby's voice came from the direction of the library doorway.

They turned, both shocked to have been caught escaping like thieves in the night by this man. Hero looked at Arthur, not certain what she should say either to the man who would have liked to be her husband, or the unfortunate one who hadn't wanted the honor but had it bestowed anyway.

Arthur replied stiffly—but still civilly, "I've received an urgent message from home."

Digby's brow lifted imperiously. "And you take your wife from her family in the dark of night?"

At that, Hero knew exactly what to say. "I insisted on accompanying him, Mr. Digby." For Arthur's benefit, as well as a partial rebuttal to his absurd statement moments ago, she added, "It is my duty as his wife now. And I am pleased to do it."

"Of course, I would expect no less of you, Miss"— he caught his mistake smoothly and corrected himself—"Mrs. Watterly. I regret that my words made you doubt my devotion to you." He truly seemed to regret his words.

"You are too kind, Mr. Digby," she answered with a tinge of sharpness. He meant well she knew. Although she did wish he had not spoken of devotion. She most definitely did not want to be worshipped from afar.

Arthur cleared his throat. "Or perhaps you have not yet adjusted to the fact that we are married. I will not hold your words against you any more than my wife has chosen to," he said. "This time."

The pained look of dismay on Digby's face made all Hero's sharpness disappear, however. "I'm sorry to be so short with you. But we must hurry, Mr. Digby. The carriage is waiting." She turned back to Arthur and could not decipher the expression upon his face. It seemed as if he'd had a revelation but not one that made him happy.

They hurried out into the dark without another word.

Her mind was so busy trying to understand all the undercurrents of the scene with Digby, she did not think to question their destination until they were well away from London. "Where are we headed?"

"We are going to follow the trail wherever he leads." He handed the note to her. It read: *You will find what you seek among the crumbling stones of Buryton Abbey.*

It was as short and cryptic as the first. "Do you know where Buryton Abbey lies?" She had never heard of it.

"As it happens, there was a reference to it among the information I used to verify Malory's letter. If the roads are good, we shall be there by this evening."

His words seemed sharp. But she dared not ask what was wrong. She contented herself with observing his behavior and trying to formulate a likely hypothesis from her observation.

He seemed a bit standoffish to her. His arm, where it lay on the back of the carriage seat behind her, was stiffly held, and she did not feel the steady, encompassing strength she had come to expect from him. That did not bode well.

She thought longingly of how right she had felt when he kissed her in their room. For a moment she had almost convinced herself that matters would be fine between them despite their rough beginning. Even when the note was slipped under the door, she had still had hopes.

But then they had encountered Digby in the library as they left, and Arthur had become quiet and his attitude colder. No doubt he had been reminded that Digby was his rival. Could the man have been spying on their actions? No, such a thought was absurd.

She considered their encounter carefully. Nothing they had said could possibly have caused Digby to know that they pursued Malory's original manuscript. So why had Arthur been so perturbed?

Perhaps, she admitted, he felt as if he had lost a step because he had been required to marry her instead of Gwen? Certainly Fenwell Delagrace had not been pleased.

Or perhaps he simply felt that having a wife along would be a hindrance to meeting his challenges? She remembered his odd statement on the staircase—that he had somehow taken her from Digby. Considering recent events, she could not help but expect that he wished Digby had won her.

There was but one way she could make amends. She must help him win his challenges. Nervously, not certain he would welcome her question, she asked, "Honor, Chivalry, and Valor. Those are the challenges you must meet. What is one expected to do to meet them, I wonder?"

Arthur took her question as a sign that she had not turned away from him in disappointment for good. Obviously, she was not too distraught over Digby's comments, as evidenced by the fact that she still had her curiosity. He answered, "A man who meets the Honor challenge must show that he can bring a high level of glory and acclaim for his accomplishments. A man who meets the Chivalry challenge must show that he takes care of those who are less able than he, such as women and children."

"A damsel in distress, I suppose?" she teased, and he dared to hope that she did not despise him, no matter that his clumsiness had cost her the man she loved.

"That is most knights' preference, I believe," he replied with an answering smile.

"And to meet the Valor challenge?" she prompted him.

There was a troublesome one, indeed. He could not summon an answering smile for her as he said, "A man who meets the Valor challenge must show that he has the bravery to lead other men by example of his courage."

"And how is one to meet such challenges in our civilized society?" She arched one brow at him in question. "I can see how men in King Arthur's time might have been able to do such things. But now, in our modern world?"

He did not know how to answer that question, and then he remembered. "Our current Arthur was knighted by the King for his bravery at Waterloo."

"But that was wartime, not to mention that it was over thirty years ago!" she exclaimed. "I hardly think you, or Gabriel Digby either, would wish to battle with swords in the street to prove your honor or your valor."

He chuckled at the thought. "Neither a battlefield nor a sword should be necessary, Hero." On second thought, however, he might not mind a chance to go at Gabriel Digby with a sword—"Words are a scholar's weapons, you know. And accomplishments as well."

Her expression was one of relief. Apparently, she had truly expected him to have to go into combat. Her next question posed a new challenge. "But how do you know what constitutes an accomplishment that will meet the challenge satisfactorily?"

He looked away, his gaze distant. "A man can do only what he believes in his heart will meet the requirements. That is the ultimate test." She had asked a question that had plagued him for years, in all his dealings with his grandmother.

She seemed to understand his dilemma, because she did not press him for a better answer. "How will they judge between you and Digby?"

How do you judge between us, Hero? But he did not speak the question aloud. "First, they must judge us individually for each challenge."

"How?"

"In three months' time, when we meet again, I

will tell three tales, one for each challenge. Digby will do the same."

"Like the medieval troubadours, you mean?" She smiled at the thought. The idea obviously entranced her. He wondered if she would choose his colors or Digby's when the time came.

"That was the intent of the founders, I believe," he confirmed. "To do well, I must tell my tale to entertain as well as to inform. I must both define the challenge I set out to meet, and prove my deed meets the requirements."

"And when you have told your tale?"

"Assuming that the other knights are still awake," he said, acknowledging his most pressing fear ruefully, "at the end of each tale, each knight of the Round Table Society will vote whether my tale met or failed the test by putting their thumb either up"—he demonstrated for her—"or down."

She gazed at him thoughtfully, silent for a moment as she absorbed what he had told her. "Can your accomplishment be drawn from the past, or must it be performed during the three months' time?"

He did not know whether to be exasperated or pleased that she asked such probing questions. "I can use past accomplishments, of course. But I suspect that more recent accomplishments will have greater weight in the minds of the knights."

"No doubt," she agreed. "Obviously, if you find the manuscript, the Honor challenge will be well met. What shall you set out to do for the other two?"

This was a question he did not want to answer. He smiled, and tried to deflect it without hurting her. "For Chivalry, as you have already pointed out, I must find a damsel in distress and help her."

She raised a brow, daring to tease him again. "Perhaps I might not be pleased about that."

She is flirting, he reminded himself. Do not take her too seriously. Lightly, he answered, "Then I must make certain that I turn my eyes away from any distressed-damsel sighting."

"Well, I don't know if I like that any better," she said archly.

He laughed. "I'm certain that distressing my wife, no matter the cause, would lead me to fail any chivalric challenge ever posed."

Her eyes lit with amusement as she nodded complacently. "And what shall you do for Valor if the sword is not the weapon of our modern world?"

"For Valor—" He sighed, not wanting to admit he wondered that himself. He decided to be truthful with her. "That I do not know. For while I do not consider myself a coward, I do not possess the courage of men who would set themselves against the odds and win out."

Her expression sobered as she took in his more serious turn in mood. "I can see that I will need to work not to be a hindrance to you in your goals."

"You are not a hindrance," he objected. It was his own nature that would win him the leadership of the society, or lose it.

She did not seem to believe him, however, because she apologized again. "I am sorry that I have made your task so difficult. I promise to do all I can to help you win your challenges."

He said softly, "You have made nothing difficult, Hero. I am the one who must be held accountable for recent events."

He sensed that she wished to argue, but she did

not. Instead, she said, "You deserve to be head of the Round Table Society, Arthur."

"Do you think so?" It was an inordinate pleasure to have her say so. But a cautious voice inside his head warned him that she might be saying so only because she was his wife. What would she have said to Digby if she were sitting across from him as wife even now?

"Your research, your discoveries, they have been of great value to the society."

"True." False modesty aside, he could acknowledge the importance of his work to the society. But he was not the only member who contributed. He asked, not certain he wanted the answer, "But do you not think that Digby's research has been just as valuable?"

Her expression grew guarded. Perhaps because she wished to be diplomatic. "He is a good scholar, I admit." Quickly, she added, "But I think you the better scholar."

"We shall see," he commented. He did not know which he cared more about the outcome of: that the society thought him the better scholar, or that he learned for certain that Hero did, and that she was not soothing his husbandly pride.

"I have no doubt." She said the words as if they were the simple truth. In that moment he could have believed her if she told him she loved him and had always loved him. Forcibly, he reminded himself not to be a fool. She had been most distressed when Digby found them leaving in the dead of night.

"I'm glad you have faith in me." He smiled and grasped her hand lightly. "But I think I will put my energies into one task at a time."

"What do you mean?" she asked, a puzzled frown creasing her brow.

"I have three months to accomplish many things," he explained. "I will do best to focus my efforts on the first one and not move on to the second until I have accomplished the first."

"I see." She nodded. "Which will be first, then? Honor, Chivalry, or Valor?"

"Well, now it is time to see if I am up to the challenge of finding the man who has the manuscript—" He corrected himself. "Who may have the manuscript, that is."

"At least he will have answers if he does not have the manuscript," Hero said. "And I would like to know why he has done what he has. Wouldn't you?"

"Indeed, I would." His moved his arm to a more comfortable position and played with a lock of her hair that had strayed from her hasty coiffure. More important, he would like the answer to the most burning questions in his mind. How much did she regret the marriage? And would she ever be more than a dutiful wife, as she had told Digby she was glad to be?

She settled against him comfortably, and he said softly, "Perhaps we shall even find some of our answers soon, among the stones of Buryton Abbey."

Thirteen

Buryton Abbey. They were going, then, Hero realized as she listened to Arthur describe the challenges he must meet within the next three months. They were set upon their quest. Where it would lead them they could neither of them say.

Still, the questions she had asked, even the ones that had turned his expression serious, had made him less cold and aloof to her. She leaned against him, enjoying the way his arm had come around her to steady her as the carriage jolted along. And she most especially enjoyed the feel of Arthur—her husband—sitting warm and solid next to her on the carriage seat.

She had not argued when he said her presence would not hamper his success. But he had only been saving her pride. She knew she must work not to be a hindrance. Fortunately, they had three months for him to meet his challenges.

Three months. Perhaps by then she would have proved she was indeed a worthy wife. She smiled to herself. No doubt she could help him meet at least the challenge of Chivalry. With that hope in her mind, his arm around her, and the dawn light beginning to shine into the carriage, she fell asleep.

She woke to find their quest to examine the stones of Buryton Abbey had led them to a small and dingy inn that smelled of old ale and badly managed privies. Still half asleep, she stared at the sight before her with dismay mingled with the odd feeling that she had not completely woken up and was trapped in a nightmare.

"I believe we are close," he said, seeing that she was awake. He pressed a kiss to her forehead. "I will return swiftly to tell you where we are." He leaped out to consult with the coachman with more alacrity than she possessed after such a long journey cramped inside a carriage.

There was still some light in the sky, so she dared to hope that this was not their destination, that they would not stop here for longer than it took to receive the necessary directions. Arthur dashed that hope when, after a quick consultation with the driver, he put his head back into the carriage to say, "This appears to be the only convenient establishment for miles. But don't fret, I will secure two rooms to ensure you are comfortable."

Two rooms. She stared dubiously at the inn but did not argue with him. Why did they need two rooms? He had seemed willing enough last night to treat her as a wife. If not for the interruption of the note—

Arthur's lips were pressed tightly together when he came back out to the carriage.

"What is the matter?" Judging by his expression, she was not certain that she wanted the answer.

"I doubt the humanity of the man who is sending us these notes" was his cryptic comment.

For a moment she thought they would get back

Introducing Ballad,
A NEW LINE OF HISTORICAL ROMANCES

*A*s a lover of historical romance, you'll adore Ballad Romances. Written by today's most popular romance authors, every book in the Ballad line is not only an individual story, but part of a two to six book series as well. You can look forward to 4 new titles each month – each taking place at a different time and place in history.

But don't take our word for how wonderful these stories are! Accept our introductory shipment of 4 Ballad Romance novels – a $23.96 value – ABSOLUTELY FREE – and see for yourself!

*O*nce you've experienced your first 4 Ballad Romances, we're sure you'll want to continue receiving these wonderful historical romance novels each month – without ever having to leave your home – using our convenient and inexpensive home subscription service. Here's what you get for joining:

- **4 BRAND NEW *Ballad Romances* delivered to your door each month**

- *30% off the cover price of $5.99 with your home subscription.*

- *A FREE monthly newsletter filled with author interviews, book previews, special offers, and more!*

- *No risk or obligation…you're free to cancel whenever you wish… no questions asked.*

*T*o start your membership, simply complete and return the card provided. You'll receive your Introductory Shipment of 4 FREE Ballad Romances. Then, each month, as long as your account is in good standing, you will receive the 4 newest Ballad Romances. Each shipment will be yours to examine for 10 days. If you decide to keep the books, you'll pay the preferred home subscriber's price of $16.50 – a savings of 30% off the cover price! (plus $1.50 shipping & handling) If you want us to stop sending books, just say the word…it's that simple.

Passion-
Adventure-
Excitement-
Romance-
Ballad!

A $23.96 value – **FREE** No obligation to buy anything – ever.
4 FREE BOOKS are waiting for you! Just mail in the certificate below!

BOOK CERTIFICATE

Yes! Please send me 4 Ballad Romances ABSOLUTELY FREE! After my introductory shipment, I will receive 4 new Ballad Romances each month to preview FREE for 10 days (as long as my account is in good standing). If I decide to keep the books, I will pay the money-saving preferred publisher's price of $16.50 plus $1.50 shipping and handling. That's 30% off the cover price. I may return the shipment within 10 days and owe nothing, and I may cancel my subscription at any time. The 4 FREE books will be mine to keep in any case.

Name _____

Address _____ Apt._____

City _____ State _____ Zip _____

Telephone (_____) _____

Signature _____

(If under 18, parent or guardian must sign)

All orders subject to approval by Zebra Home Subscription Service.
Terms and prices subject to change. Offer valid only in the U.S.

DN071A

Get 4 Ballad Historical Romance Novels FREE!

If the certificate is missing below, write to:

**Ballad Romances,
c/o Zebra Home
Subscription Service Inc.**

**P.O. Box 5214,
Clifton, New Jersey
07015-5214**

**OR call TOLL FREE
1-888-345-BOOK (2665)**

Passion...
Adventure...
Excitement...
Romance...

ll..I..I.Ill...Ill...Il..II.I.I..I.I..I.I..I.I.I.I.I.I..II.I.I..Il..II..I

BALLAD ROMANCES
Zebra Home Subscription Service, Inc.
P.O. Box 5214
Clifton NJ 07015-5214

PLACE
STAMP
HERE

into the carriage and drive away. But no, he held out his hand to her and helped her down into the unkempt innyard.

"I was able to only secure one room, but it is their best." He looked askance at the dilapidated inn building. "Or so the innkeeper assures me."

He glanced back at her as if in reassurance. "I do not think we will be here for long. One night—two at the most."

"We are on a quest, are we not?" she said, trying to demonstrate to him that she was up to the challenge.

"You are certain you would not rather be in London with your sisters?"

Hero nodded. "Absolutely certain." She had no intention of confessing to him that at that moment even London sounded like heaven to her, compared to this inn. He had said it could get rough and she had promised to withstand whatever fate dealt. She had to wonder, though, as they entered the inn, what might possibly be rougher than this.

She stood surveying the scene while Arthur spoke to the innkeeper to arrange a meal for them.

In the dim light, she could not be certain. . . . She took off her spectacles and cleaned them. The sight did not improve. The tables looked as though they had not been scrubbed in this century; the stairway was poorly lit, and there was dust an inch thick on the rickety railing and the stairs themselves—except where patrons had passed, leaving the impressions of their boots and shoes in the dust.

"I've arranged for a private supper for us, to be served in the room. Apparently, they have no private dining room available tonight." He glanced toward a door. Though it was closed, they could hear a raucous uproar from within.

"That sounds wonderful," she said, trying to sound pleased. He was working diligently to see to her comfort, and it was certainly not his fault that the inn was so dismally cared for.

"Shall we go up?" he asked after a skeptical glance around the area.

"Whatever you like," she said, hoping that he would choose to do so. She did not think she could manage to sit down there in the public room without fearing that a mouse might climb up her skirts. No matter how brave a face she was willing to put on, a mouse in her skirts was guaranteed to send her screaming to the top of the nearest table.

"I think that would be best," he said, taking her arm. As they climbed the stairs, she counseled herself to remember that she was on an adventure. Perhaps these were the very same primitive conditions that those who lived in ancient times had had to contend with. She shuddered, grateful to have been born into a modern world, even if a few corners of the countryside still had to realize it.

The room had only one bed, and that she considered promising, even though the mattress looked well worn and lumpy. He could not argue consideration for her to take another room or sleep in a separate bed. Surely tonight they would have a wedding night in truth?

Or was there some other reason he avoided it? For a moment she was convinced that he did not find her attractive. But as she examined the evidence, she was forced to discard that notion. He most certainly had proven he did not dislike kissing her last night.

And she had felt the rhythm of his heart increase when she'd been thrown into his arms accidentally by an uneven roadway along their journey.

He was nothing but a gentleman as they ate a quick and not very good dinner set up by a surly maid and a potboy, who, she was certain, had lice crawling in his hair. "I am grateful the inn at least could provide us dinner in our room," he said as he struggled to chew a tough bit of gristly meat from his unappetizing stew. "I would not have been comfortable asking you to dine in the public room. The patrons are most unsavory."

She smiled. "On an adventure, the more unsavory characters one rubs elbows with the better, don't you think?" She kept her opinion on the quality of the private meal to herself, however—the table looked like it had been cleaned within the last few years rather than the last century, at least. She had to wonder whether they used the last of the stew—when it had finally become absolutely inedible—to polish the table.

"To a degree, I suppose," he replied. He gazed at her in puzzlement, as if her answer were one he might never have considered had she not spoken it aloud.

"Did you spy anyone who could be considered as a possibility for the man who has been sending you the notes?"

"I saw only two gentlemen, but the innkeeper suggested there were more."

"How will you discover who they are?"

"Tonight I think it best if I spend the evening in the public room, nursing an ale and keeping an eye out for anyone who might suit as our mysterious friend."

"I suppose that is wise," she agreed, although she felt the sting of his rejection keenly. He would rather spend the evening in the noxious public room downstairs than upstairs in the bedroom with her.

As if he heard the underlying unhappiness in her tone, although she tried to hide it, he asked, "Are you comfortable here alone? If not, I could—"

"No. I am fine," she lied. This was his quest. To insist he spend the night with her would be doing just what she had promised she would not—hinder him. Quickly, to hide any lingering signs of her dissatisfaction with events, she asked, "How will you know him?"

"I hope he will betray himself somehow," he said slowly. "Perhaps a longer than necessary glance my way several times. Perhaps something he says. If he is in his cups, he might even confess to one and all."

"I do not think that is likely."

"Nor do I."

"Should I accompany you?"

He looked shocked. "I hardly think—"

"You are right, of course. It would not be proper." She reached out and squeezed his hand where it lay on the table between them. "I just want so much to help you."

"You needn't—"

"It is the least I can do," she said firmly. "I am your wife, after all."

Something began to burn in the back of his eyes. "That is something I am coming to believe more each day." For a breathless moment she thought he might abandon his carefully thought out plans and continue on as they had last night.

But then the flame she had seen spark to life in him snuffed out. He stood. "You must be exhausted. A carriage is no place to rest well, and I took you from your bed in the middle of the night last night." He bent to kiss her forehead. "I shall retire to the public room to allow you privacy to prepare for bed. I will have the innkeeper send up a boy to fetch the table. Shall I send you a maid as well?"

"No thank you, I am quite used to doing for myself," Hero lied. Though she had shared a maid with Juliet when in London for the Season, she was more used to having her sister help her into and out of her finery. Then they could gossip about their evenings—either in anticipation or in reflection, depending on whether they were dressing or undressing for the evening.

For a brief, sharp moment she missed both Juliet and Miranda. Miranda might have had some advice as to what a wife should do for a husband who seemed to be less than interested in getting on with the business of marriage.

Juliet had never been married, of course, but she would have had advice on how to turn a man's head, even if the man was one's husband.

Hero had no ideas at all on the matter. Even the milkmaid had not had to encourage her admirers; they had been smitten at once. In fact, her problem had been rather the opposite one. With a sigh, Hero struggled to ready herself for bed, alone. Though she thought she would not ever fall asleep in the lumpy bed, she did so long before Arthur returned.

He stumbled back into their room near dawn.

Though he appeared to those interested in his movements downstairs as if he had consumed too much ale, in truth he was simply bone weary. He had been awake for nearly forty-eight hours and he was feeling the effects despite his modest consumption of ale.

To his disappointment, he had not been able to discover who might have been tormenting him about Malory's manuscript. He had seen several men who fit his idea of the type to be the mysterious note sender. But he had been able to confirm nothing except their identities. None were men he had ever had dealings with.

Tomorrow, they would go to the abbey. Perhaps they would find something helpful there. But he could not bring himself to be hopeful. More and more, he felt he was being led on a chase that would end in fruitless frustration.

He wished he could understand the why even if he could not fathom the how. Perhaps it was someone who backed Digby as head of the society? But surely there were more reasonable ways to help a man meet his challenges?

Careless of his clothing, he undressed rapidly. He would have collapsed into the bed, but the sight of Hero stopped him. Carefully, trying not to disturb the mattress too noticeably, he climbed up beside her and lay down. Despite the lumpy mattress, he felt himself relax. Just on the edge of sleep, he moved his hand to cover hers, where it lay upon the coarse woolen blanket.

Selfish or no, he was glad she was there with him, he thought, and fell into deep and contented sleep.

He woke to sunshine. Hero had pulled back the musty curtains and opened the window. The room was much improved by fresh air, although the light served to uncover even more of the lackadaisical care.

"Good morning," she said. He glanced to where her voice came from, and saw that she sat in front of the little table again. Upon it was a breakfast that, even in the light, looked better than the dinner they had been served last evening.

"Good morning," he said, his voice rasping a moment until he woke fully.

"I took the liberty of ordering breakfast for us, since it seemed you were never going to wake."

He examined her expression, wondering if she was annoyed with him. But her smile seemed genuine. "How late is it?"

"Nearly noon."

"Good God!" he exclaimed, sitting up, prepared to leap from the bed, until he realized that he was not dressed.

Unaware of his predicament, she asked eagerly, "Did you discover anything last night in the public room?" Her eyes were on the toast she was buttering, but he dared not trust that she would not glance up suddenly if he moved to get his clothing.

"Nothing of much use," he answered. "No one stood up and confessed, I'm afraid. And I recognized no one who might wish me ill."

"I'm sorry to hear that. I suppose that means we will need to visit the abbey ruins, then?"

"As soon as I have dressed and breakfasted," he agreed. Apologetically, he added, "I did not mean to sleep so late into the morning."

"I tried to wake you," she confessed. "But you only rolled from your side to your stomach. You must have been exhausted. What time did you come to bed last night?"

"Near dawn."

"And you did not sleep last night. Did you nap at all in the carriage?"

"A little."

"You must have needed the rest, then."

He noticed that she had tidied up his clothes—they lay across the room, too far for him to reach without the risk of shocking her senseless.

In the hope of distracting her just long enough for him to dress, he asked, "Do you think you could ask directions from the innkeeper while I make myself presentable?"

Unfortunately, she did not understand what he was really asking, because she answered cheerfully, "I have already done so." She waved a piece of notepaper at him with one hand while she raised the toast to bite into with the other.

"You are a marvel," he said, meaning it despite the fact that he was still marooned in the bed without his clothing. Not wanting to waste any further time, he decided to forgo delicacy. "Hero, would you mind very much bringing me my clothes, please."

"Oh, my." She turned bright red and nearly choked on her toast as she realized, at last, his concerns.

As soon as she caught her breath, she grabbed up his clothing and carried it to him. "I have to speak to the maid," she said, not raising her eyes to meet his, her cheeks still flushed. "I will return shortly."

"Thank you." He did not think he could bear dressing under her watchful eye. He did not know how married men handled the matter. He corrected himself with a shake. He did not know how *other* married men managed to dress in the mornings without offending their wives.

He dressed swiftly, lest she return before he was finished. Fortunately, he was safely seated at the table, ready to enjoy his breakfast, when she timidly opened the door and peeked into the room.

"All decent," he teased as he lifted his napkin. His lightheartedness disappeared without a trace, however, when he discovered the folded square of notepaper that lay beneath. "Where did this come from?"

She stared at him. "I don't know. The maid set the table, I will ask her. What does it say?"

This note read only: *The sands of time run swiftly.*

She sighed. "If that is the case, then you should finish your breakfast and I should question the maid and then we should be on to the abbey immediately." Before he could reply, she had whisked herself out the door to question the maid.

She returned not long later, her expression glum. "She claims to have seen nothing. She set the table while I was talking to the innkeeper, so I cannot confirm what she says, but I tend to believe her."

"Then, how—"

"She forgot the pitcher of cream for the tea and had to run back down to get it. Perhaps then was when the note was placed?" She sighed again. "I believe her, but in the end it does not matter whether she placed it or our mysterious prankster did."

"True." He rose from the table, brushing the crumbs away hastily. "We should leave at once for the abbey ruins."

* * *

They spent hours following the cryptic directions given by the innkeeper. "Find a mighty oak; next take ten paces to the left past a rock shaped like the channel, pointing to the sky. . . ."

They were arguing over the shape of one rather large boulder when they stumbled upon the ruins of the old monastery quite literally. Hero caught her toe against something in the grass, began to fall, Arthur caught her, and they both looked down to see what they had been searching for all along.

For a while, delighted with the find itself, they explored the site, calling to each other eagerly at each overturned stone or remaining bit of wall they discovered.

"What is it that we are supposed to find?" he muttered at last as they sat to eat the bread and cheese the innkeeper had reluctantly provided them—for a pretty penny.

"Perhaps we are meant to take a stone home with us?" she offered a bit churlishly, biting into the stale bread she held.

"Or perhaps we are meant to expire out here of sheer foolishness?"

"Do you think we have been hoaxed again?"

"I fear I do."

"Perhaps we should return to the inn?"

And then what? he wondered. Would they go back to London? Should he give up his search altogether?

"After one more look," he agreed. "If we find nothing, then we will give up."

They searched for another hour, both in agreement they had been duped again. "Let us go back to the inn," he said in utter discouragement.

It was not until they had resolved that they had been sent on a fool's mission that they found the key.

Fourteen

Hero was the one who saw it. The sun, setting just
so, caused a flash of brighter glimmer to appear between two of the tumbled stones from the monastery
walls. "What is that?"

She expected it to be a bit of glass from earlier
visitors to the site. The young romantics who found
this the kind of place to share a bottle of wine and
some privacy.

But Arthur reached it first and pulled out the shiny
key. "It cannot have been laying exposed to the elements for much time."

"No," she agreed. "This must be what we were
meant to find. But to what does it belong?"

"And how can one tell?" He stared at it intently,
ran his fingertips delicately along the metal.

Watching him, Hero found herself shivering. She
remembered much too vividly how he had used
those fingertips against the skin of her cheek not
that very long ago.

He looked up into her face, his expression
thoughtful. "I feel I've seen it before."

"It appears to be a key to me, like the many that
I've seen through the years." Hero knew her comment was not particularly helpful, but she was fright-

ened by the intensity she could feel emanating from Arthur as he examined the object. "It may not even be the item we were meant to find."

He shook his head. "It is, I am certain of it."

"Then, what does it mean?"

"I should know it." He closed his eyes, lost in thought for a moment. After a bit he groaned in frustration and said, "It should *mean* something to me."

"You will think of it if you have seen it before." Hero tried to comfort him.

"I should." He clutched the key in his fist and pressed the fist to his temple. "But I cannot remember." He let out an explosive sigh of anger.

"Was there a note with it perhaps?" Hero went to the stones where the key had been lodged and put her fingers all the way into the gap. There was no note tucked in there, nor was there one anywhere nearby.

"Why do I think I know this key? Is it because I am a fool? Is it because I am not clever enough to figure this puzzle out?" His voice vibrated with his tormented doubt.

Hero could not help but worry. But what could she say? She did not recognize the key; it looked like a hundred others she had seen.

Frustrated by this next, even more baffling clue, Arthur threw it against the stones. "Perhaps it is a key some lover left here to help a tryst."

Alarmed at the frustration she could feel boiling from him, she had no notion of what to say to lessen it. Perhaps there was nothing she could say. So she touched his shoulder gently. "We just need time, Arthur. It will come to you. Give it time."

"There is no time," he groaned, sinking down onto the stones, his head in his hands.

"There is always time," she argued. "Why do we need to believe that last note? You have three months to meet your challenges. Think of that, not of the note."

Nodding, as if he agreed, he said softly, "Am I such a fool that I will follow this trail forever? Will I never know if the manuscript is a myth or a reality?"

For a moment Hero felt as if she, too, would sink into his despair right beside him. But then she chided herself for her lack of courage. As his wife she might be in the perfect position to lift him out of hopelessness and show him he was no fool.

To do so, however, she could not be a soft, sighing sympathizer. A bit of vinegar was necessary to bring him back to his senses. She retrieved the key from where it had fallen and gave him a sharp look. "Or perhaps it is just the clue we were meant to find. Perhaps we will know the answers in time because we found this key."

He lifted his head. "But how can we know?" She could not be certain if his reaction was more to her tone or her words, but she took consolation that she received a response so quickly.

Again, she did not soften her reply. "By continuing to follow the clues until we have no more to follow." It was simple enough, unless you had lost faith in your own abilities.

He stood abruptly, kicking a stone out of his path. "I hate this game. I feel as if I am being led blindfolded into a bog and soon I will find the ground giving way beneath me."

"I hate it too, Arthur," she agreed. "I hate seeing

you doubt yourself. I hate knowing that somewhere Malory's manuscript may lay waiting for you to discover it. But what else can we do but follow the facts as we find them?"

"You sound so certain of yourself." He stood and wrapped his arms about her, holding her tightly against him. "I was not meant for puzzles like this. Old books, that is what I know. Not keys and ruins and haring across the country like an adventurer."

"Nonsense! You are doing well enough so far, this is just a small setback," Hero answered sensibly as she stood in his arms with her head against his chest so that she could hear his heart beat wild and fast.

"Is it a setback, or is it a sign that I should give up such an unlikely quest?"

"I don't expect you'll know that until you have what you want," she answered. But she could not bear his frustration without offering some comfort. After a moment's struggle, she gave in to her need to touch him, to offer comfort from the heart and not just the mind. She took his hand in hers and brought it up to cradle warm against her cheek.

He stared at her for a moment, his gray eyes darkening. His hand tightened into a fist against her cheek. "I just want to know what it means!"

She answered calmly, though she understood and shared his frustration. "We do not have to look upon this as a quest that must be solved today, this very minute, Arthur."

He did not answer immediately, but his fist eased so that his palm now cupped her cheek, his fingers playing idly with the lobe of her ear. His voice was gentle when he asked, "No? What if someone tries to push you down the stairs again? Do you think I could forgive myself if that happened?"

It warmed her that he cared enough to worry for her well-being. But she did not want to think about her fall. It had been an accident. It had to have been. "We don't know that my fall was deliberate. After all, it truly makes no sense that someone would plant the letter from Sir Thomas and then try to harm me even before it has been found."

"No?" He was looking so deeply into her eyes that she felt as if she did not belong to her body. She could have been anywhere in the world at that moment and not known it.

The feel of the sun on her face brought her back to reality. She was not anywhere in the world. She was at the site of ancient abbey ruins. With Arthur. "No. It makes no sense at all," she repeated.

"I don't agree."

"Who am I to be a threat to him?" And truth to tell, no matter the logic or evidence, she would prefer to believe that her fall had been an accident. Most of the time she could even convince herself she had imagined the hand at her back, the push that unbalanced her and sent her tumbling.

She could see that he wanted to believe her, that he was tempted by her logic. Suddenly, he crushed her into a tighter embrace. His voice was hoarse against her ear. "Why should we assume this note writer is sane? Perhaps one day he wishes to tantalize me, and another he wishes to torment me? What better way than to use you as a pawn. I cannot bear that thought."

It certainly seemed as if that might be true. But she countered sensibly, "Someone is playing a game with us, that is true. But can we not treat it as such? As a game with rules, though we don't understand them?"

He released her so that he could look into her eyes again. "What do you mean when you say we don't understand the rules? Aren't we following each clue? Don't you think that is what we are meant to do?"

"Of course we are." She paused before asking, "But can we not do so without worrying that we will fail? After all, we will certainly find out the outcome of our actions soon enough."

"I see what you say," he agreed slowly. "Although I don't think I can ever come to enjoy this feeling of following blindly where I am led."

Enjoying her analogy, she continued along the same line. "Yes, but can we not enjoy the new things we discover, such as these ruins, while we play along?" It was their wedding trip, after all. And though it was not a typical wedding trip, she thought it seemed ultimately suited to a pair of bespectacled scholars with a strong streak of curiosity and an equally strong ability to dream.

A burst of anger darkened his eyes once again. "Play? You see this as a trivial amusement?" He stopped short, his temper dissolving into shock at the idea. "I suppose you are right. Someone is moving us about as if we were chess pieces. So it is a game—to whoever is behind these notes at least."

"Exactly, and if it is only a game, then we can choose to play, or we can choose to stop playing. Whenever we like. Whenever the game becomes boring, or too frustrating to be borne. Or"—she hesitated, but it had to be said—"or too dangerous to continue for either one of us."

He could see in her eyes that she thought that was a clear possibility. Arthur realized this was the first time he had ever behaved with such incivility in Hero's presence. He was ashamed for losing his temper and throwing the key. It struck him for the first time that he could have lost this newest clue among the debris.

He sighed. Her point was a good one, but he was certainly not ready to treat this quest as if it were a game. After all, he would lose to Digby if he did not meet his three challenges. "Never forget for a moment, Hero, this is a game with important consequences."

She nodded. "I know that you wish to be head of the Round Table Society and that obtaining the manuscript would ensure that outcome for you." He wished briefly she would once again put his hand to her cheek.

He waited for a moment, but she did not. He considered taking her into his embrace again, feeling her strong body against his. He could not tell whether she would welcome it or be made uncomfortable. At last he decided that it would be best not to frighten her any more than he might already have by displaying his temper.

"It would indeed be the best outcome for me if the manuscript fell into my hands and I was named head of the society."

"Say, for a moment, that we do not find the manuscript in the allotted time. Would that be so terrible?"

"Of course it would," he answered incredulously.

"If I do not meet the challenges, Digby will win by default."

"Yes." She nodded, as a teacher might with a stubborn student. "But are there no other ways for you to meet the three challenges?"

"Of course there are."

"Exactly my point."

"What?" He quirked a brow in confusion.

She laughed abruptly. "Arthur—think! Is it so important, then, that we find this manuscript within the three months allotted for your quest? What if the search takes longer? What if the manuscript does not exist? What if it is a myth? Does it matter if you meet your challenges without finding this manuscript?"

Arthur stared at her, astounded and perplexed by her simple question. Not matter? Of course it mattered, it was his whole world. But as he stared at her, he wondered what had made it matter so very much that he would risk his sanity, his life—even the life of the woman he loved.

But no. He would not risk her life. She was much too precious to be sacrificed on the altar of his base ambition to prove himself the best man to head the Round Table Society. If it came to a choice, he would stop his pursuit before he would allow her to come to harm.

"I will not allow you to be hurt."

"I know you will not." She smiled at him with a trust he doubted he deserved. But the way she stood watching him, so open to him, all he could think about was the bed they would share tonight. How would he manage to exercise restraint when he wanted her so much? At the next inn they stopped at, he would make certain to obtain two rooms, no matter what the innkeeper claimed. He could no longer trust himself.

If it were not so close to dusk, he would not hesitate to make love to her there among the ruins. The only thing that stopped him was the thought of her dismay at his ill-timed amorous foray.

Which thought made him realize that the day was long gone and he still needed to get her back to the inn and fed if he meant to keep his word. Putting aside his frustration with great difficulty, he stood and took her arm. "You are a breath of sanity, my love. Now that we have found the key, let us go back to the inn and discuss the matter in . . . relative . . . comfort."

Hero felt herself relax when he responded to her question without anger. He thought her reasons sound enough. He heeded what she said. For a moment she fought back unexpected tears. She might not have a husband who loved her, but she had one who recognized she had a good mind.

"Breath of sanity" might not be the description most women of her acquaintance would choose to be labeled with, but for Hero it felt as if he had called her the most enchanting woman in the world.

She held the key out to him. "I can trust you with this now?" she teased.

"You can trust me with anything," he replied solemnly, one hand over his heart as he snatched the key with the other and grinned at her.

Her mood was so elevated, in fact, she nearly matched his strides on their journey back to the inn, so that they walked at a good pace across the fields and paths.

Fortunately, the days were longer this time of year.

Even so, it was dark by the time they made their way back to the inn. Which meant, unfortunately, that they would have no choice but to spend another night in the wretched place.

Perhaps tonight, after the way he had looked at her as they stood in the ruins, perhaps he would share the bed with her for more than just to sleep chastely by her side? The thought cheered her almost enough that she didn't quite shudder at the thought of the supper that no doubt awaited them.

It was unfortunate that there was not another, better-quality inn close enough for them to reach that night. Now that they had found the key, she was eager to move on. Although, of course, if they had determined to go, they would still have had to decide where to go, since the key had not clarified their next direction in any way.

A key. What could it mean?

Well, of course that was a silly question. It meant there was a lock to be opened. But what lock?

It could as easily belong to a door in London as to one in Italy, Spain, or the darkest Africa. Well, no, that was unlikely. She didn't think they *had* doors in Africa. Did they?

At last they reached the inn. As they stumbled into the courtyard, she saw the most unbelievable sight. She actually removed her spectacles to clean them. But when she replaced them upon her nose, the sight was identical. She had not been mistaken.

She tugged on Arthur's arm. "Look. Look who has stopped at this inn, of all places."

She looked where she indicated, and stilled. Someone they knew—someone who should not have been anywhere near there—stood in conversation with the landlord and one of the maids. At the moment he appeared oblivious to their entrance.

Hero glanced at Arthur. He, too, seemed dumbfounded. For a moment they paused in tandem, as if each were hoping that a brief stillness might illuminate the answer for them. And then, once again as one, they moved forward.

What in heaven's name was Gabriel Digby doing at this inn? Had he followed them? If so, he must have been terribly lost. They had arrived yesterday afternoon, and he was most obviously just newly come. The dust of his travel still sat thickly upon him. Even in the lamplight they could see it clearly.

He, turning from his conversation with the landlord, caught sight of them as they neared, and greeted them with a polite nod. "Good evening." There was, however, no hiding his surprise. "I would not have expected you here. I thought you had an urgent summons from home?"

"I did." Arthur lied without blinking, which gave Hero pause for a moment. She had not realized he could be untruthful with such utter conviction.

It was unsettling to realize she must keep his ability to dissemble in mind in the future when she dealt with him.

He continued, appearing as innocent as one who had never uttered an untruth in his life, "But our carriage broke down and we have been forced to rest here until it can be repaired."

Fortunately, Digby did not seem inclined to doubt Arthur's word. Indeed, he seemed quite unfocused himself as he glanced frequently toward the door to the inn.

"I am sorry to hear that," he commiserated somewhat distractedly. "This inn is not the one I would imagine suitable for your wife."

Arthur stiffened beside her, and Hero wanted badly to chide Digby for his impertinence. But Arthur was her husband; it would only unman him for her to defend him aloud.

"We are comfortable enough here," she said with cool grace. And then she took her husband's arm, leaned against him ever so slightly, and gazed up at him with utmost trust. To her surprise, she did not find it difficult; in fact, she found that she quite enjoyed doing so.

Digby caught the motion—and no doubt the meaning—and his lips tightened briefly. With a slight bow, he excused himself. "I should not have said such a thing; I can only plead that I am worn to a nub from my rough travel. No doubt you treat your wife just as she wishes to be treated."

They watched him stride into the inn, leaving even the landlord speechless.

Arthur detached Hero's arm gently from his own. "It would be best if you go right up to our room, my dear. I will see what it is that has brought Digby here."

She could feel the thrum of his anxiety even though she was no longer touching him. No doubt he wondered, as she did, if Digby, too, sought the manuscript in order to bring his quest to a successful completion. "I'm certain that it is nothing to be concerned about. He cannot know—"

Arthur's lifted brow warned her of the inquisitive ear of the landlord, and she subsided with a quick "I suppose you are right to speak with him, Arthur."

He nodded. "I must." He turned to go.

She thought of the dreary room with dread, and blurted out as he turned to leave, "I hope you will not be long tonight, however."

His eyes once again darkened in that disturbing way she was coming to long to see. But he merely smiled enigmatically and made no comment.

He did not arrive with the dinner—just as awful as she had feared, made worse by the lack of companionship with her husband. She ate only a few bites, mostly in an attempt to entertain herself until he did arrive.

But he did not, even when she had washed in the basin, changed into her nightclothes and, finally, climbed into the unappealing bed and tucked herself into the clammy sheets.

Fifteen

She fell asleep before he had returned, and awoke choking, her lungs afire. There was something terribly wrong, and all she knew was that she must escape at once. Then she thought of Arthur. With frantic movements, she searched the other side of the bed. Was he there? Had he not woken up to the danger yet?

But no, he was nowhere to be found. He must not have come upstairs yet. What time was it? She could not tell, but at last her common sense told her that the time did not matter. Arthur was not in the room, and she must escape as well before it was too late.

Desperately, knowing that she must keep low to the ground to avoid being overcome by the suffocating smoke, she crawled to the door and out into the narrow passageway. Which way was downstairs? Right? Left? She could not remember.

From somewhere, she heard the sound of flames crackling. Her sleep-dimmed mind registered the sound—fire! It was close, she could feel the heat, but she could not tell in which direction the fire lay.

With a sob of despair she took a handful of her nightdress and wadded it to cover her nose and mouth. She began to crawl to the right, hoping that was the way that led downstairs to safety. She felt a cooler rush of air and nearly sobbed aloud, knowing by that draft that she had made the right decision.

Like a vision from the mists, Digby appeared beside her. He, too, was crawling down the hallway. But instead of heading toward safety, as she had, he was heading back the way she came. She gestured frantically that he was going the wrong way.

As he saw her, his expression grew grim. Without a sound, without a second's hesitation, he swept her into his arms, rose to his feet, and ran down the stairs and through the thickest part of the smoke.

As they entered the main room of the inn, he stopped, confused as to which direction held freedom and which would lead back to the fire. She searched for a sign that would help them through to safety.

And then Arthur, tall and serious, loomed through the smoke. Hero cried out to him, and he turned to see her in Digby's arms. She realized, then, how it must seem to him, but she did not care. He was safe. Despite the danger of the moment, she smiled with joy at him.

He came close, close enough to touch her cheek. To ask, "Are you hurt?"

She shook her head. "Are you?"

"Not now that I have found you," he answered. After a tense moment in which each man locked gazes with the other, with a wordless surrender Digby transferred her into her husband's open arms.

She buried her head against his chest as they traveled the short distance out into the inn yard. She expected him to let her down onto her feet, but he held her tightly as they watched the landlord and his staff carry buckets to put out the fire.

Digby, who had followed them out, hovered nearby. She had the feeling he was trying to restrain his urge to shoot her solicitous glances, or, worse, offer her comfort and aid.

Thankfully, he managed to keep his chivalrous urges to himself. Instead, he said only to Arthur, "I thought perhaps you were still in your room. I am glad to see you were not trapped inside, unable to get free."

For a moment she thought nothing of the words. After all, she, too, was glad Arthur was safe from the fire. And then, as his arms tensed around her, she realized the insult Arthur must feel, the stinging slap such words delivered.

The implication that Arthur had been content to stay safely away from his room— She opened her mouth to protest, but Arthur prevented her with his own curt "I cannot thank you enough for helping my wife to safety. I had been in the stables, making certain the horses were well fed, and I did not arrive until just as you came down."

"It was my pleasure," Digby answered. Though he made no comment upon Arthur's veracity, there was a clear question in his soft reply. "Miss Fenster deserves every consideration I can give her."

Hero managed an inarticulate sound of distress, unsure how to correct his address without further insult to Arthur. She expected fisticuffs at any moment.

Digby's attention diverted to her at her cry. To her amazement, his eyes widened and he interjected apologetically, "I should have said Mrs. Watterly. I am sorry for my error." He seemed to consider his transgression more serious than it truly was.

"Think nothing of it," Hero said quickly before Arthur could say a word. "We are hardly used to it ourselves, are we?" She turned her face toward his, surprised at how close he really was as he held her tight. She understood, suddenly, what Arthur had meant when he claimed words could be used by modern men as effectively as any ancient man had wielded a sword or club.

Again, his gray eyes were unfathomable. "We are not." He turned his gaze toward Digby. "But I think soon we will not remember that we were ever apart."

"I am delighted to hear it," Digby said. The untruth was almost humorous, so blatantly did his reluctant tone belie his words.

Rain began to patter down upon them, helping with the work of smothering the fire but making the yard a muddy mess. "We should climb into our carriage and wait out the rain," Hero suggested.

Arthur agreed and Digby followed. She wondered at the wisdom of the three of them in an enclosed space, but she did not want to leave Digby in the rain. He had rescued her, after all.

The three of them made their way to the carriage, which had been dragged out of harm's way, and huddled within, watching as the fire was put out by the inn workers, without a great deal of fuss and bother.

"What are you going to do about this? How could this happen! My belongings are all inside!" A portly gentleman dressed only in a nightshirt accosted the innkeeper, demanding answers. Several others, in various states of undress, gathered close, murmuring agreement.

"Happens often enough" was the only comment the innkeeper made. Which explained why the inn workers were not more excited at their fire-quelling work. "Someone sleeping with a pipe or a cigar."

"This inn should be shut down," Digby said indignantly to no one in particular. As they were too far for him to hear the comment, the innkeeper did not turn a glance upon them.

"It is not the best tended of businesses," Arthur answered mildly. "But I do not think it needs to be shut down."

Digby disagreed. "Not only are the rooms filthy, the food inedible, and the staff unkempt, they do not mind nearly burning the place down, taking a few of their paying customers with it."

"If you feel so strongly, I have to wonder why you would stop here at all," Arthur challenged.

"A recommendation." Digby met his gaze directly. "And your reason for bringing your wife to such a place?"

Alarmed at the way the two men seemed once again to be squaring off, Hero turned and pointed toward the innkeeper, who was now nose to nose with the portly gentleman. "He almost seems pleased that it took only an hour to put out the fire," she murmured to Arthur, taking his arm and catching his eye to plead for temperance. After all, Digby had carried her down the stairs and into the safety of Arthur's arms.

For a moment he didn't answer, and then the tension in his arm lessened and he sighed. "Let me go and see if our luggage can be salvaged," he said without a glance at Digby.

"I am surprised at his mood," Digby said. "After

all, he has the most important treasure kept safe from the fire."

"He does?" Hero asked the question warily. Did Digby know of the key they had found at the ruins?

"Of course." He seemed surprised that she would question him. "Unless he doesn't treasure you for a wife as he should." There was much too much animosity in his tone—and too much warmth in his gaze—for her comfort.

"Of course he does, Mr. Digby," she answered sharply. "That is why he is glum. He does not like me to go without—and our luggage may very well be unsalvageable." Watching Arthur trudge away, Hero would have been happier if she had not realized that these two men were the deepest of rivals.

"Perhaps he should consider his choice of inns more carefully next time," Digby replied, apparently unwilling to give Arthur any understanding at all.

Hero sighed. Something was bound to happen between them—unless she could find a way to turn two men who both wanted to head the Round Table Society into friends and allies. She sighed. It seemed an impossible task. Without a backward glance at Gabriel Digby, she went after her husband.

Unwilling to let him go too far without her, Hero followed him, only to hear the dismal news that their room, and the room beneath it, had been the only ones completely gutted. She shivered, looking at the remains of the room, the smoking mattress that was being pushed out the window as she stood watching. It was sobering to realize how close she had come to dying in the fire.

Arthur saw the shiver and put his arm around her. She leaned into him, grateful for his support. He held her tightly. She comforted herself against Digby's accusations. Arthur had been coming to rescue her, she knew it. He would not have left her to burn, even if she weren't the most convenient wife in the world.

Curtly, he said to the nearest stable boy, "Ready my carriage. My wife and I intend to take our leave of this place tonight." The coachman, who had been standing within earshot, put down his dipperful of water and wiped at the soot on his face. "I'll be ready in a hurry, Mr. Watterly."

Now that the fire was out, furniture and charred bedding and luggage were being dragged outdoors or dropped from windows, to be thoroughly doused to prevent another outbreak of fire.

The preparation to leave seemed to take forever in the chaotic yard. Dawn was brightening the landscape as they finally entered the carriage to make the journey. Hero had to wonder if the stench of burned wood and leather and wool would ever leave her nostrils.

As he helped her in, she turned to him, suddenly puzzled. "Where are we heading now? The only clue we have is the key. We found no note."

He said abruptly, "I am taking you back to London."

"What?" Had he decided that she was too great a liability? Had she hindered his quest one time too many? "No! I do not want to go back to London."

He was grimly determined, and she could see that he had no intention of listening to her arguments in this matter. "This is the second time your life has nearly been lost."

She was not willing to give up the battle so quickly,

no matter that he was not in the mood to listen to her. "But they have several fires a year, the landlord said so himself."

He seemed astonished at her words, his brows knit together in a frown. "I do not care how many fires they have. This one nearly killed you. And I believe it may have been deliberately set to do so."

Deliberate? "But why would you think that?" She would refuse to believe it.

He said quietly, "Because the room below yours is where the fire started." He pressed her shoulder with his hand to quiet her when she would have protested. "I spoke to the innkeeper. We both agree that you are fortunate you woke when you did." There was guilt shadowing his eyes yet again. "Especially since I was nowhere to be found to rescue you."

She considered the possibility that the fire had been meant to hurt her, then dismissed it. "I cannot believe anyone intended that I be killed in this fire. How could they be certain I would not wake and escape, as I did? Or that someone else would wake and deal with the fire before it could reach me? After all, it would have been so easy for someone to raise the alarm even before the smoke had gotten so thick."

She could see he was not inclined to believe that she was not the cause of the disaster. "There is no doubt the fire was set deliberately, Hero."

"That does not mean it was meant to kill me. It could have been meant to dislodge us from the inn."

He considered her words. She could see he did not truly believe them. "Then perhaps we can consider it a warning. A warning that you should not be here."

She climbed onto the carriage step, wondering how

to persuade him he was wrong to send her back to London. Wrong to keep her at arm's length. She was his wife. She froze in the carriage entrance. "Arthur."

He pushed gently at her back. "Get in please, Hero. I am behind you."

She swung into the carriage at once, sitting hastily in the seat as she grabbed for the folded square of paper.

As he sat across from her, she held it up.

He took it from her and read it swiftly. The look on his face was as tortured as she had ever seen. Obviously, they were set upon the chase again. Well, good, then. She hadn't wanted to go back to London anyway.

"What does it say?" she asked softly, fearing that they were heading for the wilds of Wales without proper clothing or supplies.

He handed it over to her, saying nothing.

She read it several times. The note was puzzling but clear. *Go home*, it said. And that was all.

She looked up at him with incomprehension and not a little disappointment. "London? After all this, we are being sent back to where we began? Back to London?"

He looked at her in puzzlement. "No." He shook his head. "Not London, Hero. Home."

For a moment she still did not understand. And then everything became clear. *Of course*, she was now Arthur's wife. Home for her was no longer Simon and Miranda's town house, or her brother's estate, Anderlin. Her home was Arthur's estate. A place she had never laid eyes upon before.

"Oh." She settled back against the seat. Home.

Her curiosity rose. "How long do you think the trip will take us from here?"

He frowned in thought, and then answered, "Two days, no more, if we press hard."

"Two days." Part of her was disappointed there would be more travel. Another part of her would have liked to put off the reckoning for longer. Arthur's estate would require a mistress, and as his wife the task would fall to her. On the road, she could be a simple traveler like all the rest. But once she reached her new home, she must take charge.

She sighed. Would the servants recognize that their new mistress was totally unequipped to handle the job? Would Arthur's grandmother allow her time to adjust to her duties, or would she be expected to run the house immediately?

Seeing her concern, Arthur took her hands in his and leaned toward her anxiously. "Two days, but only if we press hard."

He touched her cheek, and his finger came away stained with soot. For the first time she realized what she must look like in her nightgown, covered in grime, her hair down.

He continued, as if he thought nothing of her appearance. "If you like, perhaps we should take three, or even four. After all, you have had an ordeal."

"No, we should press on." She pulled one of the carriage blankets around her, suddenly aware of her thin nightgown. Her plain looks had never made her feel more self-conscious than she did at that moment, covered with soot and half dressed as she was. "I have clothing, since one of the trunks was left strapped to the carriage, and we will both rest better knowing why we have been sent home now."

His gaze searched hers, as if to give her a chance to change her mind. "I only want to do what is best for you, Hero." Tenderly, he took the blanket she had draped around herself and tucked it in around her more tightly, as if he thought she must be cold.

She was anything but cold. The warmth of his touch, his words, soothed through her. She enjoyed the feeling of being cared after. In the years since her parents' death she had found herself doing the caring far more often than not.

An irresistible urge to kiss him stole over her. After all, his lips were so very near hers and the carriage was a private place. But then she remembered her grimy face and thought better of her inclination. "I want to press on, Arthur. I want to see my new home as quickly as possible."

To her relief, he nodded and sat back, out of kissing range. "Fine, then, we shall press on. But I promise you, despite our hurry, we will make time to stop and find a comfortable and orderly place for you to clean up and change into a new gown."

Again, she felt cherished. "Thank you." She could come to like this feeling.

"After that, however, we will not stop until we come to an inn"—he raised his brow as he amended—"a suitable inn—to rest tonight. I will never ask you to stay in such a hovel again."

She smiled at him. Another night in an inn. One with clean sheets possibly. And good, hot food. It seemed like heaven. Especially since Arthur would be there with her.

Exhausted from her experience, she fell asleep, waking only when the carriage came to a jolting halt. In haste, and with help from a maid pressed into temporary service from the nearby inn, Hero changed into a clean gown and washed away as much of the soot and grime as she could manage in such makeshift circumstances.

They pressed on as soon as she was ready, with fresh horses and the intent to carry on as quickly as possible. Though they bought a meal at the inn, they had the innkeeper pack it for travel so that it would not slow their journey.

Washed, and dressed in clean clothing, Hero felt better able to handle the arduous trip again. It was a relief to be dressed properly, although she could still smell the lingering odor of the fire on her, but it was not so pungent as before.

She glanced once at Arthur and caught him looking at her. She could not help but hope he was thinking what she was, that tonight it was high time for them to have a proper wedding night.

But though he found a wonderful inn, and shared a delicious meal with her, he did not join her in the bed. The minutes ticked by as she tossed and turned restlessly, waiting for him to arrive, listening every so often to see if she heard the crackling sound of fire in the inn.

Though she fought sleep valiantly, the door to the room remained closed.

What was wrong with her? Instead of coming upstairs to his new bride, Arthur stayed in the public room, drinking, talking—gathering rumors, he no doubt told himself. She could no longer help but think that one motive driving his obsession to see the night out was to avoid her. How could the man be so solicitous of her one minute and then abandon her the next?

Sixteen

Arthur sat listening to the ebb and flow of conversation in the public room at the inn. Unable to help himself, he examined each and every new face, searching for a clue as to whether this was his mysterious note writer.

He had positioned himself so that he could see everyone coming up and down the stairs toward the room where Hero slept. He longed to join her there. He longed more than anything to make her his wife in truth as well as name. But after the fire at the inn, he knew he needed to watch out for her, not drop his guard.

It still froze his blood to think of it. She could have been killed in the fire. Or, come to think of it, from her tumble down the stairs. That made two accidents that could have claimed her life since they were married.

Perhaps he was being overprotective to worry that someone meant her harm. But two accidents were enough, no matter the cause. He would not allow another.

He did not retire until the last patron had departed for home or bed. He was relieved to hear her even breathing when he came into their room. Remembering yesterday morning, this time when he slipped into bed beside her sleeping form, he made certain his clothing was within reach.

He woke in the morning light to find her already alert. Surprisingly, she had not yet risen for the morning. She was gazing at him as he opened his eyes. He had the feeling she had been looking at him for a long time, and there was an expression he could not read in her eyes. Shyly, she smiled, and then looked away.

"Good morning," he said, fighting the overwhelming urge to slide over to her and pull her into his arms, her warm body next to his, few items of clothing to mask the feel of her curves from his touch.

"Good morning," she replied, glancing back at him.

Neither of them lifted a head from the pillow as their eyes met and lingered.

He could have lain like that all morning. Or, more gladly, he could have reached for her, kissed her, made love to her. But he had promised himself. He must give her time. With a sigh, he turned away from her, closing his eyes in feigned sleep. He would give her the privacy to dress that he had not been able to do more fully, yet again, because the inn could not give them two rooms.

For some reason, she lingered longer in bed even after he had arranged for her to have a semblance of privacy, but at last she rose. He enjoyed the intimacy of hearing her move about the room, washing, dressing.

After a while, she left the room. He hurriedly dressed and shaved, and was pleased that he was presentable when she returned moments after he had finished his own morning routine.

She seemed surprised, he might have said disappointed if he had thought such a thing truly possible, that he was already awake and out of bed. But she said only, "I have had them lay a breakfast in the private dining room. Will you join me?"

"With pleasure," he answered honestly as he held out his arm for her to take. After a brief hesitation, she laid her fingers lightly on his arm and allowed him to escort her down the stairs to the private dining room.

Settled across the table from her, he asked, "I trust you had a more pleasant rest than you did on your previous night."

"I found the bed quite comfortable," she agreed coolly. He could not understand the reason for her mood. Had this inn not been satisfactory? He had thought it excellent himself.

"I did not see anyone in the public room who had been at the other inn the night before last I'm afraid," he said, hoping to bring back the curious Hero he remembered from before. He did not like this silent, brooding Hero at all.

To his astonishment, she threw her napkin down upon her lap in apparent pique. "Perhaps that might be because he was in his bed, asleep, at a decent hour?" she retorted sharply.

Baffled as to why she might be angry with him, he wondered if he dared ask. "Are you certain you slept well? You seem a bit tired."

"I am well rested, Arthur, never fear." The look in her eyes was not comforting. And her next words took his breath away. "How could I be anything but rested when my own husband will not come to my bed until I am safely asleep?"

He was shocked, both by her words and her anger. What had he done wrong?

He did not know for certain, yet he could feel her distress. As he stared mutely across the table at her, he realized she was very near tears. Why? And then the reason for her upset came clear to him. "Do you wish me to . . ." He could not ask that aloud, not even in a private dining room.

She said miserably, "I am your wife, Arthur. What does it say when you will not touch me?"

"It says I respect you," he answered. Didn't it? Could she think he did not want her? Impulsively, he reached out to touch her hand. "I want to give you time to adjust."

She blinked at him, her features twisted with confusion. "Time to adjust to what?"

"To me, of course." He stammered slightly, unsure how to explain himself. "We were married so hastily, and I am hardly the kind of man women dream of. . . ." He trailed off.

"I—"

He interrupted her, afraid to hear what she had to say in the event that she used the words duty and obligation too frequently. "I see no need to rush you. There is plenty of time for that sort of thing in a few weeks, or even a few months."

A few weeks? Hero was incredulous. And then she felt the hurt flash through her. He could not feel the same desire she did if he could speak so casually of waiting weeks—months, even, he had said.

She wanted to scold him. She wanted to cry. Instead, she rose from the table. All the hope that had been building inside her died right then and there with his statement. Theirs was not now, nor would it ever be, a love match.

She managed, numbly, to oversee the transfer of their baggage back to the carriage, which was ready for their journey. Without further words, she settled herself in the corner of the carriage and feigned sleep. She could not even look at him. All she could do was wonder how much time he intended to give her. The rest of her life?

Her appetite was absent, and she only nibbled at the cheese and bread from the inn where they stopped to change the horses. She allowed herself to be lulled back into sleep as the carriage resumed its journey. She still did not want to look at Arthur, did not want to wonder how deeply his regret ran, for marrying her.

After all, she reflected, it was done. It could not be undone except by divorce, and she could not imagine Arthur ever doing something so unchivalrous, especially when she had given him no cause to dislike her.

Or, apparently, she thought sadly, to love her either.

She woke again to find Arthur beside her on the seat, shaking her gently awake. "We are nearly arrived, Hero."

She sat upright in the seat abruptly, and the look of dismay on his face brought back their earlier conversation. Embarrassment flamed over her. How had she dared to say those things to him?

"Arthur, I am sorry for my earlier mood. I should not have said anything to you. I am certain you have only my best interests at heart." His lack of desire for her was not his fault, after all, she admitted sadly to herself.

She could feel his tension ease, and he said softly, "I understand. Traveling is difficult for me as well."

"That is no excuse—"

"Let us not talk of it now." He opened the curtain at the carriage window. "Look out the window. The view is truly magnificent, you mustn't miss it as we turn into the drive."

Hero lost her breath at the first sight of her new home. It was a castle, but in miniature. A manor house with the grandest of pretensions. Turrets and towers, and battlements. Surely, they could not be real. But there was little doubt they were as authentic as the builder could create.

He turned to her, savoring the expression on her face, and said softly, "Welcome to Camelot."

The name should have been pretentious. After all, this was not the seat of some king or duke. Arthur had no title. He had only these lands. This estate. An estate that bore the weighty responsibility of its name with pride and honor.

"It is magnificent," she said softly, and he smiled in delight at her approval. She did not tear her eyes away as they drove up the long drive. She was amazed. But then, perhaps she should not have been.

After all, it was named Camelot. Whoever had commissioned it had obviously been willing to dream without limits. But the place certainly lived up to its legendary name from the outside.

"One could say that it certainly lives up to its name," she commented. Butterflies began in her stomach as she wondered what kind of mistress such a house deserved. Certainly a better one than she would be.

"Yes." He seemed a bit abashed by his own home. "I know it seems pretentious. But you have to understand, my grandfather built it for my grandmother. I got my love of Arthurian legend from them." He seemed shyly proud of the unusual history of his family's home.

Her home now.

He added, "I am certain you will love it as I do."

Dubiously, she wondered. Could one love something as impressive as this structure was? "I've never seen a house so grand."

For the first time, she understood what Arthur's grandmother had meant when she referred to his destiny. Anyone who had grown up here certainly must have a destiny to fulfill.

"No matter how grand it is," he offered as if he could sense her worry, "it will only benefit from having you as its new mistress."

"You are kind to say so." And wrong, as well. She suspected quite strongly that she would not measure up, no matter that the castle was small and Arthur had no title.

She tried and failed to imagine herself gliding graciously through those hallways, those gardens. No, most likely she would trip on the vines, fall into a rabbit hole, stumble upon the stairs. How would she ever manage this household?

No doubt such a responsibility required someone like Guenivere, the woman who had been intended for Arthur's bride. At the thought, she felt an unhappy sense of doom. Even their names suggested that they were fated to be together, just like the first Arthur and his queen had been.

And now, through an accident, Arthur had been forced to marry her instead. He had tried to make the best of it, but it was not heartening to know how easily he could grant her time, how little he minded staying out of her bed, when she could seem to think of little else.

He appeared to sense her hesitation as he handed her from the carriage. He smiled at her gently and took her hand in his. "Welcome home, my dear."

They walked arm in arm up the marble stairs that swept gracefully toward the entrance of Camelot.

Not surprised, Hero found that the entranceway, and the sweeping staircase and brilliant multifaceted chandelier, took her breath away with their beauty and style. She wondered how many other rooms would make her feel this insignificant, this out of place.

To their surprise, Arthur's grandmother was in residence when they arrived. Had she given over her chaperone duties to another London matron? Or had Gwen come home in shame, as well. That thought did not sit well in her thoughts. She would not want the girl to suffer because of their hasty marriage.

The butler asked gravely if they wished to dine with his grandmother tonight, or if they wished for trays in their room in order to rest from their travels.

Hero, not living up at all to her name, would have chosen a tray in her room rather than face Arthur's grandmother now that, seeing Camelot, she understood exactly why the woman had been so outraged at the foolish circumstances that had led to a marriage between her grandson and a woman of no feminine abilities, family fortune, or grandly titled bloodline whatsoever.

Arthur, however, said quite unwittingly, "We would be delighted to dine with Grandmama. Please inform her that we will join her as soon as we have cleaned ourselves up and dressed for dinner."

The butler nodded at the order. "Very good, sir. I will have your trunks brought up immediately." He looked behind Hero, and then out in the yard at their empty carriage.

Arthur, seeing the look, said quickly, "Most of our luggage was lost in a fire at an inn, I'm afraid."

The butler nodded. "How unfortunate, sir." For a moment his gaze assessed her. And then he turned to Arthur. "Is the lady's maid following in a separate carriage, sir?"

"I have no maid," Hero blurted out before Arthur could answer the question.

The butler stilled to the point she wondered if he had turned to marble, as so much else in this house had. And then he nodded. "I will send up young Ellen then, sir. If that will be satisfactory?"

"Excellent forethought, as always," Arthur said without a second glance at Hero.

Stifling the urge to say something sharp, and thus no doubt shock the servants again, she fumed silently at being treated like a piece of furniture. Inappropriate furniture at that.

Apparently, she now had a maid. Somehow, she did not think that small adjustment made her in the least bit fit to be mistress of the ambitious and mythic Camelot.

To her disappointment, she and Arthur had separate rooms. True, there was a dressing room that led through. But, if he had not managed to make her his wife when they slept in the same bed, would two beds, two rooms, with a dressing room and two doors to separate them, make it any easier?

Ellen was pretty and bright with a quick smile and even quicker fingers—she had unfastened Hero's dress in no time at all and was smoothing out the wrinkles as Hero washed the travel grime from her skin in the porcelain bowl provided for that purpose. She would have enjoyed a hot bath. But she dared not order one here. Not yet.

Even as she had the thought, the maid answered a light knock at the door and a bath was carried in.

"How wonderful!" she exclaimed. Had Arthur's grandmother ordered it? She could not imagine the harridan doing so.

Ellen smiled. "Your husband ordered it for you, ma'am. He thought you deserved it after your long, hard travel, he said."

Hero watched as, efficiently, three chambermaids emptied their buckets of heated water and then moved aside for three more to do the same. Her heart sang. Arthur had ordered this bath for her. He had thought of her. Perhaps there was hope yet?

No, she chided herself, *don't think that way. Content yourself with what you have, not with some fairy-tale dream of a man who loves you.* After all, his actions showed that he did not disdain her. He simply did not desire her. Their marriage would be one of friends. Free of physical passions.

She sighed. A marriage such as her sister Miranda had with the duke was rare indeed. She had known it even as she longed for the same kind of love, the same kind of devotion. But it was not to be. She must accept what life had given her, or she would drive herself mad. She sank into the bath and allowed Ellen to wash her hair. At last, she felt free of the dirty patina one always acquired while traveling.

So this was Camelot? It was sheer heaven.

She thought of dinner waiting for her downstairs. Except for Grandmama, of course. Somehow, she must win that woman's regard. But how?

Three days of living in Camelot was wearing Hero's nerves raw. She continued to get lost daily. The housekeeper had reluctantly allowed her to go over menus—after Arthur's grandmother had given her tacit permission, and then she had changed everything back to "the old way," as she said when pressed.

Arthur had been nowhere to be seen. She knew that he had to attend to the business of running the estates, but his absence had not been long—and there was certainly no need to retire each night well past midnight. She could not interpret his actions in any other way than as a clear indication he thought of her as a friend rather than as a wife.

She glanced at him, sitting down the length of the table from her at this impromptu welcome dinner that his grandmother had arranged so that she might be introduced to the "dear" neighbors.

He was deep in conversation with the elderly gentleman sitting next to him. Apparently, he was oblivious to what his grandmother was saying. Hero wished she could be so unconcerned, as well.

"Who would dream that it is proper to sit two gentlemen together?" Grandmama asked the guests closest to her in shocked tones.

Hero felt almost as if she should raise her hand and confess. But the conversation was a general one, and she would not show her ignorance now. The harridan would only use it to tear her apart for the amusement of the other guests, who presumably knew that one did not seat two gentlemen together at a table.

There was time enough for showing her ignorance when it was unavoidable. She had no need to volunteer for humiliation at the hands of dear Grandmama.

"Only poor Hattie Gower," the guest on Grandmama's right answered with high amusement. "But to be fair, she was not born to the manner, and she did try to do her husband right."

Arthur's grandmother scorned such charitable excuses. "He was a fool to marry her. A man must have a wife who shows him to best advantage, not one who needs to be kept away from the good crystal."

Hero wanted to die of embarrassment. She wanted to protest that she had not meant to drop her glass and shatter it; she had simply been very tired that first night. Although no one seemed to be looking her way an inordinate amount, she doubted that any guest could doubt that the comments were directed to her.

She tensed as Grandmama sighed once again and said, "But who can tell a young man whose head has been turned by infatuation?"

Infatuation. If only that were true. But that twist made the truth in Grandmama's words sting more. *Ignore her,* Hero told herself. *She is angry about the marriage now, but she will come around.* Great-grandchildren would soften her . . . that thought was more upsetting than anything said at the table tonight. How could there be grandchilden when he would not touch her?

Hero turned her attention away from that painful thought, when a burst of laughter came from Grandmama's end of the table. Had there been another subtle sally against women with no sense of fashion? She sighed. She had done her best to ignore the pointed conversation.

But the guest list was a bit much, even for Grandmama. Hero looked down to the other end of the table, where Arthur's grandmother reigned supreme. How dare she? Or, more to the point, what had she been thinking when she made out the guest list?

Gwen was at the dinner. Fenwell had come as well, which was astonishing to Hero. If Gwen had retired from London because she was embarrassed over the lost prospect of marriage to Arthur, why would she— or her father for that matter—accept a dinner invitation in which the unexpected couple would be present?

Seventeen

Even with the Delagraces as guests, the evening needn't have been awkward. But Arthur's grandmother apparently didn't know that. Her questions were designed to point out every weakness Hero had.

And the commentary that followed, always about Gwen, made her sound like a paragon who could commit no fault at all. As far as Grandmama was concerned, Gwen could have run Camelot with her eyes closed and her fingers strumming upon a harpsichord.

The girl herself didn't seem like such an awful person. She even blushed once or twice at some of Grandmama's more pointed comments. Once she even roused herself to defend Hero, in a way. "Not everyone can coax a rose to bloom, Mrs. Watterly. My own mother was known to have her gardens turn brown and dry up even in the wettest of springs."

Gwen's father replied sternly, "But she was excellent at running our home, Gwen. And she taught you well. You have no need to hide your light under a bushel."

"I am not, Papa. I simply meant—"

"Never mind, my dear. You were being kind. It is truly admirable for a woman to have a good heart and a kind word for those who may not be blessed with her gifts—or those who have given her cause for sorrow."

Hero sighed silently to herself. Should she take part in this conversation? Should she stand up and announce that she knew she was not adequate to the task? Give up and go home? Grandmama would be pleased. Perhaps even Gwen and her papa. But she was Arthur's wife. She dared not even wonder how he would feel if she did such an outlandish thing.

He, indeed, she noted, looking at him once more, seemed as miserably aware of the undercurrents of the conversation as she was now. It had to have been the last comment that made him realize what his grandmother was doing.

To be fair, he had not escaped his grandmother's wrath any more than she had. As host, he had striven to be polite to both Gwen and her father, despite the fact that neither deigned to address him. Each time he spoke, it was if the room went suddenly still, and then a flurry of conversation would occur—not one in response to his statement.

Her own forays into the conversation had been treated more civilly, although not to say warmly. Before dinner, as they stood in the drawing room, she had asked Gwen if her trip home from London had been pleasant. She had been told that it was "tolerable." And nothing more—from a girl who had taken ten minutes to describe the trip from her estate for the dinner invitation to Grandmama.

She could only hope the evening would end early.

With a sympathetic glance toward Arthur, she spooned up a bite of the strawberries and cream in front of her. But she tasted nothing.

She repressed a sigh, not wanting Grandmama to see that the evening was indeed wearing, as was intended.

"Are you ill?"

She looked up, startled, into the eyes of an elderly man whose name she had forgotten. "No, thank you, I am well enough."

"You have not eaten all your strawberries," he pointed out, his eyes upon her dish, still half full.

"I am not hungry," she admitted, wondering why he was questioning her eating habits.

She glanced up to the end of the table. "I have had enough strawberries and cream." Had Grandmama set him there to spy upon her? She dismissed the foolish notion as soon as she had it.

"And you are not ill? Illness often makes one lose their appetite. I should know."

She placed his anxiety now; he was one of those who enjoyed talking about illness more than any other subject. No wonder she had been seated next to him. Grandmama was punishing her yet again for not being the right kind of wife for Arthur.

She tried to stop the train of the conversation by saying firmly, "No, I am certain I am not ill."

He did not seem to understand her reluctance to carry on with the topic. "Dyspepsia, you know, that is an illness. I know a great deal about dyspepsia."

"Do you?" She suppressed a sigh, knowing that a good hostess would indulge her guest up to a certain point.

"Yes." He bobbed his head. "Strawberries help." He looked down at his own dish and sighed audibly. "But, as you can see, I've eaten all mine."

Feeling as if she had been seated next to one of

her younger sisters, Hero quickly switched her bowl with his empty one while Grandmama was making a request of the footman hovering near the table. "Here, you should have mine then as I will not be able to eat them."

"Thank you." He beamed. "You are too kind."

She wanted to cry at the comment, for it was the kindest she had heard all evening. Instinct told her to flee the room—plead a headache, or make some other excuse. But experience said otherwise. No. She was a wife now. Her responsibility was to stay and make it clear she was the mistress here.

She knew the battle with Grandmama, even with all the skills she had learned watching her sister Miranda deal with her husband's sharp-tongued mother, would not be won in one evening. And it would never be won if she fled from every skirmish, no matter how nasty.

As they retired from the table, the men to a silent, frosty smoke, and the women to chat, Hero wondered to what further tortures she would be subjected.

To her surprise, Gwen spoke to her. "How are you finding Camelot, Hero?" she asked. Her expression was warm in an impersonal manner. Her smile held no sign she was speaking to a woman who had stolen away the man she loved.

"Magnificent," she answered truthfully.

"When she can find wherever it is she wants to go," Arthur's grandmother interjected dryly.

Gwen looked puzzled.

"I have a tendency to get lost sometimes when going from room to room," Hero confessed with a laugh, as if she thought nothing of the fact.

Gwen nodded. "Oh, yes, I have done that myself sometimes."

An expression of annoyance passed swiftly across Grandmama's features. "Nonsense, child, you practically grew up here. You know the place like the back of your hand."

With a face of angelic innocence, Gwen said evenly, "I have still gotten lost at times, Mrs. Watterly." She smiled, as if to soften the blow of her defection. "Camelot has all those lovely rooms within rooms. Whoever designed it could have done well making mazes."

Personally, Hero agreed completely, but she dared not say so aloud for fear of offending Arthur's grandmother. After all, her husband had built the house especially for her. Diplomatically, she said, "I am certain I will come to know where every room is, in time."

"Oh, yes, I am certain you will," Gwen agreed.

"How agreeable you are tonight, my dear." To Hero's surprise, Grandmama was not speaking to Hero but to Gwen. Her displeasure was palpable.

"Papa says it is a woman's place to be agreeable," Gwen said sweetly, but Hero could have sworn she saw a glint of rebellion in the pale blue eyes.

"Certainly not to everyone, I should hope. You'll be carried off by the first fortune hunter to come along."

"Papa need not worry about that." There was something in Gwen's expression that conveyed her conviction. "I will only marry a man who I am certain is as perfect as can be."

"No one is perfect."

Gwen blushed. "I did not mean perfect in that sense, Mrs. Watterly. I meant perfect for me."

Grandmama asked sharply, "And what would your perfect man be? I confess I am curious to see what a girl of twenty knows of such things." Hero was ashamed of her relief at having the attention taken from herself for a while.

Again, Gwen blushed, but she did not back away from the challenge. "He would be strong, and brave, and handsome."

Arthur's grandmother allowed a longer than polite pause, then raised an eyebrow and said dryly, "My dear, there are no men who are strong and brave *and* handsome."

"Arthur is all those things," Hero protested before she realized what she had said. She hastily sent an apologetic look to Gwen.

Gwen, however, not only did not show any distress at the conversation, she also agreed with her. "Yes. Arthur is an example of a such a man."

"Indeed?" Grandmama looked from one to the other with no hint of irritation or annoyance, though undoubtedly she must be feeling a certain amount of both. "Unfortunately, he was not wise enough to avoid a hasty marriage."

Hero felt her face flame. "I apologize." She deserved the set-down for speaking out so unthinkingly. "I had not meant to imply that Arthur is perfect, of course. I'm truly sorry if I sounded as though I were." No doubt Gwen's sensibilities were still tender over her disappointment.

"As well you should be."

Grandmama's supercilious attitude at last shredded Hero's patience. She said, barely holding on to her temper, "I merely meant to point out that if Arthur exists, then there must be many other men who also would meet Miss Delagrace's specifications."

Gwen's head bobbed in a ladylike nod Hero wished she could learn to emulate. "I agree." There was a gleam of surety in her eye that had not been there until this discussion. The way she spoke told Hero something she had not know before. She wondered if Arthur was aware that Gwen Delagrace was not suffering a broken heart because Arthur had married another.

No. The girl showed every sign of being in love. The question was, with whom? And why had she not told her father?

Fortunately, Arthur's grandmother seemed oblivious to the fact. Hero shuddered to think what the woman would do if she knew. She had not yet accepted the fact that Arthur was not ever to marry Gwen. How would she feel to know that Gwen was glad of the fact?

As if she realized that she had unwittingly let Hero in on her secret, Gwen blushed and said softly, "I am afraid I must retire."

"Nonsense, the night is still young," Arthur's grandmother argued.

"I'm afraid I'm developing a bit of a headache," Gwen said firmly.

Hero, to divert the older woman's attention, quickly said, "I've no headache, shall we play whist, then?" She glanced around at the other women neighbors and raised an eyebrow in question. There was an excited murmur of agreement, and Gwen managed to escape, with a grateful smile at Hero.

At first Hero considered herself a fool, but then,

as she and Grandmama engaged in a pitched game of whist, Hero tried to find the opening that would allow her to make an overture of friendship with Arthur's grandmother. After all, they would be living in the same household for many years if the woman's health remained as strong as it was currently.

Surely, she had learned something that would allow her to build a trust, an alliance with this woman who had raised Arthur since his parents died.

Hand after hand she probed for a spot of common ground upon which they could strike a tentative friendship. It helped somewhat that she concentrated so hard on winning Arthur's grandmother over, that she lost almost every match.

She had hopes of eventual success, by evening's end, when the older woman did not purse her lips after Hero took two hands in a row at the game.

She questioned her own optimism the next morning, when a maid arrived as she was dressing, to deliver a summons to Grandmama's study. As it said nothing of Arthur, Hero wondered whether she was being wise as she knocked quickly on the dressing room door to inform him. She could not help hoping that she would catch him in the state of casual morning undress that she had become accustomed to while they were traveling. There was something disarming about the man when his hair had not yet been properly brushed back, and his shirt collar hung unfastened around his neck.

To her disappointment, he was fully dressed and groomed when he answered her knock. "Your grandmother wants to see me immediately," she said nervously, still not used to having him so near.

"Do you know what she wants?"

Does she? Hero asked silently. But she did not want to bring discord between the two. She contented herself with saying only, "The note did not specify more than a time and a place."

For a moment he seemed not to hear her words. His gaze was transfixed upon her. She realized, with a blush, that her corset was still only half laced up, and her dressing gown gaped open.

Arthur saw her blush and realized that his unintentional gaping had been noted. He stood rooted to the spot, not certain whether to acknowledge her undress or ignore it. At last he decided it would be best if he simply shifted his gaze away from her.

It took him several moments to regain his composure enough to remember that she had just informed him his grandmother wished to see them. A formal interview with his grandmother, he knew, was not good news. He wondered if Hero was aware of that fact.

He said quickly, "I will put off my business and accompany you." His duty was clear, no matter how unpleasant. The past few days had demonstrated to him just how desperately he needed to help shield Hero from as much of his grandmother's wrath as possible.

"There is no need," she protested, but he sensed an underlying relief that she did not want to admit to.

"I will accompany you," he repeated, looking directly at her, not allowing his gaze to stray down toward the open corset, or the sight it laid before his eyes. "Let me know when you are dressed and ready to go."

"Stay," she said, putting out her hand. "I have questions for you."

"Very well." He sat upon the bed, watching as her maid dashed between the dressing table and Hero to help her finish dressing. He could not help but hope it would be a scene that would eventually become a part of his morning routine. "What do you wish to ask me?"

She raised her eyes to meet his, ignoring the maid who was using a buttonhook to fasten the back of her gown. "Have you had another note?"

"No, I would have told you if I did." He chose to answer cryptically, with a wary glance at the maid, aware that no matter how cheerful or innocent she seemed, she could be a spy for his grandmother.

"Good." His reassurance brought a smile to her face. "I wondered if perhaps, now that we are here . . ." Her voice faded. And then she finished. "I was being foolish, I suppose. I apologize for doubting you."

So she had thought he would withhold his confidences to her now? Simply because they were at Camelot, his home? What had given her that impression? "We are in this together," he assured her.

There was a sadness in her expression when she said softly, "Sometimes it feels as if I am here alone."

He felt the sting of her rebuke, gentle as it was. "I have had business to attend to. . . ." He trailed off. That was not the full truth, and he should not insult her intelligence by pretending it was.

He tried not to boast as he said, "I believe I met one of my challenges yesterday."

Her eyes lit with excitement, and she waved the

maid aside as she came over to grasp his hands and look directly into his eyes. "Which?"

"I don't know if you will approve," he teased.

"Why not?" She seemed taken aback.

"Well, you are my wife, after all."

And then she realized he was teasing and said with a smile, "Does this challenge have anything to do with damsels in distress?"

"Indeed, it does." He nodded. "I have met the challenge of Chivalry."

"What maiden did you aid, then?" Did he imagine a flash of jealousy across her face, quickly suppressed? No doubt she was concerned only that he not disappoint her in meeting his challenges.

He wondered what her expression would reveal if he said he had helped Gwen out of some difficulty or another. But he would not sink so low just to try to tempt her to want to be his wife. "None, as it turns out. I helped one of the tenants on the estate to dig a new ditch, as his old one no longer carried water because the river has lowered in the last few years."

Her brow knit in puzzlement. And then, with a look of enlightenment, she broke into a smile. "So you are telling me that you, as a future leader of the Round Table Society, could find no damsel in distress and had to settle for a ditch?" She pressed her fingers against her lips but still could not prevent the chuckle that escaped her as she pictured the sight.

He found her amusement catching. "I'm afraid so," he sighed, fluttering his eyelids for comic effect. "There is only one damsel I truly wish to offer aid and succor, I confess. I am not as knightly as I should be."

Her cheeks flushed slightly as she recognized the compliment, and he considered whether she would object to a kiss.

He almost asked her.

But he did not. The maid was pretending valiantly that she was not listening to their conversation, but he knew better. He would not subject Hero to an intimacy she did not wish in front of a servant she barely knew.

After all, he still had small pleasures left to him. Instead of a kiss, he would content himself with enjoying the way she moved about the room while she was preparing for the day. Enjoy the privilege of being able to observe her in a way no other man ever had.

Unfortunately, as he watched her, his thoughts returned once again to kissing her, touching her neck with his fingertips, his mouth— To divert his own wayward imagination, he asked, "Have you any other questions for me?"

"Which broach should I wear with this dress?" She smiled, and he had the distinct impression that he could choose a twig from the ground and she would not mind. She asked his opinion only because she did not want him to leave. It pleased him that she craved his company, for he certainly was hungry for hers after these last few days with so little sight of her. He wished that her desire did not stem only from being a stranger here, though. He would have to hope that one day she would want his company because she had grown to want him for her husband.

Eighteen

Hero held her breath, wondering if he would dismiss her request. But no, he came to stand next to her, peering down into her jewel box with a frown on his face. "What will suit you best?"

You, she thought. But he had made it clear that he needed time to adjust to the marriage. She must give it to him.

No matter how much she longed to lay her cheek against the smooth material of his sleeve and feel the warmth and strength of him, she must not do so.

Still, she reflected, it was sheer pleasure to have him this close. Though she could not deny she would have much preferred having him even nearer. Nevertheless, she did not want to give him an excuse to move farther away from her.

Using her index finger, she stirred through the jewelry his grandmother had sent up to her on their second day there. Idly, she asked, "One more question for you—have you any advice on how I can make amends to your grandmother for whatever she holds against me?"

He plucked out a pretty little ruby pin that went

well with the dark rose of her gown and handed it to her. "Amends?"

"Thank you," she murmured as she took the pin. "Yes, amends. I know you have been busy about your own affairs, but surely you cannot be completely blind to the extent to which your grandmother resents me." She had not meant to be so sharp with him, but the situation was wearing on her.

"Time is the best remedy for my grandmother's tempers," he said philosophically.

"Then time I shall give her," Hero answered, trying to hide her own doubts about the wisdom of such action—or inaction, as it were. She moved to pin the broach, but her fingers were not steady enough. Ellen stepped forward, but Arthur waved the maid away and took the pin up himself.

As his fingers brushed against her breast while he pinned the broach upon her, she had the urge to reach up on tiptoe to press a kiss against his mouth. If Ellen had not been present, she might have even done so.

Instead, recognizing that she was ready at last for her meeting with Grandmama, the pit of her stomach grew more and more unsettled. His offer to accompany her was gallant in the extreme. But perhaps she should be brave enough to face the woman alone?

"Are you ready?" he asked, holding out his arm to her.

She hesitated, knowing that she could tell him she preferred to go alone. He would most likely respect her wishes, ultimately, even if she needed to argue a bit more. "I am," she answered, deciding that she would prefer reinforcements in this battle.

After all, she had never met anyone so formidable as Grandmama, and she would never be able to make Arthur proud that she was his wife if she could not even bring harmony to his household by quickly and decisively winning this battle with the harridan.

"I see now that I have missed the advantage of your escort these last few days," she said as they walked to the study.

"In what way?"

"Well, in addition to the pleasure of your company as escort, I will not waste fifteen minutes today trying to find your grandmother's study."

He paused, holding lightly to her arm, so that she would also, and turned her to face him. With an utterly serious expression, he gazed down at her. "Surely it has not been that awful?"

"It has." She laughed, to show him that she did not mean her words as a criticism. "You cannot imagine how freeing it is to have you beside me so that I don't have to ask the servants for direction."

"They have not been disrespectful, have they?" His eyebrows lifted in surprise.

"Of course not," she answered quickly so that he would not think he had cause to investigate. He might perceive the cook's failure to follow her menus disrespectful and she would not want to get the woman fired. Such an action would not win the confidence of the rest of the servants. "I am always directed in a most polite manner."

"Are you certain?" He searched her face as if looking for the truth behind her words.

"Yes." She added, knowing that it would disarm him, "Once, even a parlor maid named Ann took me to the music room herself, just so I wouldn't lose my way."

"Very well, then," he said. "For a moment you had me imagining I must fire the whole staff."

"You would do that for me?"

"Do you doubt it?"

She answered sensibly, "Well, yes. It would be highly impractical to replace an entire staff this size. Your breakfast would likely be served cold for a good week or more."

"I will have no one on my staff who shows you disrespect. Remember that, Hero." He sighed. "I know my grandmother has not made the transition easy for you, but you are the mistress of this house and I will not have you treated with less than full respect."

Except, she thought sadly, by the husband who would not share her bed. "But it is only natural for a servant to wonder about the possibility that I might very well have difficulty running a household this size when I cannot even navigate it without becoming hopelessly lost."

His lips turned up in amusement. "Perhaps I should escort you every day." When he smiled at her like that, she almost believed he could love her.

"I'm afraid I must learn sometime," she demurred. The last thing she needed was to have him watch her trial and error as she learned to run the household. He would be firing her, not the staff, if he saw her true abilities. Although, she supposed, it was not truly possible to fire a wife, no matter how much one wished to.

"Feel free to call upon me for assistance at any

time," he said softly. "I want you to feel at home here."

"I may, it has been especially pleasurable today not to have to schedule extra time for the inevitable minutes that I must spend wandering about totally lost."

He laughed aloud, and then, as they reached the study door, he sobered abruptly. It was not promising to see how quickly the thought of his grandmother and her summons had wiped the joy from his expression.

The study, which was used exclusively by Arthur's grandmother, was a revelation to her. It was an opulent room with a generous fire and well-cushioned settees draped with exotic scarves that had come from lands far distant from England. There was a hint of an exotic smoky scent as well, one Hero could not identify, but which put all her senses on alert.

All the same, it was not a restful room; the shadows seemed in permanent residence despite the sun from the arched window behind the teak escritoire. There was a darkness here that defied her experience. No wonder the woman never smiled.

Eustacia Watterly seemed unsurprised to see Arthur at Hero's side. Indeed, she seemed almost pleased as she waved them both to sit.

Hero sank into the chair, feeling as she had when she was a small girl and her father had called her before him to administer some punishment. She tried to smile, to lighten the mood.

Arthur's grandmother waited, as still as a sphinx as they settled themselves before her. Her hands played idly with a small crystal ball she had taken from its pedestal when they arrived. There was no answering smile from her.

She did not start gently, and Hero knew she would have to become accustomed to this style. Abruptly, she replaced the crystal ball upon its pedestal and said, "Do you think your wife too inept to handle a simple meeting with me, Arthur?"

"Not at all, Grandmama." Again, Hero marveled as he lied without compunction. "Hero and I had planned to go for a ride this morning, and rather than cancel our plans when your summons arrived, I thought we would both come to speak to you, and then go riding."

She frowned at his answer.

He half rose as he said, "If you prefer that I not be present—"

She waved him back to his seat, to Hero's relief. And then, again ready for battle, said, "I am most disappointed in the both of you. You have managed to turn an ally of this family into an enemy."

Arthur tensed beside her and protested. "That is an overstatement, Grandmama."

"Is it?" She questioned him sharply, an eyebrow raised in disdain. "Did you not notice that you were conspicuously not addressed all last evening?"

He sank back in his chair, as if he had been struck. "I noticed, of course." He sat forward, more stiffly, as he added, "But that does not mean that Fenwell and I are enemies."

"Does it not?"

"No."

She asked in challenge, "Then, what does it mean?"

"He is angry, that is understandable." Arthur argued, his tone raised despite his obvious effort at self-control. "But the simple fact is he came to dinner, nonetheless."

Unwilling to let go of the upper hand, his grandmother said plaintively, "He came at my invitation, but I cannot say whether it was to enjoy my company or to disdain yours."

He sighed, running his fingers through his hair despite his grandmother's frown of disapproval. Hero said quietly, "It takes time to heal certain breaches, Mrs. Watterly." They both stared at her as if they had forgotten she was in the room. "No doubt Arthur is right, and it is a sign that Mr. Delagrace will eventually reconcile with him."

"And how will you ensure that this breach is healed? Or are you willing to sit back and wait, willing to let my status in our society wither because of this betrayal of yours?"

Arthur flinched at the word "betrayal" and said slowly, "Certainly it will be some time before he can forgive me, but he knows that circumstances were completely out of your hands, Grandmama. He does not blame you—"

"Of course he does not blame me. But you do not have much time to change him back into your ally."

"I cannot force the man."

His grandmother's expression indicated she disagreed, but she said nothing to argue with him directly, instead asking, "Have you begged for his forgiveness?"

"I have expressed my regret, of course, several times." Hero could see his hands clenched tightly at his knees, out of the line of his grandmother's sight. She wished she could reach over and take his hand in hers, but she knew his grandmother would only be angered further by such a gesture.

As it was, her eyes were flinty with pure rage as she asked icily, "Have you *begged* his forgiveness for your betrayal?"

"Not in so many words."

"Then do so at once."

He nodded once, sharply. "I will ride over to see him tomorrow." Arthur seemed to find the idea a good one, but Hero had her reservations. Perhaps, she thought, it was because she did not like recognizing that marriage to her was how he had committed the betrayal in the first place.

His grandmother was still not pleased, however. "I cannot believe I must tell you such a thing. You should be on your knees to the man, begging his pardon, hoping that he will one day grant you his forgiveness. Instead, you are digging a ditch."

Hero interjected, "Arthur met one of the challenges that will allow him to lead the Round Table Society by digging that ditch."

His grandmother's expression softened somewhat as she paused for a moment and then asked, "Is that so?"

"I have." He glanced at her as if perhaps he wished she had not said anything about the challenges to his grandmother.

"Which challenge is it that digging a ditch satisfies?" The contempt in her voice was not disguised in the least.

He said calmly, "Chivalry, of course, Grandmama." He paused, and then added, "You know— the virtue of giving aid to those less fortunate than yourself."

"Virtue indeed," she said dryly. "I should have kept a closer rein on you when you were younger," she added for good measure. "You are out digging ditches when you have fences to mend. I cannot believe you have single-handedly made an enemy of this man who has been a friend to our family for years."

Arthur interrupted sharply. "I remind you, if he is anyone's enemy, Grandmama, it is mine and mine alone—not this family's or yours."

For several tense seconds, his grandmother simply stared at him, as if he were an unusual specimen she wished to categorize but could not. And then she said abruptly, "He is set upon Gabriel Digby to win out as head of the Round Table Society."

Arthur blinked at the blunt announcement. "After the meeting, I had suspected as much, but I can understand—"

"Understand! Please don't waste my time in understanding, Arthur." She leaned forward. "This is your chance. You can prove your worth. You can win. But you need to do more than dig ditches, my boy."

"We are both good men, both good candidates. It would be no shame to lose to Gabriel Digby." Arthur added, "Not that I intend to lose, of course."

"Lose?" She sighed. "Have I not passed on my knowledge of Arthurian legend? Do you not have your grandfather's and your father's scholarly research? Their library? The stories you took in with your mother's milk and those at your grandfather's knee?"

"I do." He nodded.

But she went on, impatiently. "There should never have been a competition between the two of you. If you had been more forceful, more commanding, there would have been no choice to make."

Hero wanted to protest the unfair criticism, but Arthur warned her not to interfere with a swift glance. He tried to fight his own battle. "But—"

"If you lose this, you are no grandson of mine."

"Grandmama, Digby and I are both equally respected scholars; it would be no shame to lose to him."

She sagged in front of them as if she had become boneless, and then she straightened once again. Hero braced herself for some new attack.

With an arch of her brow, she questioned him sharply. "Have you met either of the other challenges yet?"

He shook his head. "No."

She paused a moment, holding his eye with hers for a longer time than absolutely necessary. "Digby has."

Arthur became completely still in the chair beside Hero. She did not take a breath until he did. And then he said only, "He has?"

"Yes."

"How can you be certain?"

"Is it not enough that I am certain?"

He sputtered, "Did Fenwell Delagrace tell you this? He might have reason to lie—"

Her laughter was pure scorn. "With his rescue of your bride from that fire, Arthur, he has met the challenge of Valor."

Arthur sat stunned and silent.

She did not stop her scornful scourge, however. "He risked his own life for your bride." Her gaze, on Hero, was blazingly angry. She could not imagine any worse punishment.

Or so Hero thought, until his grandmother turned to her own grandson and said bitingly, "Worst of all, you will be the one to bear witness to his tale. Admit to the whole society that your wife helped your rival to win."

"That is no dishonor to either of us that he happened to be the one to rescue Hero."

"Then you do not see any shame in having to bear witness to Digby's deed? For doing so could well bring about your own failure if you do not begin to meet your challenges in as glorious and memorable a way." She added, "It is unfortunate the man does not have a bride of his own for you to rescue."

"I cannot wish that he did not rescue Hero," Arthur said softly, turning to look at her as if he thought she might need assurance on the matter. It did not please her that she did indeed need the confirmation she saw in his expression. "No matter that it means he has met a challenge, or that I must bear witness to it."

"Then you are a fool, and you will feel it keenly when you stand to tell your tales and be judged for them."

"So be it." He shrugged with a nonchalance that Hero doubted he truly felt. "I will do as I must. I will apologize to Fenwell Delagrace, and I will meet my challenges."

"Then do so," his grandmother snapped. "And exercise some control over your own wife."

"My wife is not an issue." Arthur stood, his own anger at the fore. "I will do my best, as I always have, to make this family proud."

"Good." Her attention turned with no warning to Hero. "And will you help him, girl, instead of putting boulders in his path, as you have been?"

"Of course I will," Hero answered without hesitation.

"Very well, then prove the mettle of your words with action. Begin with turning the Delagrace family back into our allies, please."

Arthur uttered a strangled protest. "How is she to do that without allowing time to facilitate the necessary cooling off of tempers?"

"I do not care."

"Grandmama—"

"I expect you—the both of you." Her eyes were sharp upon Hero. "For mark my words, you will fail if you are not both working relentlessly toward this end—to begin tomorrow."

"Tomorrow?"

"Yes. In addition, we are invited to a small dinner late next week. I expect you to have met at least one of your challenges by that time."

"I have met one."

"Digging ditches? I hope you can do better than that."

He bowed. "I will do my best."

She sighed softly. "I wish I could believe you this time." She turned her attention back to the letter in front of her.

Apparently, that action served as their dismissal, because Arthur held out his hand for Hero. She gripped it tightly as she rose, glad to be leaving the opulent and oppressive room, where darkness hovered in the very corners. She was suddenly grateful for her own large and loving family, despite the distance between them now. Poor Arthur. How awful to have such a woman as your sole remaining family member.

Nineteen

There had been no more notes in two weeks. Not since their arrival at Camelot. Each morning Arthur carefully checked to make sure their mysterious note writer had not dropped another missive while he was occupied about the business of his estate. He had tried not to care, had tried not to let it matter to him. But for a while he had felt so close, seeing the words in Malory's own hand.

He sighed, putting the frustration from his mind with a force of will. There were still over two months left to fulfill the challenges and outshine Digby at the meeting of the Round Table Society. Finding the manuscript in that time was, for the most part, a fruitless exercise in worry.

He would be better served to put his mind to meeting his challenges. He was an excellent scholar, that he knew. And he was proud of the ditch he had helped Nat Turner to dig. The man was eighty, with five widowed daughters, and twelve as yet unwed granddaughters. Perhaps if he'd not waited until forty to wed, he'd not have been in his predicament, but how could anyone in the society argue that he was not a fellow in need of a knightly good deed?

Chivalry was accounted for. Honor and Valor must be satisfied in two months' time.

The manuscript, as it would reflect upon his Honor challenge, would mean leadership of the society. He did not doubt it for a moment, no matter that his grandmother scorned ditch digging as an act of chivalry, and Fenwell Delagrace had accepted his apology with the frigid grace—and sincerity—of an ice statue. But if there was no further word—he must not rely on one possibility to meet his challenge; he knew that would be a mistake he could not afford.

Perhaps he should consider this silence a good omen. With no more notes, he would be forced to put aside his quest for the manuscript and concentrate on fulfilling the challenges to win the leadership of the Round Table Society. That would please his grandmother.

He resolved, then, to do nothing more to track the manuscript than he had already done. The men he had hired to investigate would report back to him if they managed to find out who was writing the notes. Otherwise, he would concentrate only on meeting the two challenges left to him. Honor, which he thought, barring the manuscript, could be won with a new translation he had put aside to track the manuscript. And the challenge that gave him the most worry—Valor. That was the one he must pursue most fervently—though he hadn't an idea how to begin.

Feeling as if a weight had been removed from his shoulders, he went down to luncheon expecting a pleasant meal with Hero. To his shock, he discovered that an unexpected guest had arrived. Gabriel Digby sat boldy and unapologetically at the table.

"Watterly." Digby greeted him civilly with that grin that showed all his perfect teeth.

"Digby." His new resolve to devote himself to meeting his challenges allowed him to say the man's name calmly, masking completely the astonishment he felt. He did not, at first, even glance at his grandmother.

He took his place at the table, noticing only then that Hero was not yet present. "Grandmama, where is Hero?"

He could see the question surprised her. No doubt she had expected him to challenge Digby, perhaps even call him out. She answered the question he had asked, though, after a slight hesitation. "She is being fitted for new gowns."

"She cannot take time out for a meal?"

"She lost half of her entire wardrobe in the fire. She has many gowns to replace."

He knew the message she was sending to him. She wanted to remind him of the fire and the challenge Hero had met for Digby. Apparently, she did not even mind that Digby sat consuming their prime salmon, oblivious to her rebuke.

"I will see that something is sent up to her," he said mildly, gesturing to the footman.

"As you wish," his grandmother replied snappishly. He hoped some of her irritation was in response to his cool acceptance of her perfidy. "She is mistress of the house, after all, and perfectly capable of ordering her own meal sent up."

"And well you should remember it," he agreed. When she did not seem sufficiently abashed, he added sharply, "And I am master and may be solicitous of my wife, if I wish."

Digby, who had been watching the exchange with the polite boredom of the genteel eavesdropper, said heartily, "I applaud you, sir, both for seeing promptly to the replacement of your wife's unfortunate loss of her wardrobe, as well as for seeing that she is fed during what I imagine must be quite a traumatic undertaking, if I am to believe the tales my sisters have told me."

"Thank you, Digby." He wanted to throttle the man, but the way his grandmother glanced at him, he had a feeling she was hoping he would. So instead, he said shortly, "I intend to see that my wife wants for nothing."

His grandmother was clearly displeased with his statement. But instead of inciting any further argument, she turned to a new and well-loved topic. "How is your translation on that French tale coming, Arthur?"

They talked of King Arthur, as his grandmother wished. Much to his chagrin, the conversation was stimulating, all three of them experts. Digby knew the subject as well as Arthur. Not to mention that he had rescued a woman from a fire while Arthur had only dug a ditch.

His decision was only confirmed more absolutely—he could waste no more time on Malory's elusive manuscript. He must concentrate on meeting his challenges. After he succeeded in removing Digby from Camelot.

Under his breath he asked his grandmother, "Grandmama—did you not just tell me yourself that Digby has the support of Fenwell Delagrace himself?

How can you allow him into the house knowing that?"

She smiled, not bothering to keep her voice discreetly low. "I invited him. Such a charming young man. I can see why the Round Table Society would consider him to lead them."

Digby, ever the gentleman, excused himself politely as soon as the voices about him began to rise.

Arthur watched him go, his thoughts in confusion. Why had his grandmother really summoned his rival? Could she, too, be planning to side with Digby as head of the society?

He wondered if his last failure had truly been the final one she could tolerate. Had she decided that he would never make something of himself? Without consciously deciding to, he asked the question aloud. "Have you decided to back the man as well?"

Her lip curled in disdain, and he knew that somehow she was again disappointed in him. "Don't be ridiculous. Have you never heard the adage 'know thy enemy'?"

"How would such an adage apply to inviting Gabriel Digby—a man who is currently my rival for the head of the Round Table Society—here to Camelot?"

She sighed. "You have stiff competition, my dearest grandson. It is best that you learn to appreciate it and treat this challenge as seriously as you must."

"If you say this because you doubt me," he said calmly, "then don't. I am up to the challenge."

"By digging ditches?"

"By digging a ditch for an eighty-year-old tenant with no son and no grandson to help."

She lifted an elegant eyebrow as if to say that his tale would not move her.

"I assure you, Grandmama, winning the challenge is all in the way the tale is told," he said, though he was beginning to doubt that truth himself. Digby might have the charm to tell a boring tale in the most entertaining of manners. "The fellow I helped was a true character, and the society will see that."

"Perhaps." She added, "I hope your choice of wives does not put you from the running altogether."

About Hero he had no hesitation. "If it does, I shall not regret it, Grandmama."

She looked at him sharply. "I wish I could say that sentiment of yours surprises me, but it does not."

"As it should not. Did Grandfather ever regret marrying you? I think not."

"Your grandfather had no reason to regret his marriage to me. I brought with me a fortune, and a dream." She shook her head, her expression almost tender. "What has your bride brought you but scandal and dishonor."

"She had brought me no dishonor. And the haste of our vows might have been news for the gossips, but it was certainly not a scandal."

She sighed. "Despite all my tutelage, you still do not know what is most important."

He knew in his heart she was wrong, though her words still stung him deeply. "A wife is most important, Grandmama. And Hero is my wife. That is never going to change."

"No? I confess to a bit of selfish disappointment when I heard that she nearly perished in that fire at the inn." She paused. "You know, the one where Digby met the Chivalric challenge."

Her words stunned him. He knew that his grand-mother had a ruthless streak—but to suggest that she would have welcomed Hero's death? She must be overwrought. "I will forget you said such a thing, Grandmama. It must be that your nerves are too tightly strung with all the changes we have had here in the last few weeks."

"That is kind of you, Arthur," she said, though her tone was not sincere. "But it will not change the fact that your wife helped Gabriel Digby meet one of his challenges. Or do you not remember the event?"

He remembered quite well. But suddenly he won-dered where she had heard that little tidbit of gossip. "How did you hear about the fire? About Digby res-cuing Hero?" It had certainly not been from him-self—nor likely would Hero have mentioned it.

She looked at him as if the answer should be self-evident, and once again she was disappointed in his lack of cleverness. "Servant gossip, my dear."

He had not expected such a claim. "The servants gossip about such things?"

"One can learn much of value listening to one's maid or valet. I always keep an ear out for anything that might disrupt the smooth running of this house-hold."

"And how, exactly, does Digby rescuing Hero from a fire at an inn disrupt your household, Grand-mama?"

She did not answer him directly. "The delicate ability to question your servants is a useful skill to have."

"It appears to have served you well."

She frowned fleetingly, as if he had yet again

missed something obvious. "It is a skill I expect you should cultivate, my dear, considering whom you have married. After all, your bride is not likely to be competent to manage your life and household yet. She can barely handle putting cream in her tea, and I have to remind her daily to wash the ink from her hands."

Arthur took off his spectacles to add to his sincerity as he frowned warningly at her. "If you say one more word against my wife, Grandmama, I will order the guest house readied for you and move you into it within a day."

His grandmother hitched in her breath in outrage. "You would do that to me after all I've done for you?"

He sighed. She had taken him in, she had loved him. Still— "I would indeed if you continue to undermine Hero and her management of my . . . our . . . household."

She looked at him speechlessly for a moment, and then asked in an ominously quiet voice, "For that . . . that . . . girl?!"

He replaced his spectacles and stood. "For my wife, Grandmama."

"I suppose she is your wife and there is nothing to be done about that now." Her tone was more speculative than he would have liked, as was her gaze as she stared into his eyes with the mesmerizing intensity that many through the years had found so unsettling.

He forced absolute sincerity into his voice, as well as into his expression. She would not see him waver on this, he was determined. "Yes, she is." He wondered, though, how much Hero wished she was

Digby's wife instead. He sighed. "And you will do well to remember that."

"As you say, then." She turned her cheek for his kiss as he came near her chair. "I suppose I have no choice, if you wish it."

He kissed her cheek gently. He knew it was a blow to her pride that he had chosen Hero over her. But it was her actions that had driven him to have to make a choice. "No, I'm afraid this time, Grandmama, you have none at all."

He saw her expression reflect the crashing loss of her hopes and dreams. And then, in a plaintive tone he had rarely heard from her, she asked, glancing down at her folded hands, half covered by the sweeping lace of her sleeves, "Does that mean you will turn my guest out into the cold?"

Wouldn't that be a shame? Arthur stifled his impulse to do just that. "Of course not. In fact, I must thank you. This luncheon conversation reminded me that Digby is a good man. One I have long admired."

She glanced up at him briefly, but he could not tell what emotions she felt at his statement. Fury? Approval? Hope? "I think you are wise, Arthur." Her compliment was deliberately vague, as sincere as it sounded.

"I know, Grandmama. Know your enemy." He pushed back his plate, surprised to note that he had eaten little. He would take something with Hero, as she was being fitted. "But you must understand that Digby is not my enemy. We are merely rivals for the same honor."

"And for the same woman?" Her eyes met his, and he saw that she had not truly been cowed by his threat. She had only been softening him for this moment.

He hardened his heart against her. "She is my wife, Grandmama. Digby, of all people, would not think of overstepping."

"I hope you are right in that."

"I am. Just as I am right in allowing him to stay as our guest." He added, hoping that she did not misinterpret his caution, "But he must not visit long."

"I agree." She nodded. When had she regained control of this conversation? he wondered. "I had not intended a long visit when I invited him."

"I understand now why you did so. But one question remains for me, one that I hope will be answered before he leaves Camelot."

"What is that?"

"Why did he accept your invitation, which requires him to travel so far from home this time of year?" And why did he seem to show up every few days, just behind Arthur himself?

Her eyes flickered in a way that told him she was hiding something. He wasn't certain he wanted to know what secret lay behind that gaze. "I told you, I invited him. Why else would he come?"

He pressed her, determined to have an answer. "I can understand why you might want the company of a charming man like Mr. Digby, Grandmama. What I cannot understand is why such a charming man would want to be buried out in the country with the likes of us, when London is the place to be this time of year."

"Perhaps you should ask him?"

"Perhaps I should." He could not resist adding,

"But I thought perhaps the servants' gossip might have told you what I want to know."

Her eyes flashed with annoyance or amusement or approval, he could not say, despite the years he had lived with her. "I'm afraid I have heard nothing. I cannot profess to know his motives." Her eyes flashed with emotion. "Perhaps he has set his sights on Gwen now that you have jilted her."

A flash of guilt spilled through him, but then he crushed it. "I did not jilt her, Grandmama." And he thought it would be an excellent thing for Digby and Gwen to fall in love—it would certainly ease his guilt on several scores. But no, on second thought, the complications of such a thing were too dreadful to imagine.

"As good as jilted her, then, if you must. You have had an understanding—"

When would she stop lamenting? It was not as if wishing it weren't so would change the fact that he and Hero were married. "You have had an understanding with Gwen's father. Gwen and I had nothing to do with it."

She grasped his hands tightly when he would have turned away and left the room. "You were told what it would mean to the family. I never heard you protest."

"I did not—"

The pain in her eyes was genuine. Still, there was nothing he could do to remedy her distress. "I could have explained it more thoroughly if you had," she whispered. "I could have shown you why it would have made you into the man you have always wanted to be—the man I have always believed you could be."

"I don't believe you could have convinced me of

such a thing, Grandmama. I am glad that I married Hero. And I suspect Gwen will be as well, one day."

She closed her eyes, her face pale, and he realized suddenly that age had rendered her more fragile than she allowed him to see most of the time. "You could have had a woman trained to handle Camelot."

"But I have—"

"You could have had a woman of great beauty. But no, instead, you choose to marry some milk-and-water miss in a hasty, nearly clandestine affair."

He wondered how long he would be defending his bride and her reputation from his own grandmother. "It was hasty, but it was hardly clandestine. Half of London came to the wedding."

She sniffed. "Only to see if Gwen would squirm under their stares, wilt under the pressure of being jilted—"

He made a sound of impatient protest.

She broke off, and then continued. "Oh, all right, if you insist, of having the understanding between you dissolved without her knowledge or consent."

"It is the truth." It was more than the truth, indeed, that his heart had not been in the understanding since the first time he had met Hero Fenster. If he had had the courage to tell his grandmother that—to tell Gwen—

Her voice was ice down his spine as she said, "And the truth may cost you what you prize most."

"I will not let it."

"No? Then you must discover the will and courage of Sir Balin to find the deed that will atone for your mistake and make amends to her father—or you will find Digby with the prize that is meant for you. And what will your little wife think of you then?"

Arthur felt his heart go cold at that thought. He had hoped perhaps Hero had been coming to see him in a more favorable light. But now, with Digby nearby, how could she help compare what she might have had with what she had ended up with?

Twenty

"Arthur!" Hero was visibly astonished when Arthur entered the room where she was being poked and prodded and pinned for new gowns. Her first action was to cover her somewhat bared breasts, but the seamstress muttered sharply and slapped her hands away.

"Good afternoon, my dear." He quickly suppressed the urge to put his lips where her hands had pressed but a moment before. To do so might convince her she need never cover herself from his eyes again, or it might frighten her and make her distrust him.

"What has brought you here?" She blushed, evidently realizing how her actions could be interpreted. For the exposed skin, though delicious and tempting to him, was only what a ball gown would reveal. And Arthur was, after all, her husband.

A question formed in his mind—would she had moved so if it were Digby who had entered the room? Ridiculous. What had put such a thought in his head? And why did he want to erase Digby from her memory? She was his wife. His. He found himself fighting hard to keep from making a gesture of possession. He could only suppose that his primitive reaction was caused by his jealousy at Digby's presence.

Pretending that he had not noticed her discomfort, or her desire to cover herself, he said cheerfully, "Grandmama told me that you were being subjected to torture today." The seamstress and her minions glared at him as he spoke, whether at his words, or simply at his presence he could not say. "So I brought you some sandwiches."

"You needn't have done that, I could have rung for something from the kitchen," she protested.

"So my grandmother said," he replied, wondering if he had made a blunder. He set down the plate he had carried by his own hand, to the amusement of the scullery maid and the shocked disapproval of the cook.

She blinked rapidly several times, as if she realized her words had hurt him. And then she said, "How ungracious of me. I am so touched that you would think of me, but you needn't . . . I mean . . . it was too much trouble . . ."

He tried not to let his grin spread too widely across his face. He did not want to offend her. He had not expected to fluster her so thoroughly with such a simple action. Still, it was somewhat pleasing to know that he could. "It was no trouble, I assure you."

He borrowed Digby's phrase but turned it to his own advantage. "After all, I well remember the days of fittings you and your sisters suffered through when your family first came to live with the duke for the Season."

She smiled, and her discomposure faded at last. "Thank you."

He watched the fitting for a while. She glanced at

him from time to time with a more puzzled glance each time. It was obvious she could tell he had something on his mind.

He made idle conversation. But he had no idea how to broach the subject he most wanted to discuss. Especially not when she was so intimately acquainted with the sheer volume of pins the seamstresses had overladen her with in their zeal to fit her new gowns perfectly.

Had she known that Digby would come? Or would she be just as surprised as he had been?

At last, just when she was having her corset tightened more than she could bear, more to distract her from the discomfort than because he thought she would want to know, he blurted it out. "Digby is here."

"Digby?" Her face was a study in expressions. Puzzlement, comprehension, curiosity, and then, at last, dismay. He wondered what that expression boded. For she could be dismayed to see the man she loved but could not have, or she could be dismayed to see her husband's rival. He wished there were some way he could tell which reason put the expression on her face.

"Yes, I'm afraid he has come to call here at Camelot," he said, hoping he would see something more in her face that would tell him what he most wished to know.

And then he watched as she fully comprehended what he had said. "Here? He has come to call?"

He nodded. "He has come to stay at my grandmother's invitation, no less." He was watching her closely, as if he did not know what her reaction might be. Did he suspect her somehow, since she had unwittingly given Digby a way to meet his challenge? She hoped not.

"But why has he come here?" She could feel her jaw gape, the news was so surprising.

"I have no idea, but I thought I would warn you."

"Warn me of what?"

"I think Grandmama is up to some game of her own." He touched her cheek gently. "I don't want to see you hurt by it."

With those words, he pressed a kiss against her cheek despite the seamstresses' clucks of disapproval, and departed.

Hero watched him go, disappointed. She had hoped when she first saw him that he might stay until the fitting was over, but apparently, as usual, he had business to attend to and she was left alone with the seamstresses, whose only words seemed to be "Hold still, please" and "Turn, please."

Hero could not believe Digby had arrived at Camelot. It was more than coincidence that he seemed to appear a few days behind them at each location.

His puppy-dog looks toward her were beginning to draw her nerves tight. What did he want from her? She was a married woman now, he knew that, and yet he still looked at her as if she were an eligible woman he wished to make his wife. It was most annoying. She had been exceedingly glad to be rid of him when they left the inn.

She was glad for Arthur's warning later that day when she ran into Digby himself in the library. She had meant only to get a book to read in the garden. But she could not be openly rude to a guest in her home.

He greeted her first, with delight. "Hello, Mrs.

Watterly." She was relieved to see that he did not have that infatuated look on his face today.

"Hello, Mr. Digby." She had never felt nervous around him before, but this was too much. Knowing that Arthur was competing with him, knowing that Grandmama might be colluding with him for some unfathomable reason. Her palms were damp with perspiration and she had only said hello.

His words were innocuous enough, but his expression changed to the one she dreaded to see. "Married life seems to agree with you." The glance he gave her was unnerving in its intensity.

"How kind of you to say so." Although his eyes were sending a different message altogether. Hero moved away, careful to keep a discreet distance between them.

"Are you happy?" There was too much intensity in his gaze when he asked.

"Very," she said sharply, belatedly aware that there was not a scrap of sincerity in her tone.

"I—" The look in his eye was too hopeful.

She interrupted him to add, "Arthur is a wonderful husband. I can ask for no more than what I have been given. And I do not appreciate any insinuation otherwise." This time, she managed to infuse her statement with the truth, for he backed away from her, and the intensity of his gaze disappeared.

"I assure you I did not mean—" He broke off. With a faint tinge of color in his cheeks, he said quickly, "I hope you don't think I've been following you."

She remembered now why she had liked Gabriel Digby in the first place. He was an exceedingly honest man. She met his honesty with her own, hoping she would not have cause to regret doing so. "I had wondered."

"No. I came to the inn by chance only. I had no notion that you and Arthur would be there. I had received an"—he hesitated over the word—"an invitation from Mr. Delagrace to join him here for a week or so."

"Why would Fenwell Delagrace wish to call you from London at this particular time?" The memory of how convincingly Arthur had lied to his grandmother, and to Digby himself, gave her a touch of caution. Hero was not willing to trust to her instincts that Digby was indeed telling the truth. It occurred to her, though she loathed the idea, that he could be Arthur's mysterious note sender.

"His decision is key in who will be the next head of the Round Table Society. He wished to discuss the matter with me in privacy, and he had been called home unexpectedly, so he invited me to join him."

"And you agreed."

He shook his head, and again her instinct was to believe him. "Actually, no. I told him I would follow him in a few days. And that is when Mrs. Watterly kindly invited me here, so that it would not look as though I had allowed Fenwell Delagrace to buy me the position—if I were so fortunate as to attain it."

"Indeed?" Hero had not known that fact. Delagrace had been outspoken at the society meeting in London, but he was just a member like any other, wasn't he?

But no. She thought back and realized that many members had deferred to his opinion. She wondered if Arthur knew. He could be unobservant as to others' motives. But one so critical to him? No, he must know what the lack of support could mean.

Certainly his grandmother knew. And she was not one to keep such a thing a secret.

Perhaps that was why he was so hesitant to be around Gwen and her father? He suspected that their hasty marriage had dashed his chance to become head of the society. Perhaps he felt that nothing he did could overturn that insult to their family.

Noticing that Digby was again gazing at her a bit too avidly for her comfort, she said quickly, "How kind of him to invite you out for a personal interview, especially since he has known Arthur forever." When he showed no reaction, she added, "Shouldn't you be involved in meeting your challenges though?" A part of her hoped he would agree with her so strongly that he would leave Camelot at once. Another part of her wished he would stay just long enough for her to confirm or deny whether he was the one playing the game at Arthur's expense.

"Yes." He nodded without hesitation. "But Mr. Delagrace has offered to help me find just the right task to meet a challenge."

"Is that necessary?"

"Yes, just the right challenge is essential." He watched her carefully as he added, "After all, I am vying with your husband. You would agree that he is stiff competition?"

"Arthur is a great scholar as well as a wonderful man." And it was certainly not his fault that he had been saddled with a wife likely to ruin his chances.

"I agree." He leaned forward earnestly and she leaned back in her chair. "That is where Fenwell Delagrace believes he can help—to find the perfect challenge for me to meet that will win it for me."

There was less enthusiasm in his expression than she would have expected for such an offer. She heard something more beneath his words and, after a moment's thought, realized what it was. "And you do not want to insult him by refusing, I take it."

"Indeed." He smiled ruefully. "I cannot afford to make an enemy of Fenwell Delagrace."

"I can understand that." Unfortunately, all too well, she thought, since she was the one who had managed to put Arthur on the other side of Fenwell's good wishes.

He put his hand on hers as it lay on the arm of her chair. "There is no need to be frantic, I assure you."

She removed her hand to her lap, certain he would not pursue it there. "What do you mean?"

"That Arthur will be unfairly bested. After all, Fenwell will offer me only advice on the best challenges to pursue. And Arthur has his grandmother—as well as you—to help him."

"That does seem to make it even, then, doesn't it?" she said in agreement. But Digby, bless his steadfast heart, was not aware that Hero was a liability to Arthur rather than a boon.

"Of course, Arthur and I both need to be watching for challenges. Most especially Valor." His eyes contained the almost childlike optimism she remembered well from his courtship of her.

She smiled. "You worry over Valor?" She found it impossible to think of him as a schemer, a puzzle master, or a gamester. No. If she had said she was unhappy, she had no doubt that he would have happily acted as her knight in shining armor and run away with her to the Continent.

"I consider it to be the most difficult challenge, yes."

"I would wish you well, if simply for the sake of our past friendship"—she would not categorize it as more—"but I am afraid all my support must go to my husband now. I can only hope you meet all three of your challenges well, and that Arthur wins in the end."

"Of course." He looked unhappy at her words even as he struggled to be hopeful. "We have both met at least one of the challenges already, and in that the difficulty of the competition is clear."

"Which challenge have you both met?" She would scratch his eyes out if he dared mention the fire to her, she vowed.

"We have both met the Honor challenge."

"How?" Certainly Arthur did not seem to agree. Otherwise he would not be so downcast that there had been no more notes from their mysterious friend with Malory's manuscript.

He said with certainty, "I, for the set of Arthurian stanzas I uncovered in a monastery in France last year. Arthur, for his translation of a rare French copy of a tale of Launcelot that must date back to fourteen hundred."

"Around about the time of *Le Morte d'Arthur*, then?" she asked with as innocent a lilt in her voice as she could manage, but her gaze was avid. She did not want to credit it, but cowardice should not blind her to the truth. If he was the one tormenting Arthur, she was determined to find him out.

Unfortunately, if Digby flinched, he did so so faintly that she could not observe it.

"That is my favorite of the Arthurian books, you know," she pressed on, determined to elicit some reaction.

"Mine, as well." He smiled, but his expression remained devoid of guilty starts or ruinous blushes. "I am especially fond of the Launcelot and Guinevere tales of late. It was a tragedy that they could not be together because of her marriage to Arthur."

"Yes, well, I've never understood those tales myself," Hero said sharply. "Arthur was a perfectly good husband and Guinevere was a fool to betray him with another man."

"They were in love. Even Arthur understood the purity of their love. If Mordred had not forced his hand—"

"They were still fools," she interrupted him, feeling as if the conversation were going to a place she might regret tomorrow morning.

"Perhaps I simply feel an affinity to Arthur's finest knight," he said mildly, allowing her to win the skirmish, though she had no doubt he had not changed his mind. "Have I ever mentioned to you that my middle name is Launcelot?"

Hero was left speechless at that for a moment, and then she grabbed up the first book she could reach and hastily excused herself, convinced that Gabriel Digby—Gabriel *Launcelot* Digby, was a madman—an amiable madman, but a madman all the same.

The dinner that Gwen's father called intimate, Hero called oppressive. Thirty people—laughing, chatting, curious people who knew Arthur well and Hero not at all.

Half of the guests were Round Table Society members, the other half people Arthur had known for a lifetime. Neighbors, who were all of them partial to Gwen since she arrived, a small blond angel, in their midst.

Unfortunately for Hero, aside from the staid Round Table Society gentlemen, not a one of the guests ever heard Hero's name spoken aloud until she appeared at the table and Arthur introduced her around. She had spent enough time in London to know that the quick glances exchanged among the guests did not suggest they approved of Arthur's choice of bride.

She felt like a hothouse flower brought out to be admired but found to be too dangerous to come close to. They smiled at her as if she were a rare creature, totally untamed, around whom they must be on their best manners as well as on their guard from. And they spoke to her in short declarative sentences, a trifle loudly, as if she might be deaf, or simple.

Worst of all was the false, solicitous kindnesses they offered. The gentleman seated to Hero's left had made more than one remark about Arthur being a "good boy," discussed his need to "pull his head out of his books now and again," and admitted candidly that he "had thought Gwen would bring him around sooner or later." She wanted to scream. Or, more truthfully, to cry.

More pressing than her need to scream was her desire to run away, to find privacy and solitude and deal with the wounded feelings she could not contain. But that was not to be.

She had spent enough time at Camelot to know the consequences of her actions. Where in London, her retreat would be seen with humor, spiteful or not, to leave this dinner party would be so much more. It would mean that she had conceded defeat to Gwen's father.

For herself she did not mind. She had never been truly accepted by society. She loved her books and her scholarly pursuits too much for that. She would not miss the social invitations, nor care too much for the social snubs she was certain to incur.

But for Arthur, as badly as he wanted—deserved— to be head of the Round Table Society, she did not dare. She had already been the cause of so much difficulty for him, she would not add one more black mark to her record.

No. She must face the music like a grown woman. She thought of her older sister, who had shown tremendous courage with seeming ease. What would Miranda do in a situation like this? No doubt she would charm Fenwell Delagrace into backing Arthur once more, and give her altered versions of classic fairy tales to convince everyone in the room that Arthur had made a well-fated marriage. But Hero was not Miranda.

If only she could pull one of the decorative swords from the wall and run it through the guests. Not all of them, of course, only those who would make unkind comments in the quietest way, and with the sweetest smiles, so that at first she thought her ears deceived her.

"They were such boon companions in their early age," reminisced one elderly matron.

Hero wondered at the veracity of the memories. She could not imagine a twelve-year-old boy finding much of interest in a toddling child. But such was her insecurity, that she could almost believe the two had been inseparable since birth.

She reminded herself of the look in Gwen's eye when she spoke about the perfect man. She did not speak in the abstract, Hero was certain. Perhaps it was her own experience with her sisters, but she trusted her instinct. Gwen Delagrace was not in love with a shadow hero, but with a real flesh-and-blood man.

Twenty-one

Restlessly, only pretending to be listening to the conversations about her, Hero let her mind wander over the possibilities. So who was the man Gwen loved? Was he here tonight? She quickly scanned the table but saw no one whose gaze lingered on Gwen, lovelorn or otherwise.

Perhaps he did not yet know of her feelings? Then she must not expect him to give *her* a clue, but Gwen. Unfortunately, Gwen herself was looking only at her plate.

Hero endured her torture, sat silently nodding and smiling as the memories flowed forth without encouragement from her. Arthur as a small child, destined for great things. Arthur saving Gwen from the lake, Arthur bringing Gwen the sweetest berries as they ripened, so that she should not be scratched by the brambles. Arthur, coming up just a tad short at everything he tried as he grew older.

Would this night ever end? she wondered, smiling at a woman who had just called Arthur a "trembling milkweed" in the sweetest of voices.

And then the next note came, from where she could not say, though she looked about the room as discreetly as possible as soon as she realized what had happened. One moment she was pretending with all her skill to listen to the conversation. The next thing she knew she looked down to her lap as she idly smoothed her skirt, and there was a note.

She stared at it in disbelief for a moment. How could— She blinked, thinking she had conjured it from her own boredom. But no. The small white square of paper was in her lap, and she had no idea how it had gotten there. She snatched it up into her fingers and looked around to see if anyone was watching.

No.

She read the note. *A good book can unlock any mystery, if one knows how to read.*

Again, it was so cryptic as to mean almost nothing. It puzzled her. But the handwriting was familiar. She looked at Arthur, down the length of the table, seated beside Gwen's father and across from Gwen herself.

He was too far away for her to discreetly make a gesture to catch his attention, especially since he had taken off his spectacles at his grandmother's request. She thought it made him look less than leadership material. Hero found it distinctly annoying because it made him unable to see her.

Fine, she would take care of the matter by herself. Though she might not be able to run a household like Camelot without mishap, surely she could make her way to the library of Gwen's home, as the note directed.

But first she had to wait until the gentlemen retired to their brandy and cigars. As the women began to gather for conversation, she saw one flinty-eyed matron bearing down upon her. Hastily, she left a message with the footman, in the event she had not returned before Arthur and the gentlemen rejoined them, and exited the room quickly, before she could be snared. She hoped that the other women would assume she was simply freshening up and her absence would not be questioned. Or, better yet, that no one would come to seek her out.

After only a few wrong turns and helpful directions from a maid hurrying on an errand, she found the library and quickly slipped inside, hoping no one had remarked upon her destination.

The sight that met her eyes left her gaping. For in the library with its towering walls and full shelves of books, was the famed Round Table. It could be nothing else.

For one moment, she actually believed it to be the actual round table from King Arthur's time. But then she realized her folly. She ran her hand over the smooth wood. Someone, Fenwell Delagrace no doubt, had gone to the trouble of commissioning a replica of King Arthur's famed Round Table. But why?

The beauty of the work was undeniable. Mesmerized, she walked the circumference of the circular table, noting the names carved into the table by each seat. Sir Kay, Sir Launcelot, Sir Galahad . . . She rubbed her hands over her eyes. Still, the table remained.

Was this what the note had meant to expose? Surely Arthur, who had spent a great deal of his youth here, would already know of its existence? She looked at the line of books that filled the shelves. Or was she to discover the next clue among all of those?

* * *

"May the best man win, eh, Arthur?" Digby was smiling, and it only made matters worse that Arthur suspected the man truly meant what he said.

"May the best tale win," he said in answer, more to amuse those standing around them than in hopes that he might influence any of the society members who were still unbiased.

For Digby's charm had certainly turned the heads of the Round Table Society members. The tales he told were amusing and lively in turn, and none could be condemned as idle boasting. For the man had indeed done well in his life. Arthur fought the urge to compare his own life to Digby's. Now was not the time or the place for such foolishness. Though there was no question that Digby's charm gave him a definite edge.

That, and Fenwell Delagrace's money and influence. Arthur could not believe the arrogance of the man—to have spared no expense to bring everyone out here was probably against the rules. Although no one would claim that they had been influenced to vote any way but the way they believed right.

He knew it was too soon to believe that the challenges had been won by Digby before they had even been met. There were more than eight weeks left until the day they must tell their tales. He had time to ensure that his challenges were met to the best of his abilities. But his heart was not in the race tonight. He fought the urge to stand and remove himself from consideration.

No, that would be the coward's way out. He must do his best, no matter that he no longer had faith in the outcome. He sighed. It must not have been meant to be, he tried to console himself.

But he had wanted it. He had wanted to see the admiration and recognition on the faces of the society members as he was chosen to head the society into the future.

Unless, however, *Le Morte d'Arthur* appeared in his hands immediately, that was highly unlikely.

He hoped Hero would not be as disappointed in him as he knew his grandmother would be.

Merton Danton slapped him sharply on the shoulder, so that he nearly spilled his brandy. "Arthur, Gabriel, how fortunate we are to have you both here with us."

Arthur, mindful of the need to mend his quarrel with Delagrace, said only, "Yes, it was good of Fenwell to give us this opportunity."

"I hope the quests go well?" The question was asked out of curiosity by a particularly unpleasant member of the society. No doubt the man wished to hear they had both failed miserably.

"Our three months have barely begun," he answered mildly. "But I am pleased with my progress."

"As am I," Digby answered modestly.

"One third of the time has passed. What have you done?"

Fortunately, they were both spared answering the question by the interruption of one of the oldest members present, Winfield Standish. Five feet two and bone-thin with a thick head of white hair, the man had the air of a impatient hummingbird.

Raising his old-fashioned monocle, which Arthur privately thought he should trade in for a good strong pair of spectacles, Standish quavered in excitement. "I am glad to have you both here. I have a scrap of an old manuscript I wish you to look at."

Arthur's heart began to pound. "Manuscript?"

"Yes, from a 1782 printing of—"

Arthur heard no more. It did not matter anyway. With a sigh, he reached into his pocket and retrieved his spectacles.

He would do his best with whatever he was shown, although he had no doubt the work would be less than satisfying. Still, it did not make sense to insult anyone while he was on his quest.

In boredom, he wondered how his wife was faring. She had been seated with some of the older people from the area. Those with long memories and even longer tales to tell. He hoped she had managed to stay awake. It would not do to insult Fenwell just as he was beginning to make amends.

It turned out, to Standish's grave disappointment, that the manuscript had been forged within the last two years—the ink gave it away even before the paper, which carried a watermark of a company new to the business. But the perusal, discussion, and rather lukewarm debate served to fill the time until they were allowed to rejoin the ladies.

He did not see Hero immediately. He wondered for a moment if she had fallen asleep and slipped to the floor without notice. But then, seriously, as he craned his neck, he realized that she was truly gone.

It should not have alarmed him—she could easily have withdrawn to the ladies' salon to refresh herself. But a niggle of worry ate at him. After all, her life had been threatened twice in the last month. It would not do to be too complacent.

With a twitch of his fingers, he called over a footman. He had intended to send a note to his room, but it turned out not to be necessary. The footman informed him that his wife had retired for the evening with a headache.

He wished she had told him, but perhaps she had expected that the footman would volunteer the information rather than wait until he was asked. An urgent need to make certain that she was well overwhelmed his intentions to be the perfect guest at this gathering.

He knew he risked losing Fenwell Delagrace's goodwill if he left the gathering before time, but he could not shake the feeling that he should be with Hero now. Before something awful happened. Knowing there was a possibility that she would be fine, he decided to check their room, make sure she was only suffering from a headache, and then return.

Even Fenwell would not be offended by such behavior. No one would . . . except— He located Grandmama at the whist table. She was holding court, as she sometimes did at these gatherings. He watched his grandmother's face anxiously for a moment. She was busy in conversation and had not glanced his way—or Hero's—even once.

Good. He could slip out and go upstairs to check on Hero, then. No one would be any the wiser if he returned quickly enough.

For a moment, as she passed the seat marked for Sir Balin, Hero felt as if she were being watched. She whirled toward the leather chairs by the fire, but there was no one sitting there. And no one in any other corner of the room. She sighed. Whom had she expected to find? The man who was behind these infuriating games?

She could see no manuscript lying out for her to take either. Who sent her the note, then? And why had the note led her here? Just so that she could see the table? Or was there a note in this room somewhere? A clue she was meant to find and bring to Arthur?

Her headache pounded even more insistently. She wished she had somehow managed to catch Arthur's eye and bring him here with her. Perhaps he would understand what it was they were meant to do.

She sighed. The only thing to do was to bring him here. However, she did not want to rejoin the ladies. She could not weather any more of that chatter about Arthur's childhood.

She could, however, send a footman to him with a note. She smiled. She would tell him about her note at dinner. Hopefully, this time the footman would deliver the note, not drop it into Arthur's lap, as her note had been delivered.

Again she wondered how the paper had been placed in her lap. Could one of the footmen have dropped it while they served her dishes? Had it been tucked in the napkin and she hadn't noticed at first?

She looked about for a piece of notepaper, eager to call Arthur to help her solve this latest mystery. She wondered if he would be pleased or dismayed that the notes had started again.

Though she no longer had the eerie sense of being watched, she still felt uneasy, felt there was something wrong about the room. She could not quite place what it was, so distracting to her mind was the giant table in the center of the room, and the fact that the note had led her here.

And then she heard the chattering noise. It seemed to be coming from one of the large windows on the far wall. As she looked, she noticed that the curtains were moving in the breeze. Someone had left the window open.

She began to go over to close it, when she saw that it was not simply the breeze that was moving the curtains. There was an animal there. And the animal was the one making that odd, chattering noise.

She began to move slowly toward the animal, not wanting to scare it away if it was injured. "Have you hurt yourself, little one," she cooed softly to soothe it, to let it know that she meant no harm.

At last she was close enough to see that the animal was a fox. It was curled up in a ball, and the odd, chattering noise was coming from the vibration of the animal's jaws.

"What's the matter, little fox?" she asked.

It lifted its head at the sound of her voice.

It looked like any other fox she had ever seen. However, unlike any fox she had ever seen before, this one did not run in terror at the sight of her.

At first she thought only that it had been hurt so badly, it could not move. But then she saw that there was foam coming from its jaws.

He had hoped to find her curled up reading in bed. Or, at the very least, sipping a toddy to ease her headache. When he opened the door, he did so quietly, so that if she had fallen asleep, he would not wake her. But all his cautions were in vain. She was not in their room.

An intense pang of jealousy seized him as he thought of her in a tryst with Digby. But that was unworthy of him. She had given him no cause to think such a thing of her and every reason to refuse to believe it.

He might not have been so easily soothed, however, if Digby had not been clearly visible, surrounded by a group of society members when he left the room. His own susceptibility to jealousy surprised him.

The nagging feeling grew stronger. He had to find Hero and make certain she was well. Remembering her penchant for getting lost, however, he checked with the butler, who checked with the servants, and found the one from whom Hero had gotten directions. He relaxed a bit when he heard where she had gone. The library.

Of course. He should have tried that haven first. Hero, as was her wont—he could not help a swift smile of understanding—had sought peace from his family's neighbors in the Delagrace library.

He sought her out there, still needing to see her, to make certain she was well. Perhaps they could find a volume to read to each other. He enjoyed her voice, soft and gentle, but carrying enough that he did not need to strain to understand her. He could listen to her read for hours at a time.

A thought flashed before him of Hero, dressed as she had been that morning, her corset only half laced, looking fresh from bed. That was how he would like her dressed as she read.

And the book—one of those from Mr. Beasley's shop. He stopped his thoughts abruptly. She would be outraged, no doubt, if she knew where his mind had wandered and what his baser instincts were doing to her character.

No. If she consented to read, he would be grateful. He would, of course, remember to treat her gently and with respect. After the reading he would only kiss her chastely and retire to his cot in the dressing room, as was fitting.

A treacherous dissent clamored at him. Or perhaps he should treat her more passionately, as Digby would do, no doubt, were their places interchanged.

He imagined the scene if he were to pull her into his arms, declare that it was more than time for— But how could he expect her to accept him when he was failing so miserably at his quest. Still, it was a pleasant fantasy. . . .

All thoughts of fantasy fled when he entered the library. Hero was not curled up in a comfortable chair. She had no book in her hand. Instead, she stood frozen. Her face was pale and bloodless and her eyes were filled with panic.

When he would have moved into the room, she stopped him with a shaken indrawn breath and a mute plea in her eyes. He heard the low growling then, and his eyes lit upon the fox that sat upon the windowsill.

"Don't move," he whispered, barely daring to move his lips lest the fox leap.

"Believe me, I shall not," she replied shakily.

"I will get help," he said softly, withdrawing as slowly and quietly as possible, excruciatingly aware that if he made a noise, or startled the fox, Hero would suffer for his mistake.

"Hold, Watterly." He heard someone at his back,

felt a light pressure on his shoulder but had no time to turn and give a warning before an arm came over his shoulder and a pistol leveled at the fox.

Digby. Again.

Arthur could not allow Digby to rescue his wife once more from danger. He reached his hand up carefully, so that the movement would not startle the growling animal, and took hold of the pistol.

"There's no time for debate," Digby whispered fiercely.

"I'm a crack shot," he whispered back truthfully. "I don't want her hurt." He did not know what he would do if Digby refused to release his grip on the pistol, but fortunately, he did not have to find out.

Hero had watched Arthur back away, stop, and she had seen the puzzled expression appear on his face. But at the sight of the pistol that appeared over his shoulder, as if from a great and dizzying distance, she squeezed her eyes shut and said a swift prayer.

She looked toward the fox when the animal snarled again, louder this time. She whimpered shamelessly as the wounded animal, disturbed by the commotion at the door, leaped toward her throat.

Twenty-two

Just as her panicked senses began to clamor for her to dive out of the animal's path, a shot rang out, and the fox, with a single muted snarl, fell at her feet.

Was it dead? Hero stared down at the still form, afraid to touch it in the event that the shot had not killed it.

Shaking uncontrollably, she turned to move away but found herself unable to take a step. It was all she could do not to fall to the floor in a faint. Arthur rushed toward her, pulling her into his arms. She looked into the turbulent swirl of his gray eyes and said what was foremost in her heart. "I love you, Arthur."

He heard her, she knew, but for a moment he did not react, and then, with a low groan, he bent down to kiss her, just as she'd hoped. She reached up to wrap her arms around his neck and return his kiss. She never wanted him to stop—

Raised voices grew louder in the hallway. "I heard a shot. Who has been shot?" Reluctantly, they came apart, but his arms still cradled her protectively as they watched the room fill with Fenwell Delagrace's houseguests.

Digby stood in the doorway, a smoking pistol in his grip. He looked as pale and shaken as she felt. She wanted to thank him but felt that to do so might be an insult to Arthur yet again.

She looked into her husband's worried eyes. How had he found her? "What are you doing here?" she asked.

"I noticed that you had retired early," Arthur said stiffly, his eyes focused on Digby and his smoking pistol. "I wondered if you were ill."

"There was—" She paused, realizing that anyone in the room could be listening. She would have to tell him about the note later. "I had a headache," she said, which was true enough. She truly did have a headache, and it seemed to be growing by the second. "I thought if I came in here for some quiet, I would recover more quickly."

She tried to convey with her eyes that her words were only a partial truth. Arthur did not seem to understand, however. "A headache! You should have gone up to the room directly and had the maid bring you some tea or a toddy to soothe you."

"The pain wasn't that severe, and I did not want to have Fenwell Delagrace thinking that I did not enjoy his society."

He seemed to understand exactly what she had hoped to preserve with her actions, for he said nothing more.

Gabriel Digby came toward her. The look on his face was one of a man waking up who had been asleep for a long time. "I'm glad you were not hurt."

"Thank you, Mr. Digby," she said, trying to maintain as formal a tone as possible while she was still trembling from fear. "I appreciate your quick dispatch of the fox."

"I wish I deserved your thanks. But I do not." He shook his head. "It was your husband, not I, who killed the animal. He said he was a crack shot, so I gave him my pistol. Evidently, he was not telling tales."

He looked to Arthur. "I believe you are the best shot I have ever met. I hope you will teach me what you know, one day."

"I would be happy to," Arthur replied. She wondered if he was simply being polite, or if he truly meant what he had promised. Somehow, the thought of Gabriel Digby and Arthur on the shooting range did not soothe her shattered nerves.

Digby crossed the room and examined the carcass of the fox.

"Is it dead?" Hero asked anxiously. "It had foam coming from the mouth, and it was not afraid of me as it should have been."

"Yes, I am happy to say." He looked at the startled maid who had come as far as the doorway and paused, unsure of what to do to help. "Call a footman to remove this. It should be best burnt, I suggest. But I will leave that up to your master to decide."

Fenwell shouldered toward the animal's body and then said authoritatively, "Yes, girl, call a footman immediately. This must be removed at once."

Arthur's arms tightened around her. He knew the danger of a wild beast as well as anyone did. Still, she felt pity for the poor creature and its madness. "I think it may have been rabid, Arthur." For what else could have caused it to behave in that fashion?

She leaned against him and closed her eyes. "Thank you for shooting it so cleanly, Arthur. I could feel its breath on my face just before it fell."

"I'm sorry that you had to be frightened at all."

He looked at Digby. "Whatever would have made it attack my wife like that? Do you see foam in its jaws?" He had put mild emphasis on the word "wife," which pleased her somehow.

Digby prodded the fox with his foot, turning it this way and that as he completed his examination. "Rabid, I would guess."

Rabid. If she had been bitten— "Thank goodness you shot him before he could bite me."

Arthur cradled her head in his hands and kissed her eyelids. "I would have put myself in front of you if I had not had the pistol. I intended to do so anyway, if only he had not leaped when he did. I did not intend to fail you one more time."

Fail her? How could he imagine that he had failed her? "I'm glad you were the one to fire the pistol to rescue me, though I would not have considered that you failed me if Digby had done so."

"A man should not need others to rescue his wife from danger," Arthur muttered.

Of course. The fire at the inn still rubbed at his pride. "I have never needed anyone but you, Arthur. And I trust you with my life, always." She understood how important it had been to him that he be the one to shoot. In his mind he had evened some invisible score between himself and Digby.

"But more, I'm glad you came searching for me," she said softly to him.

"I was concerned for you."

"And I love that you are concerned for me, Arthur." She put the emphasis on the word "love." Would he understand that she meant it from the very tips of her toes?

He touched the top of her head with his lips. She had said the word again. *Love.* It could not be a mistake. He could not have misheard it. It was not just the emotions of the moment. She had said it twice.

"But most of all, I love the way you have always shown your care and concern—even when we were only friends. You have always taken good care of me."

"It is my responsibility to make certain you are safe, especially now, when—" He broke off; the room was too full of potential eavesdroppers. Today he considered he had righted a balance. He hoped she thought so as well. It was not proper for a husband to leave the rescue of his wife to others.

"And that is why you came looking for me?" She kissed him on the lips, right there in the room full of Fenwell Delagrace's guests. "I love you, Arthur."

Four times—there could be no doubt she knew what she was saying, but he could not stop himself from asking, "You do?"

She smiled and kissed him again, heedless of the eyes watching them. "Of course I do."

He wished he had known earlier this was the way to win her affections. "Well, then, I should save your life more often."

"No." She shook her head. "I do not love you because you saved my life."

"It does not matter why you love me," he said. "I only care that you do."

"It matters to me that you know why I love you," she insisted. "I love you because you were concerned about me and you sought me out. You have always done that, Arthur. Even in the inn. Even in the fire— you were there to take me from Digby's arms."

He wished it was as simple as she was trying to make it seem. "But a husband must—"

"Don't you understand? When I looked to the doorway, I saw Digby with the pistol. I did not know you were the one to shoot the animal. But still, you were the one I was glad to see."

How could she not care that he had made the shot? That he had protected her? "I—" he began to interrupt

But she would not let him. "You were the one I wanted to hold me and comfort me."

He stared at her, trying to comprehend what she was telling him, but it seemed impossible. A wife must want a husband who could keep her from harm. No doubt she was speaking now from the kindness of her heart, not her head. Still, she had said she loved him. That was a start he could build on.

"She is not hurt?" Digby asked quietly as he approached them.

"No, I am not, thanks to Arthur," Hero replied.

Arthur could not in good conscience take all the credit. "And thanks also to Digby, who had the good sense to carry a pistol."

"It was not mine, Watterly," Digby protested, as if he, too, were not willing to take credit for something that was not his doing. "I found it lying on the table outside the library, and I had just picked it up, when I heard your exclamation."

"What brought you to the library?" Arthur asked, suddenly realizing what a coincidence it was.

Digby seemed disconcerted for a moment, and then he said quietly, "I received a note."

"A note?" Hero sat up in his arms, suddenly tense. "What did it say?"

"Merely that someone wished to meet privately with me in the library." Digby seemed embarrassed. Arthur wondered why. Surely Hero had not sent the note? He did not want to believe it.

Gwen came over to them, and he could see tears in her eyes. "What has happened?" There was a tiny frown between her brows. And a slightly larger pout upon her lips. Arthur knew her well enough to guess that something about this situation displeased her, but what?

He answered, to ease her mind, "There was a rabid fox in here, but it has been dispatched safely. No one was hurt."

"I am glad, then," she said with a sincerity Arthur suspected only he, who knew her from childhood, could tell was not complete. She turned a tremulous smile upon Digby. "Mr. Digby, please let me get you some brandy for your nerves," she offered.

"I am fine, it is Miss—Mrs. Watterly who needs the brandy, I fear." Digby brushed her off.

"But a hero deserves a reward—"

"Then you should offer the brandy to Mr. Watterly. He is the one who shot the fox."

"Arthur?" She turned astonished eyes upon him.

"I am a crack shot, as you well know," he reminded her. But he could not bring himself to be angry. It was all too obvious to him that she had feelings for Digby. Poor girl. First the man she expects to marry is abruptly married to Hero Fenster, and then she has the worse luck to fall in love with a man who still loves Hero as well, despite her marriage to another man.

"He was very brave," Hero said indulgently with a smile that warmed his heart.

Gwen's eyes narrowed. "What were you doing in the library, Mrs. Watterly? Were you lost?"

"I was hoping to find a quiet place to ease my headache," Hero answered. Arthur could feel her tense beside him again, and he wondered what there was to worry her in the simple answer.

"I'm sorry that you did not." The phrase might have been graciously meant, but Gwen's tone was a bit abrupt.

Fenwell Delagrace's angry tones penetrated their corner. "How did the fox get in here?"

"This window has been left open," the footman answered as he investigated. He turned, a puzzled look upon his face and a rope dangling from his hand. "It appears the animal was staked here but managed to chew through its restraint."

"Who would do such a thing?" Delagrace looked around the room, but no one volunteered an answer. With a heavy frown, the man lifted his hands and motioned for his guests to leave. "I will find out. And be assured, whoever it is will pay."

"As well they should," echoed Digby.

"Do you not think perhaps someone might have had an innocent reason for tying the fox there?" Gwen asked, her eyes wide and her face pale.

Arthur wondered if she had— "Digby, do you have the note that summoned you here?"

The man pulled his startled gaze from Hero and said, "Yes, I do." He pulled the paper from his pocket and handed it over. Arthur saw at once what he had feared. He might perhaps have said something, fueled by his fear and anger at what had almost happened to Hero.

But his wife threw her arms around his neck and rested her head on his shoulder. "Is it any wonder that I love this man, when he is so quick to gather the evidence to solve this mystery?"

Digby's face shifted into an expression so bland, it had to be controlled. "I can only wish that I might be so fortunate." Arthur understood that Hero had deliberately sent a message and that message had been clearly received.

"I'm certain you will be," Hero said lightly. She was not one to rub salt into a wound. His arms tightened around her. What would he have done if he had lost her tonight?

"The note?" Digby reached to take the note back.

Arthur, with a glance at Gwen's bloodless features, shoved it into his pocket and said, "I will give this to Fenwell. It should help him catch the fool who set this trap."

"Gwen, you are looking very pale," Hero said softly. "Mr. Digby, would you be so good as to see her to her maid, so that she does not faint dead away?"

"Of course." Digby's smile was an imitation, but Gwen's pallor was instantly spotted by hectic color in her cheeks as she took his arm and they left the room.

"I'm glad you chased me to the library, Arthur." Her fingers brushed lightly against the back of his neck. He tightened his grip and rested his head against hers, as careless as she of the last of the onlookers in the room. She had said I love you even though she thought Digby had been the one to pull the trigger.

And then she had said it again, so that Digby would have no doubt her heart belonged to Arthur alone. He closed his eyes. He did not deserve her love. "I do not want to lose you, Hero," he whispered. "I want to keep you safe."

"You have."

"How can you say that when I have almost lost you three times? I am not the best guardian of your well-being." Though it hurt to say it, he knew he must. "I am sending you back to London tomorrow."

"No—"

He released her and said without a shadow of doubt, "I must. I cannot concentrate on meeting my challenges, when I know that any moment your life might be forfeit."

All the protest in her expression died as she heard his words. "Very well," she said with a meekness he had rarely seen in her before. He had a feeling he had hurt her once more, but he could not see how. All he wanted was to keep her safe.

Hero wanted to cry. She had told him that she loved him, and he was sending her back to London. Yes, she believed he meant to keep her safe. But he also thought her a hindrance to meeting his challenges. Why else would he have said— She realized he still did not know why she had come into the library.

"Arthur," she said quietly so as not to draw the attention of the few people left in the room, "Digby is not the only one who received a note tonight."

"What?" He tensed for a moment and then

reached up to remove her arms from around his neck. "Where is it?"

He understood the puzzle no better than she. For an hour they moved aimlessly about the shelves, searching for anything that could be a clue. The Delagrace copy of *Le Morte d'Arthur* was beautifully illustrated but contained nothing that might hold the answers they sought. Nor did any of the other Arthurian literature.

Tired, and feeling the sadness that she would be leaving him tomorrow, Hero paused to survey the library again. What had she missed? She touched the magnificent Round Table and said softly, "The table—it is amazing."

"Yes, it is, isn't it?" He smiled. "I always liked playing around and beneath it when I was a child."

That fact surprised her. She had imagined it a more recent acquisition. "Then it was built before Gwen was even born?"

"Yes. My grandmother had always intended me to marry the daughter of the house. She instructed Mr. Delagrace to build it according to the best guesses of current-day scholars as to the size and position of many of the knights."

"What a wonderful addition this would be to your collection." She wondered if her dowry might even be enough to purchase the table for him. That would be a gift of generosity for the Round Table Society. In fact, she had to wonder why Mr. Delagrace had never gifted it to them.

"It is meant for Gwen's husband." Hero looked at the table again, this time seeing it as a tangible statement that Gwen and Arthur had indeed been intended to marry. Suddenly, the table seemed less magnificent.

"You mean you." She felt another tremendous surge of guilt. "Before you married me. Oh, Arthur—"

"Don't be silly. It is only a table. It was Grandmama's dream, after all, not mine. My mother thought she was daft though."

"She did?"

"Called her a witch once—right to her face." Arthur smiled at the memory.

"My grandmother didn't seem to mind."

"Still, to call your mother-in-law a witch—"

"Yes." He sighed. "My mother and Grandmama never got along." He looked up at her with a bittersweet twist of his lips. "I suspect my mother would have adored you, however."

Hero felt a breath of relief that she was not the only woman to feel such dislike for Arthur's grandmother. She knew the woman deserved respect. But somehow she felt that if Arthur's mother had not liked her, she could not be expected to either.

Arthur had begun to examine the table, running his hands across the top. And then he stopped, his gaze fixed and focused.

"What is the matter? Has the table been damaged somehow? I don't think the fox was near enough to it to do damage—" She broke off, as he was obviously not paying a whit of attention to her questions.

As he stared at the table, his eyes grew sharp. "I remember. The key. This is where I have seen a key like the one we found in the ruins!"

Twenty-three

Hero looked at the smooth expanse of the table-top, mystified. "The key? Here?"

"Yes." He frowned in concentration. "I remember. This table, with a key just like that sitting on top. Gwen and I used to slide it back and forth in a sort of idle game when we were young."

"So perhaps it belongs to something in this room?" Hero looked around. She could see nothing that required a key to open it. No boxes, no cabinets, no drawers.

"Where could it be?" she wondered aloud. To her surprise, Arthur dived beneath the table and then reappeared to take her hand and pull her under the table with him. "See?"

There was a cabinet in the thick central leg of the massive table. A cabinet large enough to hold a manuscript. And a brass lock in which a key might fit. She wanted to shout with excitement but managed to control her impulse. "Do you have the key?"

"No," he answered with chagrin after a thorough check of his pockets. "I have not thought of it in some time, I'm afraid. I did not ever truly think I would remember where I had seen it. I was not even certain if I *had* ever seen it before."

"We must get it at once."

"Unfortunately, we must wait until we arrive back at Camelot, I'm afraid."

Hero was merely glad of the excuse to leave the Delagrace household. They tried to speak of other things on the ride back home, mindful of the curious gazes of Grandmama, Digby—and Gwen, who had accompanied them to stay as their guest for a few days' time.

As soon as they arrived, without excuses they hurried up the stairs to their room.

"Where is it?"

Arthur stood, a perplexed look upon his face. "I can't remember exactly."

"Did I have it last? I took it from the site after you threw it to the ground?"

"No. Remember, you gave it back to me in the carriage."

"Oh, yes." She thought a bit. "You put it in your pocket then."

For a few moments they both searched the pockets of his waistcoats. The effort, however, yielded no key.

"Could it have fallen out?"

"Or perhaps I transferred it to a safer place?"

They searched diligently, Hero on the floor, looking for a small, shiny key that might have tumbled under the bed, beneath the dressing table, in the bed itself.

Arthur searched his own belongings, the box that held his diamond stickpin, his other valuables.

Nothing.

He pressed his lips together in chagrin. "Where could it have gotten to?"

"I wish I could remember clearly. . . ." Her temples ached, and she took off her spectacles to rub at them, hoping that would help restore her memory.

He caught a breath in dismay as he asked, "Could we have left it back at the inn?"

"No." She could remember that much. "I had it with me then."

"What about the second inn we visited, on the way home?" he asked.

"No." Again she was certain. "I remember holding it in my hand after we reached Camelot."

She sighed. "I cannot think of another place it might be." Despite an extensive search, the key was not to be found.

He paused. "It should be here."

"But it is not." She asked, almost afraid of the answer, "Could someone have taken it?"

"Yes, I suppose so." He looked as unhappy with the idea as she felt. "But who?"

They tossed the room, but the key was nowhere to be found. Excitedly, she grasped his arm. "We will find it, and then we will know, Arthur! You cannot send me away now."

"I must—" He paused. "Very well. Another few days, until we find the key and unlock the cabinet."

"You will not regret it!" She threw her arms around him and kissed him soundly on the lips.

She had expected to kiss and back away, as she had done previously.

Instead, his arms wrapped possessively around her and his mouth returned her kiss with fervor. "I cannot believe I almost lost you again," he whispered against her neck.

"Never," she vowed, her timidity gone in the blink of an eye. She felt as if she could say anything to him. Do anything with him. She turned her face into his neck and inhaled his scent.

In an instant they were lost in the joy of their discovery. Or perhaps it was the release of that choking fear when she had almost been attacked by the rabid fox? She truly did not care which, as long as he no longer wanted to keep her at arm's length. Tonight, she would become his wife in every way.

She protested when he pulled away from her, but he sat back, gazing at her with a steady intensity that made her common sense come to the fore. "What is the matter, Arthur? We are married. There is nothing wrong—"

"I do not want to rush you, Hero."

"We have been married for weeks, Arthur. Who could possibly claim that you have rushed me?"

"I want you to be certain. This step is so final—"

There was a slight release of the tension that had grown around her heart. He was not rejecting her, he was protecting her. "If that is all you want to know, then I can say confidently that I am certain."

"You are not afraid of me, then?"

"Afraid of you?" She did not mean to sound incredulous at the thought. He looked wounded at her tone.

"I do not mean of me physically, I meant afraid of the intimacy we might share." He added, "I am, after all, a virtual stranger."

"Not to me." That she knew she could say with complete honesty. "I have come to know you and trust you in the years I have known you. I do not consider you a stranger."

"But you were on the verge of marriage to Gabriel Digby—"

She put a finger to his lips to stop his words. "He was on the verge of proposing." She realized that for the sake of her marriage, she must make him see the truth. "That does not mean I intended to accept."

"No?"

She smiled, hoping that he could read the truth of it in her eyes. "You would laugh if you knew how many schemes I had to hatch, how many careful plans and near misses I had in order to make certain he could not propose."

"But he is a fine man. He would have made you a good husband."

"He is. And perhaps, with luck, he will make Gwen a good husband. But he never would have made me one. I have been in love with you since I first met you in Simon's breakfast room." She laughed at the memory. "The sheer look of horror when you saw all the Fenster females at their worst. How could I not have fallen in love with you?"

"Yes, I remember that morning well—it was the first time I discovered that females could be enchanting in bunches." He smiled, too, and then a shadow of doubt came across his expression. "But—"

"Do you not want me?" She closed her eyes, preparing for the worst. "I can understand. After all, you were not expecting to marry me. You have been all but promised to Gwen for so long. I did not understand it at first. But now, after being here, I can see that the promise was so accepted that you did not know there could be any other outcome."

"I did not want to marry Gwen."

His statement was so blunt, she wasn't sure she had heard him correctly. "But you were—"

"My grandmother and Gwen's father were quite happy with the match. Gwen and I were never actually consulted."

"She is a nice girl."

"Yes—and perhaps a good wife for a man like Digby, if he takes the blinders off his eyes. I have considered her a friend all these years. But I could not think of her as a wife, as a boon companion, as a"—his voice grew husky—"as a lover."

"Do you think you could ever think of me that way?" She knew she might regret the answer. But she had to know.

"I have since the first time I met you, though I scarcely dared admit it, even to myself." There was no doubt he was telling the truth. She could see it in his face, in the way he sat tensed, as if he strained against invisible bonds.

She began to cry.

He rose from the bed in distress. "I knew I was rushing you."

Still crying, she threw her arms around his neck and drew him back to her. "I'm crying because you have said the words I most wanted to hear. Because I want you."

"You do?"

"Can you not tell?"

His eyes warmed as he allowed himself to look full into hers, to plumb the depths without fear. Even as he gazed, his hands were warm against her cheek, her neck, skimming down her arms. With a shaky sigh, he asked once more, "You have no doubt?"

She understood his fears. After all, she shared them—what if they were both disappointed? But she did not want to play this game a moment longer;

they had played too long already. She said as softly and inviting as she could, "Arthur?"

"Yes?" His breathing seemed to become more rapid, his ribs moving up and down more shallowly with each breath.

She held out her arms to him. "Could you please just kiss me? I think you'll find your answer there."

And so he did. This time he heard no warning voices in his head telling him that he was letting his own feelings carry him away. This time he understood the message her body was sending his. She wanted him. As a husband. And as a lover.

He was gentle. At first. But she gave him no hint that she minded when his own passion made him grow bolder. At first he kissed only her lips, but then he was not satisfied with that. He moved, first to her neck, then to her shoulder, then to the delicate flesh of her inner wrists. Down to her belly, the back of a knee. He wanted to taste her everywhere, he wanted to hear the little sounds of pleasure she made. He wanted to hear them forever.

And so it was nearly dawn before she slept, warm and trusting against him.

Arthur did not sleep at once. It was not his nature to believe himself worthy of so much unconditional love. After all, he had failed her more than once. He wondered if he had made a mistake, if he would only end up hurting her in the end. But he could not believe so. Not when she slept so contentedly beside him. There had been no sign of regret in her expression—and he had observed carefully. He had seen only passion, response, joy, amazement at the sensations they had managed to coax from each other's eager bodies.

As he lay quietly contemplating his good fortune, he saw the rose pattern on the wall opposite shift slightly. He half closed his eyes and watched as the wall opened. Were his eyes playing tricks on him? No. It was a secret door!

He tensed, wondering if he should leap up and chase away the intruder, or remain as if asleep and see what the prowler was up to. He chose to remain still, but he was tensed to protect Hero if it turned out that someone was indeed trying to harm her.

The shadowy figure crept toward the washbasin on the bureau and, after a second's bustle, just as carefully crept back toward the wall, disappeared, and the wall once again appeared as normal.

Arthur leaped from the bed and lit a lamp. A little light exposed what the prowler had been up to. Another note had been left on the bureau.

He was almost afraid to pick it up and read it. He wanted no more than to rest in bed with Hero. To wake her in the morning with a soft kiss and more lovemaking. The note was more likely to send him away into the night, away from her, away from what he most held dear. And all for what? A musty old book manuscript that held no secrets a modern printed text couldn't reveal?

His cynicism shocked him. Since when had be begun to view his quest with such rancor?

He curled up again next to Hero, the note clutched in his palm. He would read it tomorrow. Nothing of importance would suffer if he spent one night next to her.

She curled into him with a soft sigh of pleasure and comfort, and he knew he had made the right decision.

* * *

When she woke, all she could think of was how right it felt to have him beside her, warm and strong.

His smile, however, was troubled. At first she thought it was just the look of a man who was not sure how his wife would greet the morning. But then she noticed the dark smudges under his eyes.

She thought the worst, of course. Perhaps he had not felt the joy that she had felt when— "What is the matter? You do not regret—"

"Never." He held her close. "Never."

She relaxed, knowing somehow that he told the truth on that matter. "Then, what has you so restless?"

He told her of the secret passageway.

At first, she thought he had been dreaming, and she laughed at his tale. "A secret passageway? Arthur, really, I would more likely believe that you had seen a dragon breathing fire outside the window."

"It was no dream. I am certain of that." Arthur could not blame her for not believing him. Even he might have doubted his story, it sounded so far-fetched in the light of day.

"I cannot believe it." She gazed sharply at the wall he had indicated held a secret door. "There? It was there?"

"Yes."

"But there is not anyplace a door could be—"

"I know what I saw." He did not know how to convince her. But there was the note, still clutched tightly in his fist. He held it out to her.

She stopped smiling, her expression growing unbearably serious. "You found another note."

"He left it. He came into the room by the secret door in the wall, left this note on the dressing table, and then left, again through the secret door."

Apparently, the note was enough to sweep away any lingering doubts she might have entertained. "What does it say?" she asked anxiously.

"I don't know, I didn't read it," he answered. And didn't want to, he confessed to himself. But he lifted it, smoothing it out, and read slowly, *"The key is the key."*

They looked at each other in amazement. "The key! Do you suppose he took it?"

"It is certainly possible."

She leaped out of the bed. "What part of the wall moved?"

He took a moment to admire her, standing as she was so adorably disrobed. He pointed to where he had seen the wall move. "Here. Why?"

She took her fingers and began to run them lightly over the wall. "We must try to find the mechanism that will open the door to us."

He got out of bed and began to look as well. But it seemed futile to him. "I don't see how that can help—"

She knocked on the wall, her ear pressed against it. "Perhaps he took the key to keep us from finding what he has hidden from us." She knocked again, a little farther down.

He realized she was searching for hollow spaces behind the seemingly solid surface. "Finding the door will not get the key back if he did indeed take it."

"Why not?" She stopped her examination to stare at him with excitement. "If we can follow him—perhaps he even hid it there, behind the wall?"

The sense of her statement appealed to him. If they found the secret door, it might very well lead them directly to the culprit—and the key. "I suppose I am very lucky to have you."

"And I am lucky to have you, as well, Arthur. My life has not been so happy in—forever!" She smiled at him, and he felt something that had been tight within him all these years spring free.

With a smile he showed his heart to her. He said, "Perhaps, though, we could spend a little more time in bed? After all, I did have a sleepless night."

She looked surprised. "Now, in the daylight?" A small sigh escaped her. "If you get me in that bed, sir, you will have a sleepless morning, I assure you."

"Perfect," he replied, lifting her into his arms. "It is just what I need to restore me to full health."

She touched his earlobe gently with her tongue, then teased it with her teeth. "Then how can I refuse you?"

It was several hours later before they resumed their search for the opening to the secret passage—and for some way to release it from this side of the entrance.

Completely by accident, Hero found the passageway. It was a simple foot trigger. She never would have found it if she hadn't been struggling into her boots and stumbled against the device.

The door in the wall unlatched with a soft click, and suddenly, she could pull it open. Without hesitating, she did.

They both peered inside. "The inside is darker than I had expected," she said quietly, a shiver running down her spine. For a moment she was sorely tempted to close up the entrance and pretend she had never found it.

"We should bring a lamp with us so that we don't break our necks," he muttered, and she wondered if he felt the same doubt as she did but could not tell from his tone.

Or simply close the door and pretend they hadn't found it, she thought. Don't be silly, she chided herself. Taking up a lantern, she decided she would not feel comfortable until they had managed to have a quick look around.

He hesitated, barring her way. "Perhaps I should go alone. We don't know what—or who—we might find."

Only sending him in alone and waiting to see if he reemerged safe and well would have been worse than going in by herself. "No doubt the prowler himself is not going to be there, not in the broad light of day," she answered. No, that kind of man preferred the dark of night.

"Very well, then. Follow me." And he plunged into the passageway, holding the lamp before him, so that his body blocked most of the light from her eyes.

She shivered, thinking of how she had been so soundly sleeping when the intruder had made his visit last night. And then she realized he could have been there previous nights as well. He might have known that Arthur had slept on his cot—until last night, that was. She came into the passageway behind Arthur and rested her hands lightly on his waist. Whenever he stopped, she allowed herself to lean against him, breathing in his scent, feeling the strength and warmth of his body against hers.

She smiled. Miranda had been right. This thing between men and women was not frightening at all.

Twenty-four

The passageway was cool and dark but clean. The stairs led steadily down for a bit, then leveled out. No cobwebs wrapped around her arms or brushed her face as she walked. There was a faintly familiar scent lingering in her nostrils as well. She grasped for it but could not bring the memory teasing at her mind to focus.

Arthur stopped. "Look." She peered around him and saw light coming from two holes at eye level on one of the walls. They each took a turn peeking through. It was the library. Gwen sat reading softly. Digby sat nearby, his eyes closed. Hero recognized the pose though. He was listening intently.

Not certain whether their voices would carry, she put her lips very near his ear to whisper, "Do you suppose we can do anything to help them along? I think they would make a wonderful couple."

He turned his head to steal a slow kiss, just a brush of lips against lips. "I don't know if he would ever forgive her for staking that fox out."

She sighed. "I explained it to you. She must have sent Digby the note, intending to meet him at the library and give him the opportunity to rescue her.

She did not mean for me to stumble into harm's way."

"It was a foolish thing to do."

"It was a desperate thing to do. But she knows that this is her one chance to catch his eye. I know how she feels."

"Do you? You have my eye." His lips pressed lightly against her cheeks, her eyes, her neck. "And more."

"Should I be so selfish, then? I stole you from Gwen. The least I can do is help her to win a replacement for you." She leaned against him in pleasure, but then, feeling as if Gwen and Digby would surely hear, she pushed him away and urged him to move ahead.

He sighed against her ear and kissed her once more, quite thoroughly, before he complied.

The next room that could be peeped into was a few twists and turns down the passageway. He peered through, and then backed away, a shocked gurgle his only sound.

Hero peeked through, and it took only a moment to understand what she was seeing. This was his grandmother's study. And Grandmama was in residence. The room was nearly dark, the drapes drawn against daylight. A small candle burned in the sconce that held the crystal ball upon her desk, making it glow like a cold moon. A strange, rhythmic, almost musical chanting filled the room.

Grandmama practiced the dark arts.

Realization struck Hero at last. The familiar scent she had noticed in the passageway was the oddly exotic one lingering in the study when they had been summoned last time. She wondered, with a bright flash of scholarly interest, what combination of herbs made such a scent—but she put her curiosity aside. For Grandmama appeared to be in the midst of something important, and she wanted to see what it was.

"Arthur," she whispered. "I think your mother meant more than an insult when she called your grandmother a witch." She *was* a witch. And not a kindly, herb-dispensing healing witch either.

He answered wearily, "And she had been in the passageway as well."

She heard the fear in his voice. Fear that he would find out his grandmother was behind the notes. Pulling away from the peepholes, she tried to offer him reassurance, though she did not really think his grandmother innocent. "Your grandfather built this place for her—no doubt she designed the passageway and has used it for years."

"That is possible." His voice did not hold much conviction, however.

She turned her attention back to the room, in which a dozen candles were eerily burning and making the shadows dance. She saw Grandmama with a deck of cards in her hand. As she stood motionless, her eyes pressed against the two small holes that allowed her to see, the woman asked sharply, "What shall I do?" and dealt three cards facedown in front of her. Quickly, she flipped them over one by one.

They were not, Hero realized, playing cards. No. These were cards of Tarot. She had seen them before, in a book that warned against falling prey to any practitioner of the dark arts.

Arthur pressed against her back, bringing his arms around her waist as he whispered in her ear, "What is she doing?"

"She is reading the Tarot, I believe."

"Why?" He tensed beside her. "What are the cards?"

"I cannot tell." She squinted into the peephole. "The faces are too hard to make out from here."

"Let me see." He pushed her gently away so that he could bend and peep through.

Grandmama moaned again, oblivious to the eyes upon her. She swept up the cards, shuffled the deck ferociously, and then dealt herself three cards again. He could make out only one of the cards, but it chilled him. Death. Ornately done. A beautiful card. He had been fascinated by it as a child. But what did it mean to his grandmother—and to Hero?

"No!" She was nearly incoherent in her rage.

Apparently, the cards were not telling her what she wanted to hear. Should he find that a relief? He clenched his fists against the wall. He knew she could be devious. But to have done this to him? He did not want to believe it.

Hero pulled at his arm. "Perhaps we should not watch. After all, we did not enjoy finding that we were being secretly observed."

"True." He glanced at the peepholes, torn between giving his grandmother her privacy and finding out once and for all what was going on.

But just as he was to turn away, a footman led Gwen into the room. She looked frightened and stubborn.

"You have disappointed me again," his grandmother said sharply.

He settled back against the wall. "At last," he whispered to Hero. "We will find out what is going on."

Gwen replied to his grandmother's charge, "Arthur is happy with his bride. There is nothing I can do to change that." Her voice was strong, although he could see the telltale signs of nervousness in her fingers, which twisted her skirts. Her glance flicked to the deck of cards in front of his grandmother. "Haven't the cards already told you so?"

"Just as they have told me that Digby could be used to turn her away from Arthur. Which would have worked—if not for you."

"It is not right—to make him suffer so."

"Digby is in love with Arthur's bride."

"I don't believe that. He is an honorable man."

"I'm not saying he has taken her to bed, foolish girl. Merely given her his heart. I only hoped to encourage what he already feels. If he ran away with her, the path would be cleared for you and for Arthur to meet your destiny. But you could not leave fate to work alone, could you?"

"I thought if Digby saw—"

"You thought he would fall in love with you. Foolish child."

"I—"

"Do you think I did not realize it was you who changed the notes so that it was Arthur, not Digby, who was trapped in that bookshop with Hero?"

"It was a mistake!" Gwen protested, but even Arthur could see that she lied. There was no doubt now. His grandmother was behind all the plotting. And Gwen had been intended to help, although she had tried to save Digby for herself and scrambled his grandmother's careful plans.

"You will not lie to me any longer, Guenivere Delagrace. I have known you since you were born. Do you not want to meet your destiny?"

"No." Gwen lifted her chin. He saw steel in her that had not been there before. "My destiny is Gabriel Digby. Whether you approve or not."

"Do you think he will want you when he knows the truth?"

Gwen's expression was agonized, and it took a moment for her answer to come. "I don't know. I shall have to ask him." She turned and left the room before his grandmother could say another word.

"Fickle girl!" With a cry of despair, his grandmother lay her head down upon her desk.

He pulled away from the wall, silent for a moment, digesting all that he had learned. "Grandmama and Gwen were behind it all."

"I heard," she said. "I could not see, but I heard every word. I hope Digby forgives Gwen. It is very brave of her to confess her part."

"If she does so, we have yet to see." He sighed. He had always been fond of Gwen, thought of her as a younger sister. But this betrayal took him hard. "And even if Digby does, I don't know if I can forgive her."

"No?"

"You can, so easily?"

She pressed a kiss against his collarbone. "If not for her, I would never have been married to you, Arthur. How can I not be grateful to her forever for that?"

He had not thought of it like that. Perhaps he should not only forgive Gwen but thank her. All he could do at the moment, however, was take Hero into his arms and kiss her. As she opened her mouth under his, he thought gratitude the best answer.

Remembering belatedly that they were in search

of the key, they followed the passageway once more. A set of stairs led them up, and they found themselves peering into his grandmother's bedroom. Disappointed that they had not found the key, they returned to their room.

He would have asked his grandmother directly about the key. He would have let her know that he had discovered her manipulation and would not allow it to continue another day. But when he went to her study, he found her there, her head still down upon her desk. She lay still when he called her name.

He called a footman to help move his grandmother to her room. He could feel her breathing, shallow and rapid. Before the footmen arrived, he removed the cards beneath her hand. Her palm had been resting flat against Death, and he threw it into the fire and watched it go up in flames.

She was not dead. Not yet, at least, said the doctor. But she could not speak, could not eat, and her eyes when they opened were unfocused and unseeing. He could not ask about the key. He could not even ask her why she had done all this. For him?

Hero held him that night, after they made love with a ferocity that shocked him and no doubt shocked her as well. She whispered that all would be right even if they never found the key. She nuzzled into his neck and said softly, "After all, we have found each other, what more could we want?"

Hero had tried to comfort Arthur. But she was not certain that she had been of much help in soothing his anguish. His grandmother's scheme had resulted in their marriage, inadvertently. But it had also made her a target for danger. If Grandmama recovered, she did not know if she would ever be able to forgive her.

She checked with the maid who was posted to care for Mrs. Watterly. The woman was failing. Hero tried not to wish her ill. This illness, this inability to speak or move, was punishment enough.

Silently, she said to Grandmama, *I have one goal in common with yours, and I hope to see it through. I will not be a hindrance to Arthur gaining what he most wants. I promise it.*

She turned to the maid. "See that she is comfortable, then, as the doctor advised you," she said as convincingly as she could manage.

When she went downstairs to luncheon, it was to discover that Gabriel Digby had met the challenge of Chivalry.

Gwen was positively glowing with the news. "He was so gallant, you cannot imagine. I would have been most devastated if he had not come by to rescue me."

Digby sat near her and took her hand. His gaze was quite adoring, and Hero wondered if Gwen had yet told him of her part in their little family drama.

The story unfolded that Gwen had been riding her little pony cart, sent by her father to fetch her home. She had gotten stuck in the mud and sent her servant back to fetch help. A storm was raging and she was unprotected from the elements.

"But," she said prettily, her cheeks pink as rose petals as she gazed up at Digby, "I could not leave little Lily there alone, and I could not unhitch her from the cart myself."

So, Hero thought a bit uncharitably, she thought she would just allow herself to be drenched by the rain, possibly subject to strong gusts of wind, and not be of a whit of rescue for herself or her pony?

"And then he came along—like a white knight on his charger. I swear, I practically saw his lance."

Hero tried not to allow her amusement with the tale to show. Nor her chagrin. For though the tale was foolishly charming and amusing, it was also true that Digby had met his second challenge surprisingly well.

"How is Arthur's grandmother this afternoon?" Digby asked solicitously. But the innocence in his tone could mean only one thing. Gwen had not yet confessed. The girl looked somewhat downcast and guilty. Hero hoped she would tell him soon, before both their hearts were once again in jeopardy.

Perhaps, she decided, she and Arthur could do something to further the relationship. If she explained to Digby— But first, Gwen must confess. Hero felt only a profound relief at the thought of the two of them as a couple. There would then be no more need for guilt that Gwen and Digby had been robbed of their hearts unsuspectingly. Obviously, they had found more than solace with each other during today's rescue.

Arthur came in at that moment, hastily and a bit abruptly. He came over to kiss her cheek and whispered in her ear, "I have found it."

They ate quickly and excused themselves indecently early, but neither of their guests seemed to take note.

In the drawing room she turned on him. "Where was it? How did you find it?"

His voice vibrated with suppressed excitement. "It was hidden in an old boot."

She looked at the key he held in his hand, an odd twist of eagerness in her midsection. "So we will try it out, then? But how?"

"We shall escort Gwen home-and arrange to stay the night."

She could not help but say, "It may be nothing, you know. Your grandmother may not have—"

He interrupted her to say firmly, "We will know tonight."

The key fit the lock and turned smoothly, but Arthur hesitated before he swung open the door. Hero gripped his shoulder and held the light high to encourage him. With a swift prayer for he knew not what, he pulled the door smoothly open.

Hero made a wordless sound of amazement, echoing his own.

Inside the cabinet, wrapped carefully, was a bundle the size and shape of a manuscript.

Gently, reverently, he took the bundle out and unwrapped it. The top page looked fairly modern, and he felt a swift stab of disappointment. The manuscript could not be five hundred years old.

But as he lifted the first page, he saw that there were older pages beneath it.

Hero shifted the light and leaned against him as they both read:

> *I have kept these pages safe for he who will walk again for many years. I believe that Arthur will return in my lifetime. In fact, I believe my gray-eyed grandson is Arthur reborn. The cards have told me so. All the signs are there to be read.*

He has but to prove himself and all will be granted him. But should fate prove me wrong, know that I valued my guardianship over my own life and I will not turn over these pages until my hopes and dreams are confirmed.

If my dreams are wrong, and I die before I can see the once and future king with my own eyes, care for this manuscript with your life. Let no eyes see it until the king returns to us.

I pray you take your duty up as faithfully as I took mine.

Below his grandmother's letter were those of a dozen others. All who had promised to keep the manuscript safe until Arthur, as promised, was reborn.

"What shall you do?" Hero whispered the question quietly. "How sad that they have hidden it for so many years. Could they truly have believed that Arthur would return?"

"They must have. Why else pass along the tradition so assiduously?"

"Do you—"

"No. I do not believe there is any reason for the manuscript to be hidden away."

She clutched at him, her whisper growing excited. "Then you have done it, Arthur! You have won the challenge."

He considered the reality, trying to make himself feel it for a moment. As they sat awkwardly beneath the table, the door to the library opened and they stilled, afraid to be caught.

Gwen's voice, subdued, as if she had been crying. "You don't understand. I had to do it."

Digby, cold and angry. "It was evil, Gwen."

"Cowardly, perhaps, at first. Selfish, I can agree. But surely not evil. Say you do not think that of me?"

"I do not know what to think." Digby sighed violently. "To trap them in that bookshop?"

"Would it have been any better to trap Miss Fenster in with you? That is what Mrs. Watterly wanted." Arthur tensed for the reply. Did Digby still have feelings for Hero?

He did not answer her directly. "You should have refused."

"Yes. I see that now." Gwen was openly crying now. "And I beg you to forgive me."

"I do not know if I can." His voice was strangled, as if he were fighting strong emotion. Arthur sagged against Hero in disappointment. He had hoped—

"Here, take my handkerchief and do not cry. We need talk of this no more." Digby's voice held little warmth, but it was clear that Gwen's distress made him unhappy as well.

"But—"

"Good night, Miss Delagrace." The door closed softly behind him, and all that was left was the sound of soft sobs from Gwen.

Arthur and Hero huddled under the table, listening to her cry, and then waited until it seemed she had sobbed herself out. But she did not leave. At last Hero shifted enough to peek out. "She is asleep, poor thing."

"She brought her own misery upon herself."

"Can't we all say that? After all, if I had told you I loved you—or if you had done the same when Simon demanded that we marry, we would have been happy from the start."

"You have a compassionate heart, Hero. I am not so—"

"We must bring them together."

He most emphatically did not agree. "Playing with fate is not a game I wish to enter. My grandmother's example is warning enough for me."

She sighed. "I do not mean to force them together but merely to give them the opportunity to bridge that distance between them."

"How?"

"I do not know."

They moved quietly out from under the table, careful not to wake Gwen. He glanced at her sleeping face and remembered the girl she had been. Remembered that she had confessed her mistakes to Digby, which took courage.

He sighed. "I know how." He left the key on the table, where Gwen could not fail to see it.

"Arthur?" Hero would have reached to retrieve it, but he stopped her by taking her hands in his own and drawing her to him gently.

"I am content with what I have, for perhaps the first time in my life. I do not want what my grandmother wanted for me. I want only you."

"But you—"

"I will stand before them and tell my tales. This is one I need not tell. For I know I have won over Digby in my heart. And that is what matters most."

She freed her hands from his and threw them around his neck, careless of waking Gwen now. "You are the bravest man I know." She kissed him. "And the wisest." She kissed him again, and he could taste her tears. "And the kindest—"

"Let us go to bed," he whispered, wrapping his

arm about her and pulling her into him as they walked from the room, leaving the key to Gwen and Digby.

was about her and pulling her throught as they walked from the room. Feeling my love take her hand...

Twenty-five

"Now, gentlemen, it is time to tell your tales. How did you fare on your quest? Did you meet each challenge?" The outgoing Arthur sat down wearily but with flair. From his seat he added, "And remember—we want to be entertained by the telling, not bored to tears." The assembly laughed a bit edgily.

Who would begin? Arthur rose and Hero tensed. Their scheme had worked. Gwen and Digby were now married, and possessed of the manuscript. Would Arthur be forever humiliated by these events? She could only pray he would not.

Digby appeared nervous, but he did not protest that Arthur be the first to tell his tale.

"I have set seriously upon my quest," Arthur began. "And in the three months since last I was here, I have met and mastered many challenges. Among them I hope you will agree are the three which were set for me by the society."

"First," he said, looking toward Hero, "I proved my honor by offering my heart to the woman who is my wife. I am glad to say that she has at last considered it a worthy enough gift to accept."

Hero felt numb. She wanted to stand and tell him that she had always considered it a worthy gift. But she would not dishonor him by interrupting him mid-tale. She would tell him so in private, later.

To her distress, there was a rustle of disapproval from the members at the table. But Arthur held up his hand and said, "Second, I have met my challenge for Chivalry. A man may plead his case before a court of knights, and they may find his deed chivalrous. But if the one to whose aid he came does not credit the deed thus, then I say it is not so, no matter the judgment of his fellow knights.

"Conversely, if the one aided finds the deed chivalrous, then it is so no matter the judgment by his fellow knights. For that is the nature of chivalry in my eyes. A knight must be truly judged by the one in need of the aid he offers.

"As Sir Galahad found, true honor is not in pretty words and idle deeds but in true aid.

"When I met a young woman who had been forced to come to live with a dragon whose fire breathed both hot and constant, I knew that it must fall to me to rescue her, whether she grant my actions the title of chivalry or not.

"This young woman—stout of heart, no shrinking violet of a maiden she—"

Hero sat back in shock. He was not speaking of the ditch he had so proudly dug, but of her. Of winning her heart. Of protecting her from his grandmother's wrath. Each tale he told, for Honor, and for Valor, had her at its heart. She heard only one tenth of the words he spoke though. For her eyes were fastened upon his, mesmerized by the light in his gaze and the smile on his lips, and he told the society in the prettiest of words of how they had come to be together.

Then it was time for Digby to tell his tale. The members, who had moments before been heartily congratulating Arthur for a tale well told, now grew silent and thoughtful again as they turned their attention to Digby.

He smiled as he stood, projecting an air of confidence and leadership that Hero knew was what had led Arthur to the conclusions he had made. She was proud of him again, for recognizing what so many men might not have. Digby was the man for the job of leader of the society.

Unless—and she doubted this outcome very much—he managed to turn his triumphs into a tale so stupefyingly boring that even the members could not see their true magnificence.

Somehow, though, she could not imagine the man—standing there with such casual command— ever doing such a thing. She settled back, prepared to hear a worthy and entertaining tale. One that she knew well, even to the added details that made known her husband for the better man, no matter that he would not end as head of the society.

The trip to Wales was exhausting. Hero was glad to have a warm shoulder to nap against when she was too tired to stay awake. The day was windy and there was a chill in the air when they came to the cliffs at Caernarvon. The crumbled ashes of the letters that had caused so much unhappiness flew into the air like bits of snow, or dandelion fluff.

"They have done their job. They do not deserve to be scorned for their beliefs, as they would be if these were read." He saw the tears in her eyes and his arms came around her.

Warm and safe in his embrace, she said, "It's good to think that someone has guarded those pages so well until now, and that they are now safe in the hands of the society."

"The words themselves have been with us for so long though. Does it really matter that we have found the original pages upon which they were inscribed?"

"True, the words themselves cannot die, they have been reprinted, translated, read aloud, for nearly five hundred years." She sighed. "Still—"

He heard the unspoken question. "I do not regret it. Digby is the right man for the job. He is the man with the heart of a lion."

"And you are the wise one. He would not have had the position if you had not been generous and wise enough to hand him the opportunity. You could have snatched it for yourself, but you recognized that you belonged elsewhere than in London, heading the Round Table Society."

"It is less wise than selfish, I think, to want to be home with you, surrounded by our books, my ears and heart filled with the discussion that only we can create between us."

"Nonsense. It is wisdom. You recognized that you are better suited to it than Digby would be. Could you see him with Gwen, stuck in a library with no one around but their servants and themselves?" She laughed. "No. You were wise. They are the London couple, the bright and beautiful couple."

"And we are the country mice, then?" He amended, "No, we are the quiet couple, the ones who don't need a whirlwind social life or admiring looks to reach our own peace and happiness."

"See? See how wise you are, Arthur? Just as you recognized that the words are more important than the paper upon which they were first written, when it came to the truth of Malory's manuscript you recognized what it meant in the end."

"The words themselves burn into the heart, Hero. That is the glory, not the acclaim that comes with being feted as the discoverer of the pages that first carried those words. The words themselves are enduring. Just like the ones you said to me not so long ago."

She smiled. "I love you."

He bent to kiss her lightly. "Yes, those very words." His lips were chilled from the wind, but still, when they touched her neck, she felt warm as he replied, "I love you."

The last bits of paper crumb blew off and were captured by the churning waves, and they stood, leaning against each other until the sun had set in a fiery blaze into the sea.

If you liked *The Unintended Bride*, be sure to look for Kelly McClymer's next release in the Once Upon a Wedding series, *The Infamous Bride*, available in October 2001 wherever books are sold.

An irresistible flirt, Juliet Fenster believes the attention of just one man is more boring than words can express. And now that she is the sister-in-law of the wealthy Duke of Kerstone, plenty of gentlemen are eager to pay her court. There is only one notable exception: Romeo Hopkins, who dares to chide her for spending too much for the buttons on her gowns! Fuming at the staid American financier's remarks, Juliet swears to her sisters that she will have him at her feet within the month. Yet her relentless campaign to win his affection meets with his exasperation—and a scandalous kiss that results in a wedding!

Put a Little Romance in Your Life With
Betina Krahn

__**Hidden Fire**	**$5.99**US/**$7.50**CAN
0-8217-5793-8	
__**Love's Brazen Fire**	**$5.99**US/**$7.50**CAN
0-8217-5691-5	
__**Midnight Magic**	**$4.99**US/**$5.99**CAN
0-8217-4994-3	
__**Passion's Ransom**	**$5.99**US/**$6.99**CAN
0-8217-5130-1	
__**Passion's Treasure**	**$5.99**US/**$7.50**CAN
0-8217-6039-4	
__**Rebel Passion**	**$5.99**US/**$7.50**CAN
0-8217-5526-9	

Call toll free **1-888-345-BOOK** to order by phone or use this coupon to order by mail.

Name _____

Address _____

City _____ State _____ Zip _____

Please send me the books I have checked above.

I am enclosing	$_____
Plus postage and handling*	$_____
Sales tax (in New York and Tennessee)	$_____
Total amount enclosed	$_____

*Add $2.50 for the first book and $.50 for each additional book.

Send check or money order (no cash or CODs) to:

Kensington Publishing Corp., 850 Third Avenue, New York, NY 10022

Prices and Numbers subject to change without notice.

All orders subject to availability.

Check out our website at **www.kensingtonbooks.com**

Put a Little Romance in Your Life With
Shannon Drake

__**Come The Morning**   0-8217-6471-3 $6.99US/$8.50CAN

__**Conquer The Night**   0-8217-6639-2 $6.99US/$8.50CAN

__**The King's Pleasure**   0-8217-5857-8 $6.50US/$8.00CAN

__**Lie Down In Roses**   0-8217-4749-0 $5.99US/$6.99CAN

__**Tomorrow Glory**   0-7860-0021-X $5.99US/$6.99CAN

Call toll free **1-888-345-BOOK** to order by phone or use this coupon to order by mail.

Name _____

Address _____

City _____ State _____ Zip _____

Please send me the books I have checked above.

I am enclosing $_____

Plus postage and handling* $_____

Sales tax (in New York and Tennessee) $_____

Total amount enclosed $_____

*Add $2.50 for the first book and $.50 for each additional book.

Send check or money order (no cash or CODs) to:

Kensington Publishing Corp., 850 Third Avenue, New York, NY 10022

Prices and numbers subject to change without notice. All orders subject to availability.

Visit our web site at **www.kensingtonbooks.com**